DEADLY
DESIGN

DEADLY DESIGN

DEBRA DOCKTER

G. P. PUTNAM'S SONS
AN IMPRINT OF PENGUIN GROUP (USA)

G. P. PUTNAM'S SONS
Published by the Penguin Group
Penguin Group (USA) LLC
375 Hudson Street
New York, NY 10014

USA | Canada | UK | Ireland | Australia
New Zealand | India | South Africa | China
penguin.com
A Penguin Random House Company

Library of Congress Cataloging-in-Publication Data
Dockter, Debra.
Deadly design / Debra Dockter.
pages cm
Summary: "Kyle McAdams races to find out what's killing kids conceived
at the Genesis Innovations Laboratory, before he becomes yet another
perfect, blue-eyed corpse"—Provided by publisher.
[1. Genetic engineering—Fiction. 2. Brothers—Fiction. 3. Twins—Fiction.
4. Family problems—Fiction. 5. Murder—Fiction. 6. Science fiction.] I. Title.
PZ7.1.D63De 2015
[Fic]—dc23
2014031154

Printed in the United States of America.
ISBN 978-0-399-17105-5
1 3 5 7 9 10 8 6 4 2

Design by Annie Ericsson.
Text set in ITC Berkeley Oldstyle Std.

To Mom and Dad
Thanks for always telling me I could

I was five years old when I found out that my older brother wasn't just my brother.

It was right after my preschool graduation. Chairs were set up for parents and grandparents in the lobby of the school. A wooden box and a microphone sat across from the chairs. We were each expected to stand up on the box, lean over a microphone, and tell the audience what we wanted to be when we grew up. One little girl said she wanted to be a mermaid. That made everyone laugh. The boy in front of me played it safe. He said that when he grew up, he wanted to be a grown-up. Then it was my turn. I was going to say that I wanted to be a fireman. Not original, I know, but Mom had just bought me this awesome fire truck at a garage sale, so . . .

I went to stand up on the box, and I noticed a photograph hanging on the wall behind me.

There were a lot of photographs, each filled with groups of graduating preschoolers, all of them wearing nice shirts or dresses and all with the same dorky grins. But there was something in that photo, someone, that almost knocked me off the box. It was me.

I looked at the kids lined up on either side of me. These were my classmates, the kids I'd learned my letters and colors with. The kids I'd chased around the small playground. But they weren't the same kids in the photograph with me. We hadn't lined up yet to take the official graduation picture. But there I was on the wall.

"Kyle," Mrs. Parks, our teacher, said as she gently took my shoulders and turned me toward the audience. "Tell everyone what you want to be when you grow up."

My mind was a complete blank, at least as far as deciding at five what path my life should take.

I didn't say anything. I stepped down from the box as a few people inhaled sharply like it was bad luck not to say what I wanted to be in the future. Like not saying something meant I wouldn't have a future.

My family didn't stick around for the punch and cookies. Instead, Dad dropped Mom and my brother, Connor, off at the house, then he took me out for ice cream—just me because I wouldn't stop asking why my picture was already on the wall and why I was wearing a green button-down shirt in the picture, when I don't have a green button-down shirt.

Dad and I got ice cream, then we walked down the block to the park and sat on a bench. That's when he told me that Connor wasn't just my brother; he was my twin brother, my identical twin brother. The picture was of him, not me. When

Connor graduated from preschool, he was five, just like I was, so we looked exactly alike.

I felt stupid. If Connor and I were twins, identical twins, I should have noticed. Twins are supposed to be the same age. That's part of being twins, being born at the same time. But we weren't.

Dad explained everything at the park. Well, he probably didn't explain all of it, not the part about him and Mom being carriers for a fatal disease called spinal muscular atrophy. Not the part about Mom having had six miscarriages. He did tell me that Chase, my other brother, whose picture sits on my parents' dresser, died when he was six months old from a very bad illness that they wanted to make certain their next baby wouldn't have.

That spring day in the park when I was five and ice cream was melting faster than I could eat it because I didn't have much of an appetite, Dad told me that Connor and I were designed in a special lab. They had a very smart doctor, and he created a baby for them who was very healthy. But then the baby split into two babies—me and Connor.

Because they wanted us so much, they decided to separate us. Mom gave birth to Connor first, while I was kept at the lab.

That threw me. Connor was at home with our parents, and I was still in some creepy lab? Then Dad explained that I was frozen the whole time, so I wasn't lonely or anything. That threw me even more.

While Connor was baking in Mom's Easy-Bake Oven, so to

speak, I was frozen. When he was crying and getting his diapers changed and people were talking about how cute he was, I was in the deep freeze.

After our talk, we got ice cream for Mom and Connor, and we went home. Connor asked if I wanted to kick a ball around in the backyard, and I said yes, but I couldn't keep my eye on it. All I could do was stare at him—at me, two years into the future. I asked Connor if he knew we were twins. He said he'd found out on his own a few Christmases ago when he was snooping for presents in Mom and Dad's closet. He found our baby books and when he started looking through them, noticed that when put side by side at the same ages, we were identical. He said he'd wanted to tell me, but Mom and Dad thought it would be better if I was a little older before I knew.

People used to comment that Connor and I looked alike, but it seemed like people had to say that. Like it was a rule or something to say, "Oh, he looks just like his brother."

I remember Connor putting his hands on my shoulders, his arms tilting downward because he was two years taller.

"I'm glad we're twins," he said. "Are you?"

I nodded. He smiled, and we started kicking the ball again.

But I couldn't stop wondering what it would have been like if we'd graduated preschool together. If we could have always been together.

"Even in that stupid getup, he looks handsome," Emma says, staring at Connor's photo displayed on the wall with all the photos of the graduating class in their caps and gowns. It's not a very big graduating class. Rose Hill High School has a total of about six hundred students in the entire school—pretty typical for a small town in Kansas. "I can't wait to see him onstage giving his speech."

I don't say anything as students rush past us, anxious to step out of the frigid air-conditioning and into the warm spring—almost summer—air.

"I'm meeting Connor at your house after school," Emma says. "You should let me drive you home."

"Doesn't Connor have track practice?"

She shakes her head, her long blond hair brushing against her shoulders. "The coach doesn't want Connor worn out for the meet tomorrow, so no practice today. We're going to hang out for a while and then grab some dinner."

Of course they are. I love having Emma around all the time. I love hearing her laugh as Connor tickles her on the sofa. I love watching him whisper in her ear right before he kisses her and my dad tells them to get a room and Mom tells them not to.

I love her blue eyes. I love her full lips and the pink gloss she lightly coats them with. I bet it has a flavor—cotton candy or bubble gum. I could ask her, but I won't. It's bad enough to be head over heels for your brother's girl, but I refuse to be that pathetic.

"So, about that ride home?"

Emma never offers me rides, usually because she's too busy with her after-school activities. Plus, I only live a few blocks from school.

"Why?" I ask.

"I want to talk to you," she says. "It's important."

"It better be," I say, not because being alone with her in a confined space could be torture, but because riding in her car is definitely dangerous. Really dangerous.

We follow the dwindling mob of high school students out to the parking lot, where most of the parking spaces are occupied by hand-me-down four-doors or old pickup trucks. Emma's car takes up half a parking space at most.

"Get in," she says, unlocking the doors with the remote.

I hesitate, looking at the dull green coffin on wheels. "I think I'll walk."

"Please," she begs. "I promise it's safe. It even has air bags."

"Are you sure?" The Smart car is tiny, and I can't help imagining a dozen circus clowns crammed into it. "Does it really have air bags, or does a whoopee cushion pop out of the steering wheel?"

"Don't insult my car. I love my car. And I love the environment."

I open the door and get in. It's roomier than I expected.

"Your mom said you might not go to graduation?" Emma says once my seat belt is buckled.

I half expect the door locks to engage, to trap me in the car for the conversation I don't care to have.

"Connor needs you there. You're his brother, his twin. This is really important to him and your parents."

"You and my parents talked about this?"

"Just your mom."

"Then why doesn't *she* talk to me?"

Emma hesitates. "You know your mom doesn't like conflict."

"What conflict? My mom and I never fight."

"You don't talk that much either. She doesn't want to push you away. She doesn't want you spending even less time with the family."

"I eat supper with them every night," I say, trying not to sound pissed, but I kind of am. "I watch movies with them on the weekend. I let you and Connor drag me around."

"Sometimes," she says.

"I'm sixteen. Eating dinner with my parents is as social as I'm supposed to be. Besides, I have *interests*."

"You mean video games?"

How can I explain to her that "video games" aren't just games to me? I'm good at them. I'm damn good at them. Online players beg to have me on their teams. They schedule their playing times around mine because no one can kick ass on *Call of Duty* like I can. But compared to Connor's history of athletic domination, who gives a shit if my kill-to-death ratio is off the charts.

"I don't want to make you mad," Emma says. "I just want everyone to be happy.

I scoff as a giant-ass pickup truck pulls up next to us.

"Will you at least think about going?" she asks.

How can I make her understand why I don't want to go? Yeah, we may be twins, but we're not twins in the traditional sense. Even if it weren't for the age difference, Connor and I still wouldn't look exactly alike. He has six-pack abs and giant biceps. And he's super smart, super athletic. He's super everything, and I'm . . . good at video games.

"Why don't you want to go?"

I look at her like it's a stupid question, because it is a stupid question.

"I'm serious. And don't tell me it's your pride, because that's bullshit. You are not supposed to be your brother. You are two different people, and that's good. Besides, if you and Connor were carbon copies of each other, how on earth would I be able to choose between you?"

She gives me a coy little smile.

"Do you have any lemon juice?" I ask. "I just found a paper cut on my finger I'd like to pour some into."

"I just meant that you're both special people. Connor is like my Clark Kent, my Superman. He's perfect." Emma's eyes stare out over the dashboard, but I know from the way she's smiling, her face beaming, that she's seeing more than the after-school traffic. "He's the most perfect person in the world, and we're perfect together." She looks at me, and she's so happy. And I'm happy for her. I really am. "And you," she says. "You're like James Dean."

"James who?"

"Dean. James Dean. He's the quiet but tough guy. He doesn't need anybody else, doesn't care about what anybody else thinks. He's a bad boy." She gives me a sideways glance.

I consider this, then nod in agreement. "Yep, that's me. I'm bad to the bone."

"Oh, yeah," Emma says. "Tell me something you've done, bad boy."

I think for a minute, but I don't have to think for long because I've been so notoriously bad. "Last week, I was playing *Call of Duty* online. It wasn't just me. I was playing on a team. I had guys relying on me, and I realized that I'd been chewing the same piece of gum for over two hours."

"Two hours?" She's already amazed, her eyes wide with disbelief.

"I couldn't leave the game. I couldn't let my guys down, but it was disgusting—like chewing on a rubber band. So you know what I did?"

"What did you do? Tell me."

"I took it out of my mouth."

"And then?"

"I stuck it on the nightstand. Yeah, that's right. I didn't put it in the trash. I could have. It was only a few feet away, but no. I stuck it there, and guess what?"

"What?" she says, like she can't take it. Like she wants to speed all the way home so she can rip my clothes off, and if I say something about Connor, she'll say, "Connor who?"

"I left it there."

"For a whole week?"

I nod and she laughs, breaking character.

"I better arrange an intervention," she says. "You're too wild for your own good."

"Yep, that's me." I turn up the volume on the radio, and she turns it down again.

"So, graduation?"

"Graduations are boring. They read a bunch of names, the choir sings a couple of sappy songs, and the band plays like shit."

"What about his speech? He's valedictorian. That's a big deal."

"I know it's a big deal," I say. "Everything in Connor's life is a big deal. He doesn't need me around to make it any bigger."

"But he does." She reaches over and grabs my arm. "It's not your fault that you were born second, and it's not his fault he was born first. He cares about you, and he really wants you there. It's important."

We stop at an intersection, and she looks at me. I can't help but wonder what she sees. I have the same eyes, the mouth, the nose, even the voice—the exact same DNA of the guy she's madly in love with. I'm just two years younger and too lazy to go to the gym.

"Think about it?" She makes a left turn onto the street where I live. "What about the state track meet?"

Now she's really pushing it. "I suppose Mom mentioned that to you too, or was it Dad? Well, like I told him, I'm busy Saturday. I signed up to help medical students learn how to perform colonoscopies. So if Connor's upset that I'm not there, if he wants to know 'what's up Kyle's ass?' you can tell him I have about a dozen medical students up it."

She growls, tightening her hands around the steering wheel. "It's his last meet."

"So I'm supposed to go cheer him on while he breaks his *own* record."

"It's also his birthday. We're going out to dinner afterward."

The car slows, and Emma pulls in front of my house. She places her hand on my arm.

"If you won't do it for him, do it for me?"

Why does she have to put it that way? Am I that transparent? Can she tell that there isn't anything I wouldn't do for her?

Connor's just getting out of his Jeep in the driveway.

Emma jumps out of the car, runs across the lawn, and throws herself into his arms. Connor spins her around, and she's flying with her arms tight around his neck and his arms tight around her waist. When they stop, they stand there in the driveway staring at each other like they're the most gorgeous people in the world, and they can't help themselves, and that's pretty much how it is. Hell, even I can't stop staring at them as I walk across the lawn toward the front door.

The windows are open on Connor's Jeep, and the wind has made his hair into a perfect blond mess. My hair is usually just a mess. My face isn't quite as full as his either. Being an athlete, he packs a lot of food away. He's always drinking protein shakes and downing giant spoonfuls of peanut butter.

He's tan too. The lamp in my basement bedroom doesn't do a lot for my skin tone, but when Connor's not in school, he's outside. Sometimes I look at him, and I can't believe we're identical twins. Even if I spent hours at the gym or running outside in the sun, no way would I look like him—like Apollo coming down from Olympus to let the mortals bask in my awesomeness.

I reach for the doorknob.

"Kyle." Connor runs up onto the porch. "We're going to go walk around the park for a while and then grab a bite. You want to come along?"

"No thanks," I say, opening the door.

"You sure? We can shoot some hoops or something. Mom texted me that she's making tuna casserole. Between you and me, I didn't get the text. Why don't you come with us?"

I look at Emma. "I better eat here. Evidently I don't socialize enough with the family."

Connor follows my eyes. He looks at Emma, at the smirk on her face, then back at me. "Did I miss something?"

"Not a thing," I say. "You two go ahead."

"We can bring you back something if you want," Connor says.

"I'm good, but thanks."

I start to step inside, but he's still standing there. I turn, and he's looking at me, looking right into my eyes. He does this sometimes, a lot of times. He looks at me like he's waiting to see if I can read his thoughts, like he wants to tell me something, but it'd be so much easier if he didn't have to use words. But I can't read his mind. Even if I could, I think I'd be afraid to. Connor's mind has to be full of amazing things, like state championships and political issues he knows inside and out because of debate and maybe even plans to someday cure cancer.

My thoughts are more of the Nazi zombie type. I just want to kill shit.

Connor sighs, his eyes finally leaving mine. I've failed the test again. If he had a better twin, a more worthy twin, we'd be able to have psychic conversations, and I'd ace every test in school because he could "think" me all the answers.

Emma takes Connor's hand, and they start to walk toward his Jeep. I start inside again.

"Are you sure?" he says, his body sideways like he's torn between coming inside with me or going with Emma. "It's *tuna* casserole. We could get a pizza."

"I'm good," I say again, and I hate how he's looking at me, like I'm rejecting him. With all his admirers, does he really need one more, and does it have to be me?

I have to get away from him. His aura, or whatever the hell it is, is too damn bright. My skin, my pale epidermis, is starting to burn. Connor needs to leave. Then I just have to get through dinner, so I can shrink back into the shadows of my basement sanctuary.

Emma pulls him toward the Jeep, and he follows. He walks her to the passenger side and opens the door, but before getting in, she looks back at me and smiles.

I remember the first time he brought her home. He was a freshman, and I was in that hell called middle school. They'd walked to our house after school on a Friday because Mom was going to serve as chauffeur for their first date. Connor and Mom went into the kitchen to discuss rules and curfews, and Emma sat down next to me on the sofa. We watched television for a few minutes and then she started talking to me. She asked me if I liked sports, and when I said no, she asked me what I did like. I started talking about gaming, and she seemed interested. Interested in the games. Interested in me.

She noticed me.

When Mom and Connor came back into the living room, Emma got up, and I thought that was it. Once the great Connor was back, I disappeared again. But as they were walking out the front door, Emma turned and smiled at me. That was four years ago, and she's still giving me that smile.

"**G**uess what I heard."

It's the voice of Teddy Eskew. As if spending the day sitting amongst Connor's adoring fans isn't bad enough, now I have to put up with the school's biggest asshole.

"I heard you and your brother were Siamese twins, joined at the dick, and when the doctors separated you, they decided to give what there was to your brother. That's why you have to piss sitting down."

Teddy doesn't ride the short bus to school, but he can't get it through his head that Connor and I are twins, born two years apart. Somehow he got the idea that I'm a sophomore while Connor's a senior because I had the cord wrapped around my neck. Lack of oxygen made me *delayed*. Teddy's a senior, and he and I are in two classes together. He's the one who's delayed. He's also the one on probation for vandalism, underage drinking, exposing himself to a minor, and attempting to grow facial hair like Wolverine from *X-Men*.

"You made any summer plans yet?" I ask as I push past him, balancing two hot dogs and a can of Diet Coke in my hands. "I heard there are lots of unsupervised kiddies at the water park if you want to show off your . . ." I lift the hot dogs.

Teddy's hair-framed face reddens. His biceps flex.

"Is there a problem?"

Officer Prater, our school's resource officer, is standing right behind Teddy. He's not wearing his uniform or his Taser, but at six and a half feet tall and three hundred pounds, he doesn't really need them to be intimidating.

Teddy walks away, but not before giving me that "I'll find you later" look.

"I really hate that this is Connor's last meet," Prater says, running a hand over his shaven head. "I've been watching him since middle school."

I know what he's thinking. He's thinking that even though Connor is graduating next week, he should be able to come watch me compete in football and basketball and track. But I'm too much of a slacker. I'm too lazy to *be all that I can be.*

"He's got a good chance of breaking his record, and I bet it stands a long time too." Prater looks off at the cloudless May sky like he's savoring this moment—the moment before Connor McAdams cements his place in the history of high school pole-vaulting. He smiles to himself, and when his eyes fall back on me, it's like he's about to reprimand me for hanging out in the hallway instead of being in class. "You better get up there. There's only one more competitor before Connor. You don't want to miss this."

"Oh"—I shake my head—"you have no idea how much I don't want miss this."

I push my way through the crowd, and the hot dogs I was craving a second ago have lost some of their appeal.

I don't want to be here!

But over breakfast this morning, Mom kept opening her mouth as if to say something, then closing it again and starting to rinse dishes or wipe counters. Dad, on the other hand, came into the kitchen, fixed a bowl of cereal, and said what he wanted to say.

"Don't come if you don't want to." His mouth was full of cornflakes, and there was a tiny dot of milk on his chin. "Your mom and I understand that watching your brother compete may not be . . ." He couldn't quite find the words, so he shoveled another spoonful of cereal into his mouth to buy some time. "It's just that this is his last meet. He wants us there, all of us. You mean a lot to him. I know you two haven't been that close, not for a long time, but you used to be. It's probably my fault. Maybe if I'd have tried harder to get you involved in sports, or maybe a little less hard with him, then . . ."

That's when I agreed to come to the meet. I hate it when my parents start analyzing the ways they may or may not have screwed up their kids. Right or wrong, Dad loves sports, and he loves watching Connor. I don't want him to feel guilty for that. And I definitely don't want him to feel like he's a bad father. He's not.

Besides, the truth is, what Connor does is pretty cool. I've watched pole-vaulting on YouTube. It's pretty amazing. These guys, they actually fly—not for long, but they do fly. And that part where the pole is bending, and it looks like it might snap in half and stab them, that's scary as hell. And Connor's not just good at it. He's the best.

I go up the four steps leading to the bleachers and notice a guy standing next to the chain-link fence. He's young, probably in his midtwenties. He's got broad shoulders, definitely the athletic type, and he's taking pictures of . . . Connor. Of course he's taking pictures of Connor. Connor isn't even jumping yet. He's just bending over touching his toes, but even that's impressive if you're a scout for some big university and you want Connor on your team. The photographer pauses to look at the shots he's just taken. He glances up for a second, and when he sees me, he looks . . . uneasy. Then it's like he remembers that somebody told him Connor had a twin, and he nods at me and looks away.

Don't worry, buddy, I want to tell him. You won't have to come back to take pictures of me in a couple of years. Not unless you're recruiting for your college's video game club.

I don't walk to the stairs. I step from metal seat to metal seat. It's not hard maneuvering around people, because most are congregated in the middle of the stands.

"Hey, Connor!"

I recognize the voice immediately, and she's not talking to Connor. She's talking to me. I turn. Cami, Emma's best friend, is sitting about three feet to my left. She's wearing an old orange *Lion King* T-shirt and cutoff denim shorts. Her pale legs are propped up on the seat in front of her like she's attempting to get some sun.

"How are you, *Connor*?"

She's doing it on purpose. She always does it on purpose. Cami, short for Camille, calls me Connor because she knows that there is an unwritten law in the universe that anyone who calls me by my brother's name will get flipped off. I've served two detentions because of her, once because she did it during my food presentation in Spanish class and once when she said it as the principal was walking down the hallway.

"Really?" I lift my full hands.

"Sorry," she says, as if she hadn't noticed. She puts down the sketchbook she's been doodling in and takes the can of Diet Coke from my hand.

I flip her the bird, and with a smile on her face, she hands the can back.

"I'm kind of surprised to see you here," she says.

"You didn't think I'd want to see my brother break his own record? Watching Connor achieve his goals is pretty much my purpose in life."

She shakes her head and tucks short curls of brown hair behind her ears. "I just figured you wouldn't want to be here— wouldn't want to spend another day in the Great Connor's shadow."

Wow. I scoff because I can't believe she said that. She gets it. The girl who constantly calls me by my brother's name just to piss me off and get me into trouble gets it. Connor is the quarterback of the football team. He's the captain of the basketball team. And when he's not breaking track records, he's walking on water. I can't compete with that. And Cami gets it.

I give her a miniature "fuck you" with the hand carrying the

Diet Coke, but this time it's meant as a sort of salute. She smiles and flips me the bird from behind the sketch pad.

"What are you drawing?"

She turns the pad around to reveal a small bird sitting amongst sparse tufts of grass.

"Over there," she says, nodding her head toward the patch of grass next to the concession stand, where tiny birds with red-tipped gray wings peck at bits of popcorn.

"Nice."

"Thanks." She smiles at me. "Any time you want to sit for portrait, just let me know. I'll even let you strike your favorite pose." She rubs her cheek with her extended middle finger, and I almost laugh.

"See you later at the festivities."

Poor Cami. She's getting sucked into everything, too, and she's not even related to him. I suppose that's the downside to being BFFs with Connor's girlfriend. I give her a sympathetic nod, and then continue up to where Mom and Dad are sitting.

"You're going to spoil your dinner," my mom says when she sees the two hot dogs balanced in my left hand. She takes her Diet Coke.

"I don't like Luigi's, so what's it matter?" I sit down in the space my parents have left for me between them on the bleachers. I don't understand why they're not sitting next to each other. I'm not five. I don't need a parent on either side of me to make sure I don't slip between the metal seats and break my neck.

She runs her hands through her short sandy blond hair. She had it cut this morning, and the hairdresser got a little happy with the scissors. Now Mom can't seem to stop touching it, and every time she does, she frowns a little.

"You love Luigi's," she says, the slight wrinkles around her brown eyes deepening a little as she processes the idea that I don't like the place they drag me to every year for Connor's birthday. If I liked it, then I'd want to go there on my birthday, but I never do. I prefer Mom's fried chicken on my birthday. She's a really good cook, except for tuna casserole, and that's more the tuna's fault than hers. Mostly, I like to stay home on my birthday because once the stupid song is sung and the cake is cut, I can open the video game that I asked for and then show my appreciation by rushing downstairs to play it.

"You like Luigi's," she says, more to herself than to me.

If my mom were Poseidon, the ocean waters would always be calm. Emma's right—Mom hates conflict. She hates anyone being unhappy. She has this Disney picture in her mind of how she wants our family to be. I'm not talking about the perfect spotless house or a garden where butterflies shit glitter over flowers that never wilt. She wants harmony. Her version of the perfect family would be one where we all played different musical instruments and sat around the living room every night singing folk songs. We used to have game night on Fridays and movie night on Saturdays. It was okay. On Fridays we'd have pizza and play Uno or Clue, and Saturdays meant a trip to the video store, microwave popcorn, and Mom and Dad curled up together on the couch while Connor and I made faces at each other every time they kissed.

Then Connor started youth football and started playing

noncompetitive basketball at the recreation center in town. Once he started running, he ran fast. And then there were practices and games and tournaments. No more time for movies or Clue, and by the time anyone bothered to ask me if I wanted to sign up, Connor was so far ahead of me, I could barely see him.

"You really don't like Italian food?" Mom asks, taking her thin-framed glasses off and wiping the lenses against her shirt.

"No," I say.

"That's crap," Dad says. "You love it. You've loved it since you were little and kept crying for more 'b'sghetti.' So listen to your mother and don't spoil your appetite." He takes one of the hot dogs from my hand and devours it in two bites. "No mustard," he mutters with a full mouth. "Who doesn't put mustard on a hot dog?"

Dad's a no-frills kind of guy. He's simple, ordinary. He wasn't a jock in school or a straight-A student. He wasn't a superstar like Connor is. I like that about him—his ordinariness. I also like that he remembers me wanting "b'sghetti." I don't like that I don't look anything like him. He's medium in height—tall enough for high school basketball, but forget college. He's also a little on the pudgy side, and his once-black, now mostly gray hair is receding faster than the polar ice cap. Connor and I have our mother's sandy blond hair, and, although both of our parents have brown eyes, Connor and I have blue eyes. Evidently Mom and Dad both have a recessive gene for blue.

"He's getting the pole," Dad says, and it's like everyone heard him. Now they are all waiting, all anxious. Emma is standing by the fence, as close to Connor as she's allowed to be.

23

She glances up at my folks, giving them a worried but hopeful smile. Mom's clenching the bleachers, her knuckles bone white. Just one more jump and then she won't have to worry so much about him getting hurt anymore.

Connor takes his mark. His right hand holds the bottom of the long, slender pole, while his left hand steadies it, the tip pointing to the sky. He starts running. The pole lowers, and for a second, it's parallel to the ground, then it lowers more. Connor plants it right in front of the mat. His legs kick up until he is completely upside down. His body twists and turns as his feet clear the bar, and somehow, he wills his arms and shoulders to pull backward, to leave the bar undisturbed.

Held breaths are exhaled in unison. Then the cheers come. Mom and Dad leap from their seats. Everyone is standing and cheering. In front of me is a row of butts, bouncing up and down and making the stands vibrate. I can't see what's happening down on the field, but I can imagine. People are slapping Connor on the back. His coach is beaming. His teammates are distracted from their own events. They're smiling and nodding to each other because they knew this was going to happen. And they knew that nothing they did this day would compare to Connor McAdams breaking another record.

His teammates are probably acting happy, and truth is, a lot of them are. I mean, Connor's not the kind of guy to rub his triumphs into the faces of everyone else. He's not arrogant, even though he has every right to be. He's likable. But for some of the other athletes, especially the seniors, I bet they wish that, just once, Connor would come in second or, better yet, third or fourth. Couldn't he trip over a shoelace or catch his foot on a hurdle? I wish he would. Just once I'd like to comfort him instead of congratulate him.

Maybe if we'd have been born together, instead of almost two years apart, we'd both be champions. Mom and Dad would have signed us up together. We'd have gone to the gym together and practices together. We'd be unbeatable. He would have been quarterback of the football team, and I'd have been his wide receiver, catching anything he threw at me and running in for touchdown after touchdown.

I know Mom and Dad thought they were doing the right thing. I know they were afraid that if they carried their perfect, laboratory-created, identical twins at the same time, they might lose us to yet another miscarriage in a long line of miscarriages. Don't put all your eggs in the same basket, as the saying goes. I lost the coin toss. I'm the one who got to be frozen. I guess I came in second then too.

If we'd been born together, today would be both of our birthdays. We'd both be eighteen, and Connor would be my best friend instead of a constant reminder that there is someone who exists in this world who will always be admired and respected and loved more than me.

We weren't born together. We never played "pass the umbilical cord" in the womb. We never lay side by side in a crib. While Connor was rolling over and then crawling and then walking and talking and getting farther and farther ahead of me, I was frozen. And sometimes I feel like I haven't quite thawed.

If calories could be absorbed through the skin, a person would gain ten pounds just from walking into Luigi's Italian Eatery. The air is thick with the aroma of pasta and garlic bread. Italian music plays over the speakers, and candlelight flickers in the center of each table.

"How's this?" the waitress asks, leading us to a rectangular table set for six.

"Would it be okay if we sat over here?" Cami says, taking hold of my arm and pulling me toward a table for two in the corner. Dad gives Mom a little grin because he didn't know Cami and I liked each other like that. He didn't know because we don't. But we're used to splitting off from the group, so to speak—the Connor and Emma group.

It's crazy how at least once a month, Cami and I get dragged along to a movie or, last month, a rodeo, because Connor and Emma both think we need to get out more. Cami's usually working at the grocery store, taking care of her little brother, or driving around in search of artistic inspiration. I, on the other hand, am usually trying to break records of my own on Xbox.

Emma always checks Cami's schedule first. If she isn't working or doesn't have to babysit, then she starts trying to force Cami to go, and Connor starts on me. They bug us until we give in and then it's like we don't exist. When Emma and Connor are together, everyone else becomes invisible. They're Romeo and Juliet, and the sun hasn't risen yet.

Cami isn't in love, and I can't have Emma, so we leave the star-crossed lovers alone and see who can get the lowest score at mini golf or who can shove the most Milk Duds in their mouth at one time.

Mom, Dad, and the golden couple sit down at the table, then the waitress takes two sets of silverware and brings them, along with two glasses of water, over to where we're sitting.

"So." I fold my hands together like I'm about to conduct a very important business meeting. "You wanted to see me."

She tilts her head and smiles at me like I'm the world's biggest pain in the ass. "As you are probably aware, today is May fifteenth. In approximately fourteen days, the love birds will be graduating from high school. They will continue to reside in their current homes throughout the summer months before moving to dormitories in Manhattan, where they will continue their educational endeavors at Kansas State University."

I nod, my expression stern because she sounds like a secret agent imparting classified information.

"Do you know what this means?" she asks.

My eyes narrow. I look around suspiciously and shake my head only slightly.

"Think of Connor and Emma as the people who arrange

your social calendar. When they're gone, who's going to come drag you out of the house? Make sure you get a little vitamin D once in a while?"

Wow. Like I don't get enough grief from Connor and my parents about hanging out too much in the basement. Now I'm going to get it from her too?

"I'm concerned," Cami says. "I'm afraid one of these days your parents are going to be looking for you and they won't find you because you'll have been sucked into one of your games."

I lean back against the chair. Doesn't sound too bad, actually. Especially if I could be sucked into the gaming system, instead of just one single game. I could battle aliens, kill zombies, and there's a hot blonde on one of my *Borderland* maps I wouldn't mind getting to know better.

She kicks me under the table to get my attention. "You need a life."

"You need a boyfriend," I say. "Then you can lecture him instead of me."

"Why do guys always think that girls need a boyfriend? My life is quite fulfilling as it is."

I pick up my glass of water and take a drink. "Then how did you get sucked into coming to this?"

She sighs. "Have you ever tried to say no to Emma? And she knows my dad doesn't work this weekend, so I can't use Josh as an excuse."

"What does your dad do anyway?"

"He's a news producer for channel five. He makes sure

stories are edited and ready to go and nobody cusses on the air. They're always switching his schedule around, so it's hard to know my schedule sometimes, since I have to take care of Josh."

"Do you ever resent your brother?"

She shakes her head, surprised, I think, by the question.

"No. I don't mind. It's not my dad's fault that he fell for a pretty blond reporter. And it's not Josh's fault that she bailed on both of them when she got a chance to move to a bigger network. I was seven when my mom died. At least I got to know her, and I know she didn't want to leave me. Josh doesn't have a single memory of his mom. For him to know she doesn't want him—I can't imagine. I don't ever want him to feel like a burden. I want him to feel loved."

I look at Cami. She's simple. She never wears makeup, but she actually looks good without it. I mean, some girls . . . face it. They need the stuff and lots of it. But Cami doesn't. Her eyes are large and brown and deep set. Her skin could be in an ad for Proactiv—the after picture, of course. She's pretty, not glamorous, but pretty. And she's a good person.

"Thanks." I lift my glass, motion for Cami to pick up hers, and we tap them together.

Her eyes narrow. "For what?"

"For not wanting me to become one of those people who never leaves the house or throws anything away and ends up eating old discarded food and peeing in plastic buckets."

"You're welcome."

I look over at Connor and Emma, their shoulders constantly

touching as they lean into each other. Cami looks over at the golden couple too. Emma is gorgeous. She's wearing a dress with inch-wide straps instead of sleeves. Her tan skin glows in the candlelight, and the low-cut fabric of the neckline gapes just above her breasts.

"Keep your eyes above her neck," Cami says, giving me another little kick under the table. "You should try being a little less obvious."

My face heats up. I am obvious, and pathetic. And the worst part is I think Emma likes it. It's like Connor's the first-string boyfriend and I'm eagerly waiting on the bench. That's why she smiles at me the way she does, touches my arm every once in a while, even offers to rub my neck if I look tense. She likes the power she has over the McAdams twins. But it's not like I'll ever get my chance. She'd never give up Connor. Why would she want an inferior version of him?

"Connor looks especially handsome tonight," Cami says. "That thick, wavy hair of his is just inviting someone to run her fingers through it. And those piercing blue eyes and that strong jaw." She sighs, glances in my direction, and then looks startled. "Oh, wait," she says, like she's never seen me before. "You look just like *him,* only maybe not as ripe."

"Ripe?"

"You know. You look like you need a little more time on the vine. Need to mature a bit. Maybe start appreciating what you see when you look in the mirror."

I almost laugh. I mean, people never appreciate what they see in the mirror. We barely even acknowledge to ourselves that it's us reflected back. We just look to make sure our hair isn't too much of a mess or there isn't something stuck in our teeth or poking out of our nose, but we don't really *look* at ourselves. At least, I don't.

"How is everyone?" a booming voice asks. Luigi himself is standing beside the table where Mom, Dad, Connor, and Emma sit, and he's giving them his best Disney-inspired Italian accent. Lou's from Kansas City, not Rome, but he's sort of Italian. His great-grandfather came over in the early 1900s. He taught his daughter how to cook, and she taught her daughter, and her daughter refused to teach her son because, in America, men should be doctors or lawyers and shouldn't obsess about countries they've never been to. So Lou took an extended trip to Italy to learn how to cook, and he came back as Luigi. "Do you know what you'd like this evening?"

Actually, he sounds a little like an Italian version of Dracula.

"Wait," Luigi cries just as my father starts to order. "I know what you want. I know what you all want. You want . . ." His eyes dart from side to side like he's waiting for something. "To celebrate!"

And then it comes. People rush out from the hallway leading to the kitchen and the bathrooms; others pop up from behind the long wooden bar where Luigi lets adult patrons sample different wines. Within seconds, the scarcely occupied restaurant is packed with people throwing balloons and holding signs that say HAPPY BIRTHDAY and CONGRATULATIONS and STATE CHAMPION.

I slouch in my seat and seriously think about slipping under the table. Cami reaches over and takes my silverware. She unrolls the white cloth napkin, removes the knife, and hands me back the fork and spoon.

"I wouldn't want you to . . ." She takes the knife and does a slicing motion across her wrist.

"I appreciate that," I say and hand her my fork too.

"Wow. That bad? I can't even trust you with a fork?"

I pick up the spoon. "Looks like I'll be having soup." Truth is, I don't want anything. Not minestrone, not lasagna or "b'sghetti." I want to get away from the fans who have crammed themselves into the restaurant. I should slip off to the bathroom and call the fire department. I'm sure the fire marshal would have something to say about the hundred plus people crammed into a room that shouldn't hold more than fifty.

I feel a hand against mine. Cami's looking at me. She's the only person who is. Everyone is staring at Connor, talking to Connor, praising Connor. Dad's beaming, enthralled by the magnificence of his eldest son, while Mom dabs at her eyes with her napkin. She's touched, no doubt, by the idea that all these people would go through all this trouble to surprise them—to surprise Connor.

"He'll be going off to college soon," Cami says.

I nod. "But the legend will go on." I try to smile at her. Try to show that I appreciate that she's talking to me, acknowledging me. But I just want all of this to be over.

Killing zombies is stupid. I mean, really. They're already dead; that's why they're zombies. So why does shooting them over and over again, or exploding a bomb next to them, kill them? I know they're *undead*. Like they were dead, then they became "undead" and now I have to make them dead again, so that I can move on to the next level and get better guns and scarier zombies. It's so stupid, but I'm so good at it. Like really, really good. I actually got invited to a tournament last month in Ohio. Only two hundred people in the entire United States got invited, and I was one of them. It's crazy to think they actually have scouts watching online players. Sometimes players even get sponsored; they get paid to play Xbox and go to tournaments.

What I really can't imagine is Mom or Dad missing one of Connor's sporting events or forensic tournaments to take me to Ohio so that I can play in a *Call of Duty* tournament. I never told them about the invite to play. I didn't want them to feel bad when they chose Connor over me.

I imagine that every zombie on the screen was at Connor's

surprise party. I imagine them dragging their rotted limbs between the tables at Luigi's. I imagine them singing "Happy Birthday" out of rotted mouths, their words nothing more than mumbled, melodic moans. And I shoot them. I shoot them over and over and over. I let some of them morph into crawlers, so that they are dragging their legless bodies across the wooden floors and cracked sidewalks as I finish them off.

What would Dr. Phil say?

A monkey slapping those eerie little cymbals sits at the top of the stairs. It's just about to explode when someone knocks on my bedroom door. I pause the game. "What?"

The door opens. It's Connor. He's changed since we got home. He's wearing an old T-shirt and a pair of gym shorts. He hesitates, unsure if it's okay to come in. Like I've got landmines buried under piles of dirty clothes, just in case someone dares to enter my inner sanctum without my permission. I used to have a DO NOT ENTER sign taped to the door. The tape hardened like thin glass over the years and finally shattered. I'm not sure what happened to the sign, but by then I knew everyone had gotten the message, especially Connor. I can't remember the last time he came into my room. It's been a few years at least.

Connor's holding a package wrapped in balloon-covered paper.

"Nice place you got here," he says and then he laughs. "How do you know when you're going to run out of clean clothes to wear?" He glances at the assortment of soiled socks, shorts, and underwear strewn around the room.

"It's easy. When seventy-five percent of the floor is covered,

I know I'm down to two days' worth of clean clothes. That's when I gather it all up and head for the laundry room."

Connor nods and smiles like he admires my organizational skills. He comes toward me and sits on the edge of my unmade bed. "I, um . . . got you something." He holds out the package.

"It's your birthday, not mine."

"I've been thinking—you should get presents on my birthday, and I should get presents on yours, or maybe we should pick a date right between our birthdays and celebrate then. We're not just brothers, right? We're twins. It just seems jacked up that we don't celebrate together." He puts the present in my hand. "It's really more for me than you, anyway. Open it."

I can already tell what it is from its odd shape. I don't want to unwrap the present, but I do.

"I thought maybe we could play together."

I hand the new controller back to him. "No." I nearly choke on the word, but I'm going to get this out. I'm going to say this, even if he doesn't like it, because I have to. "I don't want to play with you. You have *everything*. Everything out there belongs to you. I'm good at *this*." I lift my own controller. "*This* is all I have. Can't you just—"

"I understand," Connor says, cutting me off. "I just thought . . ." He takes the controller in both of his hands and stares at it like it's much more than a video game controller. And it is.

Connor's eyes turn even bluer as tears gather in them. Why does he care if I play with him? Why does it matter? He's had the most amazing day, a day like most people never ever get,

35

and he's crying because I won't play stupid video games with him.

Connor leans forward, his elbows resting on his thighs. "Do you remember when we were little, and I'd build these towers out of blocks, and you'd knock them down as fast as I could build them?"

I try to remember, but I don't. "Bet it pissed you off."

"No! Are you kidding? It was a blast. That's how it's supposed to be. Big brother builds 'em, and little brother knocks 'em down. It was all you could do to give me time to finish a few stories of blocks before you started throwing Hot Wheels at them."

A spark of a memory comes to mind of Mom yelling and threatening us with a time-out if we didn't calm down. We were laughing, and pretty soon Mom was laughing too. She even knelt on the floor and helped Connor build faster so I wouldn't have to wait as long to demolish their crooked towers.

"I kind of remember."

"How about when we'd go to the park? We'd pick up sticks and handfuls of dirt to throw down the slide?"

"And Mom would get mad because we'd go down and get all dirty."

"Yeah." Connor grins as a tear slips down his cheek. "I remember when it changed," he says. "When we changed."

I don't know what he's talking about. There wasn't a moment, an event when suddenly things were different between us.

"It was one of my first basketball games at the community center. I was in sixth grade, and I was on fire that game. I couldn't miss. All the parents started yelling and clapping. My teammates kept throwing me the ball because they couldn't believe it either. No matter where I shot from, the ball went in. I kept trying to pass the ball so somebody else would shoot, but they'd give it back to me. I got so scared."

I do remember that game. All the moms and dads and grandparents were on their feet, like they were seeing something amazing. Like someday, years in the future, they'd talk about the day when the town realized that Connor McAdams was something special.

"What were you afraid of?" I ask.

"What if I missed?" he says, and I can't believe he thought that was even a possibility.

He stands, wading through my clothes like they're waves at his feet. He stares at the gaming posters on my wall and a petrified piece of pizza on my dresser. He looks like a psychic trying to get the vibe of a missing person, but I'm not missing. I'm right here.

"After the game, it was crazy. My teammates tried to pick me up and carry me into the lobby, but they dropped me and then all these adults were everywhere, talking about me and how someone should call the newspaper and 'how many points did he make—it has to be a record.' I was just a little kid, and all of a sudden, I felt this pressure. I wanted to quit basketball, but Dad was so excited. And all I could think about was the next game and the game after that and the game after that. What if I bombed? What if people were disappointed in me? What if I let them down?"

Connor gives me that look again, like he wants something from me. Every time he looks at me this way, I feel like I'm disappointing him, because he wants me to be somebody I'm not. He wants a brother, and so do I. But I don't exist in his dimension. I don't belong on Mount Olympus, any more than he belongs in the basement.

"This isn't about me," he says. "It's about what I saw after I stopped hiding out in the bathroom. I saw you on the court."

I shake my head because I don't want to talk about this. I don't need to remember this.

"All the grown-ups were in the lobby or had already left. A bunch of kids were shooting around. You were holding a ball."

Now my eyes are burning.

"You held it for so long and stared at the basket like everything depended on you making that shot."

It did.

Connor made every basket. Every shot sailed through the air as if delivered by celestial hands into the net. He could do that, and we were twins. Identical twins, even if we weren't the same age. Mom and Dad were always amazed at how fast Connor learned to tie his shoes or skip or bounce a ball or read. Sometimes they'd look at me, and I knew they were wondering if I was going to be like Connor. If I was going to be exceptional, and just the fact that they were wondering told me that we could be different. He could be better.

I stood there, holding the ball that felt like a boulder. I remember staring at the basket and thinking that this would decide it—this one shot.

"I missed."

"One fucking shot," Connor says. "You missed one fucking shot. And everything changed. But who gives a shit about one shot? I just wish . . . I wish you'd taken another one. I bet you'd have made it."

Maybe I would have. But it's too late now.

Connor gestures toward the screen. "Doesn't this shit give you nightmares?"

I look at the brown and gray images of bony zombies frozen in grotesque positions, and I have to smile because I'm really fond of them, of killing them, anyway.

"I suppose we could play for a while and see if it gives you nightmares."

"Really?" Connor grins and jumps on the bed as I plug in the controller. "I've never played, so . . ."

I roll my eyes like teaching him is going to be a royal pain. And I hope it will be. I hope he's not a natural at aiming guns and placing bombs and building barriers. I hope he sucks. I hope he dies a hundred times, and I hope he loves it, because we're too old to build towers and knock them down.

I walk into the kitchen, and Dad's sitting at the table reading the Sunday paper. Mom's combing through the coupon section. She's still wearing the oversized blue nightshirt with polar bears on it that she's slept in ever since I can remember. Dad's wearing his usual Sunday attire—a faded SeaWorld T-shirt and paint-stained sweatpants that declare that he will not be leaving the house today.

I pour a glass of orange juice and open the cupboard to see what sugary cereals we have.

"I can't believe Connor's not up yet," Dad says.

I smile. About one A.M., Connor and I decided to play story mode. We'd stayed up until three protecting the Pentagon from the undead.

"We stayed up pretty late last night," I say, and both my parents look at me. "We were playing video games."

They look at each other, and while my dad does a good job camouflaging his smile with a fake yawn, Mom beams. I bet we could have played all night, could still be playing now, and she wouldn't get mad at us or force us to go to bed.

"Could you go wake him up?" she says. "Emma's coming over this morning, and I doubt he wants to be in bed when she gets here."

"Sure."

I take out a box of store-brand, sugar-coated cornflakes and set it on the counter. Connor's room is halfway down the hall, next to the bathroom. I lift my hand to knock on the door, but hesitate. I can't remember the last time I went into Connor's room. Maybe it was to race Hot Wheels around a track or to bash Godzilla's head in with King Kong's fists. We were kids. I know that much. The last time I went into Connor's room for anything, we were kids.

I knock on the door, wait a second, and then open it. He's on his stomach, one leg sticking out from beneath the covers and one arm hanging off the side. His room is *so* clean. Of course the toys are gone, but there is nothing on the floor, not even a discarded sock. I have a feeling that if I open the closet doors, his closet will be clean and neat too. I'm pretty sure if I opened my closet, a Saint Bernard would have to come rescue me from the avalanche of shit I've shoved into it. I can't help myself. I open one door.

His clothes aren't arranged in any specific manner. As a matter of fact, there's a nice pile of dirty laundry in the middle of the floor. What strikes me is the row of trophies lined up on the closet shelf. They aren't in his room, not displayed anyway. They're all in here, all crammed together because there are too many. I take down a shoe box, and inside are ribbons and medals won during track or debate tournaments. I glance back at his room.

The only thing on his dresser is Emma's senior picture sitting in a frame made of looping metal hearts. On one wall is a bulletin board where he keeps the schedules for all of his meets and tournaments and his work as a lifeguard at the recreation center. He's got a few photographs pinned to the board, mostly ones of Emma. And there's a photograph of our family taken on the water ride at Six Flags in Texas about eight years ago. It's a horrible picture, one of those taken by a camera right as you plunge down a steep decline. Normally our parents wouldn't have spent the money to buy it, but Dad's baseball cap is flying off his head in the picture, and the expression on his face is hysterical. That was one of our last vacations before life got too busy for trips to theme parks and campgrounds.

"Time to rise and shine," I say as cheerfully as I can.

He doesn't move.

"Connor, time to get up." I nudge the mattress with my knee. "Come on. You don't want Emma to . . ."

Something's wrong. The sheets on his bed are black and against them his skin looks . . . it looks gray.

"Come on, Connor. Quit messing around!" I grip his shoulder and then recoil.

His skin . . . it's cold.

"Connor!" I yell and start shaking him like it's not too late. He can hear me. His spirit's standing by the bed or hovering below the ceiling and when he hears my voice, when he sees how desperate I am for him to be alive, he'll come back. His spirit will enter his body, and it won't matter that his skin is cold and turning hard; he'll be alive. "Connor!"

"Connor?" Mom rushes toward the bed. She grabs his shoulders, feels the cold, but instead of recoiling, she pulls him to her. "No! Connor!"

I back up. I keep backing up until I hit the wall and there's no place to go. Dad's there, calling 911, but there's no use. The operator knows it too, because even though she can't see the grayness of my brother's skin or feel the hardness creeping into his muscles, she can hear my mother's sobs. They are the worst sounds I've ever heard. They are the sounds of a living heart being torn from a warm body. They are the sounds of a mother who has lost her child.

It's hot outside, bright and hot. In movie funerals, the weather always matches the mournful mood of the characters. But there are no clouds, no rain today. The only dampness is from tears and sweat. The church parking lot is boiling over with cars. Trucks and compact cars and piece-of-shit cars driven by teenagers line the main road and side streets. People, all dressed in the appropriate drab colors, filter in through the double doors, past a life-sized crucifix hanging on the wall. The church hall is actually the Catholic school's cafeteria. Once all the sack lunches and fish sticks are devoured, the tables fold up against the walls and the basketball goals come down. It's table time now, and the goals are tucked high against the faded blue ceiling. I could go for a little basketball right now. I could go for jumping up and crashing down and plowing through sweaty bodies and running. Running until I collapse with exhaustion. Running until I drop . . .

I didn't go to the funeral. I couldn't, and I don't think people could have handled seeing me there. A person can't be dead and alive at the same time. There can't be one of you reposing in a coffin while another one is sitting in a pew singing or praying or . . . existing. It's weird because I always thought about how different Connor and I looked. It wasn't until last year that I had a growth spurt and caught up to his six-foot-two stature. My muscles—and my tan—have never caught up. But I see him now when I look in the mirror. I see the same sandy blond hair, the same nose, same chin. I see the same eyes and how mad they are that we lost our chance.

We had one, a chance to be brothers again, like when we were little. We felt it. Hell, we lived it the night before he died. And it was so simple. We played a video game. Connor reached out his hand, and for the first time since I'd missed that fucking basket, I took it.

We played—together. And we saw it, the years ahead of us. The trips I'd take to see him in college, the beer he might let me drink as long as I promised not to tell Mom and Dad. I would have been best man at his wedding and uncle to his kids, and even if it took years to finally be the brothers we were sup-posed to be, we'd have gotten there. But now it's too late.

We missed so much in the past, and now the future's been taken away. From both of us. And I see the pain and anger in his eyes when the mirror looks back at me.

I take a deep breath, standing in the doorway to the cafete-ria. Mom and Dad understood that I couldn't go to the funeral or the cemetery. But Dad suggested I come to the dinner.

I walk in, and there they are huddled against the back wall, my dad shielding Mom from the onslaught of condolences that threatens to bury them. Suddenly the hum of conversation stops. A hundred eyes are staring at me, and almost every pair is asking the same question. "Why couldn't it have been him instead of Connor?"

I start to back up, wanting to get away from the stares and the whispers. Suddenly a hand takes mine and pulls me hard, back into the entryway and then out into the sunlight.

Emma yanks me past the two-story brick building that serves as the elementary school, and once we reach the playground, she drops my hand as abruptly as she'd taken it. Her blue eyes squint against the white, glaring sun as her hands search out something new to hang on to. Her hand falls on the ladder of a tall metal slide, and she grabs it like she's about to collapse. She doesn't look like she's breathing. She's pale, her skin ghostly against the black dress she's wearing. I see her start to fall, and I rush forward, catching her in my arms and lowering us onto the grass.

My back rests against the hot metal slide as she sobs. The metal is burning me through Dad's thin dress shirt, the bottom rung of the ladder branding my lower back. I think about that, about the heat and the pressure and the pain as I stroke Emma's hair.

She cries for a long time, long enough for me to watch the shadows of trees moving slowing across the grass. Long enough for Cami to come looking for Emma and see me holding and soothing her. She smiles sadly and sweetly at me before she returns to the dinner; I expect to see gratitude on Cami's face because she knows I'm comforting her best friend. But her face, colored only by the slight sunburn she'd gotten at the track meet, is full of concern, and somehow I know it's for me, because no one is holding me.

Finally, Emma stops crying, and I don't know if it's because she's temporarily out of tears or because she's just too tired to give birth to any more. I hold her awhile longer, the trembling of her body coming less and less, until she's still.

She looks up at me. I know what she's realizing. She's realizing that the arms that are holding her are made of the exact same DNA as the arms that she's missing.

"It's so strange," she says, her voice mostly air and little tone. "You're him. Your eyes. Your mouth." She combs her fingers through my hair, making my spine tingle. "That's better," she says. She looks at my lips, her fingers gently touching them. "You're him, but you're not."

Her eyes shine with tears, and it kills me inside. I'd do anything, anything to lift the pain from those eyes. Not just because she's Emma, but because she's Connor's Emma. She needs him, and they were supposed to be together.

For a second, I see myself running to the cemetery, pounding against the casket, and telling God that I'll take Connor's place. We won't even have to switch bodies. My soul can just go wherever, and Connor's can jump into this body and then Emma can be happy again. They can both be happy.

"I miss him so much," she says.

I swear her blue eyes aren't just glistening with tears; they're turning into tear-filled orbs.

"I wish . . ." My voice falters. "I wish . . ."

Emma knows what I'm trying to say, what I'm feeling. I mean it too, I really do, but what I really want is for her to shake her head and tell me not to wish for that, not to wish that I could take Connor's place. But she doesn't. She just stares at me and wonders, like everyone else, why I'm alive and Connor isn't.

I open the refrigerator and scan the contents. There are five glass bowls and pans wrapped in plastic. Most of them haven't been touched. I don't get the whole tradition anyway. Someone in the family dies, and friends and neighbors suddenly get paranoid that everyone else in the house is going to starve to death, so they make casseroles that even a starving person wouldn't want to eat. Not to mention worrying about which casserole came from which neighbor.

Mrs. Carson, three houses to the south, has at least seven cats. Her three mutt dogs are always getting into the neighborhood garbage, and rumor has it, she just bought a pet rat. Does anyone really want to eat something out of her kitchen? And Denise Parker, across the street and two doors to the north, has been rumored on more than one occasion to have cooked meth in her kitchen. *That* casserole might be interesting to try, but . . . I don't think so.

If Dennis Kingsbury baked something up, I'd be inclined to eat that. He's been diagnosed with obsessive compulsive personality disorder, which basically means surgery could be performed on his kitchen table with no fear of the patient getting an infection. If he brought something over, though, he forgot to place a crisp yellow sticky note with his name and precise heating instructions on it.

There is a bar of plastic-wrapped cheese covered in green mold and numerous bottles of nearly empty condiments, but not much else.

"There was plenty of food at the church. You should have eaten something there," Dad says, startling me. He's wearing his lounging pants. Connor gave them to him last Father's Day. They're a thin, navy flannel with four-inch trout swimming up the legs. He's also wearing the "Just Fishing" shirt I bought him. Connor and I actually coordinated gifts. Dad looks exhausted. The bags under his eyes have bags.

"I didn't feel like it," I say, knowing that he and Mom evidently hadn't felt like it either.

"You and Emma have a good talk?"

"Not really."

Dad peers over my shoulder into the fridge. "Slim pickins."

"That's okay." I shut the door. "I'm not that hungry."

He stares at me through bloodshot eyes. It's more than just staring, he's . . . examining me, but he can't *see* what he wants to know. He can't see inside of me. He can't see what it's like to lose a brother, a twin, just like I can't know what it's like to lose a son.

"What have you eaten today?" he asks, resorting to what he can deal with: the physical.

"Counting breakfast and lunch?"

He nods.

"Nothing."

"That's what I thought." He nudges me out of the way and opens the refrigerator door again. "There are eggs. I can whip up one of my not-so-famous omelets. Besides, I need to talk to you about something."

"What?"

Dad starts cracking eggs into a bowl. "I talked to the principal today. She wants you to do her a favor."

"Drop out or transfer?"

Dad pours the eggs into a pan, shakes salt and pepper over them, and shuffles them around with a big wooden spoon.

"She wants you to give Connor's speech at graduation."

The little appetite I'd worked up vanishes. "What?"

"You don't have to memorize it. He gave her a copy last week. She'll give it to you at graduation. All you have to do is read it."

"But . . . why doesn't she just read it, or you?"

"She said it needs to be you. It's what Connor would have wanted."

"How does she know what Connor would've wanted?" I know what he'd want. He'd want to give his own goddamned speech. He'd want to be alive.

"She said it has to be you."

Dad takes a plate and nudges the eggs onto it, then he stares down at the pile of yellow mush. He's thinking about all the eggs Connor used to eat. He's thinking about carrying a plate over to the table and setting it down in front of his other son, the one whose head will be forever resting against a satin pillow. Lavender, I bet. Or maybe they chose blue, blue for their baby boy.

"Okay," I say, because I can't tell him no, even though I don't think I should do it.

Connor worked his ass off for the honor of giving the graduation speech. I have a straight-C average and a piss-poor attitude when it comes to school. He got straight A's—in honor classes. I don't deserve to stand up there and speak his words.

I don't want to eat the eggs. They look curdled now, like they've gone sour just like my stomach has. And I don't want to give the speech. Einstein should come down from the spirit world and shove a graphing calculator into a stone. Whoever pulls it out is worthy to give Connor's speech. But it wouldn't be me. Same DNA or not, Connor was and will always be better than me.

I'm sitting on the stage with the principal, vice principal, and the school board members. They're wearing black robes with various colored ropes draped around their necks. Before me is a sea of green robes and caps dotted with eager faces. I'd watched them file in through the gymnasium doors. Some looked nervous. Others were flashing smiles at their parents or their friends. A few students, fellow members of the basketball team Connor led to State, looked up at the black scoreboard like it was a symbol of Connor's passing. Like the buzzers and the referees' whistles and the screaming coaches had all been silenced forever, because two weeks ago, Connor had been silenced and now nothing would ever be the same.

I'm not shrouded in the uniform of graduation. I'm wearing black dress slacks and a white button-down shirt. I was wearing a thin black tie about fifteen minutes ago, but I swear it was constricting my throat like a damn snake, so I took it off and chucked it behind the makeshift stage.

I hear a deep, rattling cough and know immediately that

our neighbor, an aircraft worker forced to retire early because of emphysema, is in the audience. A few days before Connor died, Connor came up to me while I was taking the garbage out, and we'd had a conversation about him. Connor asked me if I'd seen Dick Barber lately. I did what I always do when I hear our neighbor's name: I laughed. Then he asked me if Dick had wished me good luck at the state meet because he thought I was Connor.

"He did," I answered, causing Connor to grimace even though he already knew what I'd done. He had to, or he wouldn't be asking me.

"So that's why he called Dad and asked if I was okay." He shook his head. "You know you don't have to flip off *every* person who accidentally calls you by my name."

I told him I did. I absolutely did. But I didn't tell him that while gesturing "fuck you" was my standard response, there was a part of me that meant it as a thank-you because it felt like a compliment. If somebody wished me good luck at the meet or told me what a good job I'd done at the forensic tournament, or if someone simply waved and smiled because they thought I was Connor, it made me feel good. Made me feel like shit too, because I'm not Connor, but just knowing that somebody thought I could be . . . it felt good. But I didn't tell him that. I wish I had.

There is silence, real silence. There are hundreds of people surrounding me. Hundreds of people breathing and fidgeting and thinking. And staring. The principal has said something. She's introduced me, and the gymnasium has filled with the silence of waiting.

I stand, then walk, taking a second to look at my parents. They're sitting in the first row behind the graduating students, and while I know they want to give me encouraging smiles, smiles to settle my nerves, they can't. I reach the podium, look down, and start reading. It's typical stuff, at least what filters through the haze in my brain. Motivational, fortune-cookie shit. "Work hard and you can accomplish anything. Don't let the difficulties of life dissuade you from your dreams, blah, blah, blah." And then there's a space between paragraphs and a handwritten note. It reads *Find Kyle in the audience. Look at him. Don't say another word until he sees you.*

I glance back at the principal. She nods her head knowingly at me and smiles with trembling lips. I look up at the crowd of faces staring down at me. I'm searching through them, but for a second, I'm not sure if I'm looking for Connor or looking for me. I go back to the words.

"Kyle," I read, "I don't believe in regrets, at least most of the time I don't. I don't regret that we were born separately, because the truth is, if Mom had tried to carry us both at the same time, we might both be dead now."

Everyone is quiet, breath-held kind of quiet. No one fidgets against the hard chairs; no one fans themselves with their programs or turns through the pages to see how much longer this will take. Even the quivering cries of a discontented infant stop. All anyone can hear are the electric fans moving back and forth to aid the school's ancient air-conditioning system.

"I guess I do regret a few things. I regret that I didn't wait for you. I arrived on the path first, and I ran ahead, so far ahead that you couldn't catch up. I shouldn't have done that. To make it worse, being twins, I should have figured that people would always be comparing us. It was up to me to set the bar, and I set it too high—for both of us. There's always been this thing inside me, pushing me to be perfect. And once it started, it was like running down a hill, and you can't stop, because if you try, you'll fall, and the hill is so steep you know you won't survive.

"I'll never forget when you were in first grade. We were walking home, and you wouldn't talk to me because the teacher made you miss recess when you didn't get a perfect score on your spelling test. She thought that because we have the same DNA, we'd have the same brain, the same likes and dislikes, the same drives. But the truth is I *had* to learn those words. Maybe it's that oldest child syndrome or something. I had to get them right, but you didn't. You could have if you'd wanted to, but you didn't, and that's okay. Hell, that's great, as long as you know you could have.

"I regret now that I studied for those stupid tests. I mean, really, who cares if a seven-year-old can spell *umbrella* or a ten-year-old can recite the fifty state capitals? It doesn't say anything about who we are. Not really. If I had to do it over again, I wouldn't have taken Calc 2 or Spanish 4. I don't think I would have even gone out for track or football. Not because I don't think education is important or because I don't love sports, but because there's no achievement in my life that means as much as being able to walk the path with you. You are my brother . . .

and I love you." I say these words slowly because they are for me. They are mine. "Nothing means more than that. And to all of you out there who have ever called Kyle 'Connor,' and especially to all of you who ever judged my brother for not learning his spelling words or his state capitals or his quadratic equations, this is for you."

It doesn't say anything else, but I know exactly what Connor intended to do. I look out at the young and old and middle-aged faces. I take a deep breath and, with tears burning in my eyes, extend my middle finger to the crowd.

I hate doctors and doctors' offices. I hate needles, X-rays, and nurses who say this will only hurt a little as they jab giant syringes filled with radioactive isotopes into your veins. I hate being injected with something called radioactive isotopes. It just sounds like a bad idea. The dentist puts that lead jacket over you so your organs won't absorb the radiation from your annual bicuspid photo, and the cardiologist thinks it's a good idea to put nuclear waste right into my veins. Of course I'm reassured that it's not harmful; I just have to avoid using public restrooms for the next twelve hours lest I spray someone with my radioactive pee. Peter Parker gets bitten by a radioactive spider, and he can scale buildings. I get injected with the stuff, and I have twelve hours to stop bad guys with my *stream of death*.

The autopsy report, which took almost three weeks to get back, confirmed that Connor died of a heart attack. The report also showed that his arteries were clear. It was like his heart stopped for no reason. So now a machine is taking continuous pictures of my heart. It's just a precaution; Mom and Dad both said so. Just a precaution to make certain everything inside me is working fine. But according to the autopsy, everything inside of Connor had been working fine, until it suddenly wasn't.

This last test is supposed to take forty-five minutes.

The walls are a dingy green. The molding has been stripped from around the doors and the floor, and there are signs everywhere apologizing for the mess while they remodel. IT'S ALL FOR YOUR COMFORT the signs read. Do they think a new paint job will make people comfortable *here*? I feel like I'm in some sci-fi movie. Or worse, one of the docudramas Mom likes to watch where some beautiful woman finally meets the man of her dreams, only to discover he has a rare disease. I don't have a rare disease. I'm fine. At least, I'm pretty sure I'm fine. Connor was fine.

But there had been something.

Maybe if the skinny nurse with smoker's breath had pumped shit into his veins, he'd be alive now. Maybe if he'd been told to stay still, with his left arm bent over his head, for a mere forty-five minutes while a giant machine inched its way around him, they would have found something. A doctor could have fixed it, and Connor could have given his own speech at graduation, and we'd have made it to level forty by now and saved the Pentagon and the world from the zombies I can't stand to look at anymore.

But he didn't get the chance to have someone look under his hood to make sure his engine was fine. I may hate this room and this machine and the radioactive shit in my veins, but I don't hate them that much.

"**H**ey," Mom greets me when I get back from picking up an application from the Sak & Save. Since my tests came back all right, I get the pleasure of finding a summer job, and what could be better than sacking groceries?

I show her the two-page application. She glances at it, then puts it on the kitchen counter.

"I'm not sure I like the idea of you pushing carts all day out in the hot sun," she says, more to herself than to me.

"It's cool in the store. I'll be inside as much as I am out. It'll be fine."

"Of course." She smiles, then wraps her arms around me and hugs me tightly, starts to let go, then tightens her arms again. At night, I hear her crying. It's been a month, and she still cries herself to sleep every night. She has a job as a receptionist in an insurance office, but she hasn't gone back yet. I'm not sure she ever will.

Dad's boss offered him time off, but he didn't take it. He seems okay. He gets up, goes to work making airplane parts, calls home a couple of times a day to check on Mom, and spends every night holding her while she sobs. He cries too, but he's sneakier about it. He cries when he's mowing the backyard. He'll walk back and forth, his shoulders shaking, his hand wiping his face every once in a while. I'm sure he cries other places, too. Sometimes when he comes home from work, his eyes are red and puffy. Allergies, he says. But I know better.

I cry, mostly when I'm driving Connor's Jeep. Mom and Dad gave it to me, hence the need for a job to pay for the insurance. But sometimes when I'm driving, I look into the rearview mirror and see Connor. I think about how his hands should be on the steering wheel, how he should be the one picking music from his iPod to listen to. I keep mine on shuffle, and sometimes a song will play that reminds me of him, and the waterworks will start.

Mom turns her attention back to dinner, and I head for the living room, where Dad's watching the local news.

Another "Hey, how was your day?"

I don't answer, because the news is starting, and I know Dad wants to hear the leading stories. I'll tell him about my boring day during the commercial break.

Two guys in a dark pickup truck tried to abduct a ten-year-old who was walking home from the park with her babysitter. Another politician is being pressured to resign after having relations with prostitutes; he claims he was trying to reach a new class of constituents. Dad scoffs at that one.

"A girl collapsed during a youth soccer game. Seventeen-year-old Alexis Warren, a recent graduate of Bishop Carroll High School, was helping coach a team of twelve-year-olds when she collapsed and was later pronounced dead at the scene. Heat is not considered to be a factor. Apparently Warren, who would have been eighteen tomorrow, died of cardiac arrest, but the cause of death will not be certain until an autopsy is performed."

Dad and I are silent, then we notice Mom standing in the doorway. Her naturally pale face is bleached white; her mouth hangs open. She's still holding the wooden spoon in her hand.

"Honey?" Dad stands. "Are you all right?"

"Did they say Alexis Warren?"

Dad looks at me and nods as if I can confirm that he's right. "I'm pretty sure that's what they said. You know her?"

Mom leans her back against the wall and slides toward the floor. Dad rushes forward, catching her and helping her to the sofa. "Connor's baby book. Get his baby book," she says, waving her hand at the built-in bookshelves.

Dad gets the book and hands it to Mom, and she frantically looks through the pages of handwritten notes and snapshots.

"Here," she says, taking out a photograph. It's her and another woman, sitting on the edge of a hospital bed. Mom is holding Connor, and the other woman, still in her hospital gown, is holding a baby wrapped in a pink blanket. She turns the picture over and looks at what's written on the back: *Bethany Warren and baby Alexis*.

"How did you know her?" I ask.

"Bethany and her husband were carriers of cystic fibrosis. They already had one child who was very ill. Like us, they'd heard that Dr. Mueller at this new fertility clinic, Genesis Innovations, had a way of removing certain genes. That's where we met. We were both having our eggs harvested, and we were so nervous, so hopeful." Mom stares at the picture, at the two beaming mothers with their healthy babies. And now both babies are dead.

"Is that the doctor who 'tweaked' us?" I ask, seeing another photograph taken in the same hospital room, on the same day, only now there is a man in a gray suit standing beside them. He's medium height with broad shoulders and a long, narrow face. His beaming grin makes him appear to be as happy as the new mothers, maybe even happier.

"Yeah," Mom says. "That's Dr. Mueller. He made sure you'd be healthy. And then you, the fertilized egg, split." She looks up at the television screen, a new sort of horror on her face. "What did they say about her birthday?"

"She would have been eighteen tomorrow," Dad says.

"That's so weird," I say. "What are the odds that those two babies would both die within a day of their eighteenth birthdays?"

"A weird coincidence," Dad says, but there's something in his eyes—his slight, dismissive smile doesn't match the darkness gathering in them. "It's just a coincidence."

"Yeah," I agree, wanting desperately for the color to come back into Mom's skin. "Stuff happens sometimes. She was a soccer player. It was hot outside. She probably got dehydrated."

Mom looks at me, and I know what she's thinking. She's

thinking that she loves video games. That she loves that she's never sat on hard wooden bleachers and yelled because the refs said I traveled or double dribbled when I hadn't. She's glad that I always came right home after school, instead of going to football practice or running laps around the track. And more than anything, she's glad that I'm sixteen.

After dinner and an awkward hour of watching television with my parents, I head downstairs, not to play video games, but to get online. I have a feeling that as soon as I left the living room, Mom and Dad jumped online too. I wonder if they're looking at Alexis Warren's Facebook page. Probably not. Neither of them use Facebook, so I doubt they'd think of that.

She's beautiful. Her page is blocked, so all I can see is the photo on her cover page. It's eerie as hell. Blond hair, blue eyes, a soccer uniform, and a lean, toned body with one foot balanced on a soccer ball. She's perfect, the female version of Connor. Connor was perfect, physically and mentally. While Emma is gorgeous, Alexis Warren was . . . goddess-like. Put her in a swimsuit and stick her on the cover of *Sports Illustrated,* and she would look right at home amongst the supermodels. But I bet the other models didn't take trigonometry in high school, and I bet Alexis did. I bet she was a straight-A student.

I search Bishop Carroll High School and find a link to the school paper, and there she is. She's on the front page, standing at the podium, giving the graduation speech. The article says that she'd have attended the University of Kansas, where she had received both academic and athletic scholarships. An active member of the choir and drama club, she recently starred in her school's production of *Godspell.*

I do a search for Genesis Innovations Fertility Clinic, and three different ones come up. One is in Wichita. There is another in Arizona and yet another one in Anchorage, Alaska. When I click on the Wichita clinic, I get a homepage showing a mother and father cozying up on the sofa with their precious infant cradled in the mother's arms and the dad smiling adoringly. I almost expect them to be high-fiving each other. After all, they did it! They created life! With the help of "a highly qualified staff."

There are tabs along the left side for potential parents wanting information on financing and insurance, lab services, treatment options, and the ever-important testimonials. I click on staff and see a photograph of two doctors: Dr. Hodges and Dr. Preston. No Dr. Mueller.

I click on treatment options, then services. It talks about in vitro fertilization and intrauterine insemination, but there's nothing about genetic manipulations. There's no section on tweaking genes, on removing sequences for things like cystic fibrosis, or in my and Connor's case, spinal muscular atrophy.

I start another search: *genetic manipulations*. Lots of university sites pop up boasting research being done in various areas.

And there's a blog.

The partial quote starts off, "Are you genetically engineered?

I was, and I'm looking . . ." I click on the post. A photo pops up next to the title: Superior Beings Unite! The guy can't be more then seventeen or eighteen. He's got dark brown hair and blue eyes. What's up with the blue eyes? And they aren't merely blue. They're bright and deep, like the waters off some pristine beach.

His eyes are just like mine.

"My name is Triagon Summers," he says.

If I were a girl or gay, I'd be instantly smitten. I'd be sending him a friend request on Facebook and moving quickly from acquaintance to stalker. I can't help but wonder if his name is made up, a way to keep the would-be Triagon worshippers from finding his high school and setting up surveillance across from his locker.

"I wasn't created like most people. I was created in a lab in Wichita, Kansas, and I'm searching for others who might have been created there too. I'm great at sports, but I don't particularly like them."

I stop reading for a second. Triagon doesn't like sports. He could be a superstar at them, like Connor and Alexis, but chose not to play. I wonder what Connor's life would have been like if he'd chosen not to play. He told me the night before he died that after the game where he couldn't miss, he wanted to quit. It was too much pressure, and he was just a little kid. But Dad was so proud and excited. Hell, the whole town was. He felt like he didn't have a choice. When you're so good at something and people have such high expectations, you can't let them down. I wish Connor hadn't cared so much about other people and their expectations. I wish he'd spent his eighteen years doing whatever the hell *he* wanted. I keep reading.

"I love chess and foreign languages and playing Brahms concertos on the piano. I'm not trying to brag or anything. The truth is, I'm not normal, and it kind of freaks me out. Were you created in a lab? You might not know. My parents didn't tell me. Not until I wore them down with questions about why my brothers have hemophilia and I don't, and why I have blue eyes when no one else does, and why I can sing and play music when both my parents are tone-deaf. When I started searching for my birth parents, they cracked, finally telling me that while I am theirs biologically, I wasn't conceived the typical way.

"A Dr. Mueller from Genesis Innovations had contacted them. He told them he could give them a healthy child, and he did. But I know there's more to it. I'm more than healthy. Please let me know if you relate to any of this. Maybe you have some super skill. Maybe you're exceptionally good-looking. (If you're female and this applies to you, then please, please, get in touch with me!) But seriously, it's kind of lonely being so . . . superior. I'm not sure how else to say it. Normal would be nice."

I look back at his picture again, then open another tab and Facebook him. His profile picture shows him seated at the piano. It wasn't taken onstage, but in a living room, and he's hamming it up for the camera. His mouth and eyes are wide open and while his two hands are poised over the keys, so is one foot. He looks like a goofball. He looks like someone I'd love to meet. He lives in Nebraska, if his page is accurate. Went to Lincoln High School and will be attending Eastman Conservatory on a full music scholarship in the fall. Wow. I send him a friend request, then Google his name.

I bet anything that Triagon Summers was the valedictorian of his graduating class. His name pops up, and there it is—he's dead.

He died April 12 of heart failure. His father found him slumped over the piano. He was rushed to the hospital but never revived. He died on his eighteenth birthday.

Part of me wants to run upstairs and tell Mom and Dad—a big part of me, because they're supposed to fix things. They're supposed to be able to make everything all right. But I don't want to tell them, not yet. Not until I know more. To be honest, I don't think my legs would carry me up the stairs anyway.

I go back to Triagon's blog and check for any responders. There's one from "Anonymous," requesting that any genetically modified "babes" be passed on to him after Triagon is done with them. There's one from Holly Stephenson sympathizing with his feelings of isolation and saying that while she isn't "superior in the looks department," she has a "superior personality" and would love to get to know him better.

James M. writes, "Couldn't believe it when I read this. I'll send you a friend request on Facebook. Accept it. We need to talk." It's dated April 13. Triagon never accepted his friend request, but James M. must know that, because there's another response on April 15. It simply says, "RIP."

James M. Why couldn't James M. put his whole name? Hell,

what if *he's* dead too? It can't be a coincidence that three babies all conceived at Genesis Innovations have died. How many of us are there, anyway?

But it's got to be a coincidence.

There could be Genesis babies all over the place, celebrating their nineteenth and twentieth and twenty-first birthdays.

I go back to the blog.

"James, my name is Kyle McAdams. *We* need to talk. You already know about Triagon, but there are others."

I stare at the screen, at the words I've just typed. Then I slump back in my chair and run my hand beneath my T-shirt. I press it against my chest, against my ribs. I want to feel my heart beating. And I want to make sure it doesn't stop.

"**D**id you drop your application off?" Cami asks, coming toward me in her orange Sak & Save shirt. She looks good in orange, especially with the noon sun shining down on her. The summer is drawing out the freckles on her face, and they go well with the earthy tones of her hair and eyes.

"I haven't filled it out yet," I say, leaning against the front of the Jeep.

Her eyes narrow. "Why? I thought you had to get a summer job. School's been out for a week. There aren't going to be any openings left if you don't get your application turned in."

"I don't think I want a summer job."

She looks at me like she knows something's wrong. Shit, this was a bad idea. I wanted to call Emma, to have her go with me, but Emma's been through so much, and the last thing she needs is to hear what I have to say. I could go alone, but the truth is, I don't want to.

"Kyle, what is it? Are you okay? Why did you want to know what time I got off?"

"You probably have to go watch your brother, don't you?"

"Actually he's at his grandparents' for the next few weeks."

I nod a couple of times and watch some sorry-ass boy in an orange shirt trying to push a cart with a gummed-up wheel across the pavement.

"Spit it out," Cami says.

"I need to go somewhere, and I'm kind of nervous, so I thought maybe you could go with me." I rush the words and wait for her to come up with some excuse why she can't.

"Sure." Cami starts toward the passenger side of the Jeep.

"Don't you want to know where we're going?" I ask. We both get into the Jeep.

"If you want to tell me." Her hand lands briefly against my arm. "Are you all right?"

"Yeah," I say, honestly. "And no," I say, honestly again. "A girl died yesterday. She was the same age as Connor, and she was conceived at the same fertility clinic. She was fine one minute, dead the next. Heart attack. And there's another one. A kid in Nebraska. Same thing, same age, same clinic. That's three people, all dead, all conceived where Connor and I were."

Cami stares out over the dashboard for several seconds, processing what I've told her and trying to think of something to say. Finally, she looks at me. Her brown eyes don't look brown anymore. They look black, and I'm not sure if it's the absence of direct sunlight in the Jeep or something else, something like determination or fear. "So where are we going?"

I start the engine and decide that it's determination. "We're going where it all started."

. . .

"Shit." I start to duck down when I see my dad stepping out the front doors of the Genesis Innovations Fertility Clinic. That's really dumb, because there's no way he won't recognize the Jeep. But he barely looks up. His eyes are fixed on the pavement as he walks toward his truck. He's not carrying anything. If he asked for a photocopy of the files, they didn't give him one.

We wait for him to leave, but for the longest time, he just sits in his pickup. He hasn't even turned on the engine, which is crazy because it's June, and the temperature is already in the 90s. With the doors and windows shut, he has to be cooking without the air on. Finally, he starts the truck, and with a hauntingly blank look on his face, pulls out of the parking lot.

It's Wednesday, and the place is pretty dead. There's a middle-aged couple sitting in the waiting room. They're both, as my mom would say, on the fluffy side; the angles of their bodies are all round, except for the crisp shoulders on the man's blue suit. His hair is mostly gray, but hers is only gray where it's parted down the middle.

"I don't know if I can do this," he says, leaning close to her.

"I'll help you. You don't have to do it by yourself. Not that I'm sure you haven't done it a thousand times by yourself. That's probably part of the problem."

"Shhh," he hushes her.

Cami and I glance at each other. They look like somebody's grandparents.

The receptionist scoots her chair closer to the window. "I

think you want Planned Parenthood," she says. "This is a place for people trying to get pregnant, not for ones who think they already are."

Cami and I immediately take a step away from each other. "No," I say. "It's not like that. I was . . . my brother and I, we . . . That was my dad who just left."

The expression on her face changes immediately. "You're Kyle?" she asks.

I nod.

"And she's . . ." The woman looks at Cami.

"A friend," I say.

"Your friend can have a seat. Why don't you come around, and I'll get Dr. Preston for you."

Cami gives me an encouraging smile. A heavy wood door opens up to my left, and I step through it.

"Just wait here," the receptionist says. "I don't think he's gone in with his next patient yet."

There is a water dispenser in the wide hallway, and I take one of the cone-shaped cups and fill it. I down the chilled water, then smash the cup in my hand and toss it in the trash. There is a long, narrow table pushed against the wall. On it are pamphlets describing different procedures. I pick one up and open it to a picture of a couple holding their newborn. The mother is still in her hospital bed, and there's a large bouquet of flowers on the nightstand and a balloon announcing IT'S A GIRL!

I have to wonder if they wanted a girl. Our biology teacher said that parents can now choose the gender of their child if they have enough money. Doctors just isolate a sperm carrying the right chromosome for the desired sex and inject it into the egg. They squash its tail first. They do that so that the sperm doesn't swim around all crazy in the egg and destroy all the genetic information. By the time most sperm reach the egg, they're a little worn out from the race, but not these guys. They get sent right to the finish line, if, that is, they're carrying the right chromosome to determine the right sex. X for a girl and Y for a boy.

"Hi." The doctor is tall with broad shoulders and thick hair that's mostly black on top but gray around his sideburns. His hand is extended as he approaches in his white lab coat. "I'm Dr. Preston. I believe I just spoke with your father, Mr. McAdams?"

I nod and give his hand a firm squeeze.

"I'm afraid I'm going to have to tell you the same thing I told him. There's not much help I can give you, other than to direct you to Dr. Hodges. He's the only doctor I've ever worked with here, and he didn't start until after you and your brother were conceived. He retired about six months ago. I took down your family's information and phone number. I told your father I'd pass the information on to Dr. Hodges and have him contact you."

The man has a slight scar above his lip, probably left over from a surgery to fix a cleft pallet. I was born perfect. No cleft pallet, no clubfoot, but then, I've probably got less than two years to live.

Dr. Preston turns away from me, and I grab his arm. "That's

it? Did my dad explain the situation to you? Three of the people conceived in this lab are dead. They were all only eighteen. Can you explain that?"

Dr. Preston smiles and leads me farther down the hall, away from the waiting room.

"How many other kids were conceived here? How many are about to turn eighteen? How many have already died?"

He lifts a hand. "Your father told me everything. But there's nothing I can tell you. I wasn't around back then. Dr. Hodges barely was. He started working around the time . . ."

"What? Around the time what?"

"Look, I haven't been here that long. You really need to speak with Dr. Hodges."

"Where does he live?"

Dr. Preston lifts his hands, signifying his inability or unwillingness to help. "I can't give you that information. But I promise, I'll call him and pass everything along to him. He'll get back with you and tell you whatever he can."

"Call him now. Ask if we can meet today. I've got some free time. I suppose if I don't talk to Dr. Hodges, I could maybe . . . talk to the press. I'm sure they'd be interested in knowing how many people from this place have died. It is interesting, isn't it? Even if you weren't employed here at the time, I can't imagine a scandal would be very good for your career. Especially if there are lawsuits involved. Lots of lawsuits."

Dr. Preston has that look adults get when they don't want to give in. But I'm not asking to stay out late on Friday night. This is about my life and the lives of others.

"Fine. Just . . . wait here."

I watch him disappear down the corridor. With each step he takes away from me, I feel my lungs constricting. I bend forward, doing the whole head-between-the-knees thing, and try to take in a few deep breaths. When I stand up straight again, I'm dizzy.

I lean back against the wall, take deeper breaths, and notice a sign posted next to a door. LABORATORY ONE. I can't help myself. I was created somewhere in this building, stored for almost two years. I can't imagine any normal person wanting to see the scene of the crime, the place where they were conceived. I can't imagine a single person who would look nostalgically at their parents' mattress, amazed that this is where it all began. But I'm not normal. I wasn't created by nature. I was created by science. Not by some Dr. Frankenstein, sewing together corpse parts and zapping them with electricity, but I was created all the same.

Laboratory One is nothing like Frankenstein's castle laboratory. There are bright fluorescent lights and straight lines connected to more straight lines. There are machines, microscopes like nothing I've ever seen in biology or chemistry. I open a cabinet to see instruments sealed in plastic: petri dishes and metal tools, boxes of gloves and boxes of vials. Syringes and beakers. There are machines on the smooth, sanitized counters, with various sizes of holes in which to place varying sizes of vials. I don't know how it's all done, but in a weird way these tools are like my parents, or at least like my pre-conception nannies.

Dr. Preston opens the door, and, though I think he means to rip me a new one for being in here, he knows that I'm not messing around. I'm not touching anything. I wouldn't do that. I know how important this place is, how important this room is.

"Here." He hands me an address written on paper torn from a prescription pad. "You might give your father a call. I'm sure he'll want to meet you there."

I know the area. Wichita's only fifteen minutes from Rose Hill, and when we were kids, Mom and Dad used to take us to the ritzy areas of town to drive by old mansions decked out in Christmas lights that blinked to synchronized music.

"Science is an amazing thing," Dr. Preston says. "If it created a problem, it can fix it."

We watched a documentary in my science class about the nuclear accident at Chernobyl. The film showed the town where families of the nuclear plant workers lived. The place was completely deserted: apartments and businesses. They'd just built an amusement park, and the scene I remember the most was a shot of the Ferris wheel. The seats were hanging, suspended in the air against a blue sky. A radiation-filled wind rocked the rusted metal seats back and forth, like some ghost boy was throwing his weight around, trying to get his ghost girlfriend to cling to him. But no one was sitting in the cold metal seats. No one can live there now. The earth's population is growing like crazy, and places are getting x'ed off the map because science can't always tame the monsters it creates.

The doctor's house is a two-story square made out of gray brick. Branches of giant cottonwood trees reach out over the black-shingled roof. The spacious lawn is green and glistens from a recent dousing from the sprinkler system. Dad's already in the driveway as Cami and I pull in.

He looks like he wants to hug me, but seeing Cami, he squeezes my shoulders instead. "Good job getting this meeting."

"I can be pretty persuasive sometimes," I say, wondering how much he knows.

The house's front door is a glossy black. Dad lifts his hand toward the doorbell, but the door opens before he can push it. An older man stands staring at us like he hasn't merely been expecting us, he's been waiting.

"Welcome," he says. Dr. Hodges has a tan, slightly wrinkled face and wisps of gray hair hovering over a mostly bald head. There's a tan line on his narrow forehead, probably from the hat he wears to keep his scalp from burning when he's golfing or doing yard work. He's tall and slender and wears a yellow pullover with an insignia over the pocket, probably the logo of some country club.

"I really do remember you," he says, offering his hand. My dad takes it, and the two engage in a firm handshake. Dr. Hodges turns toward me. He focuses in on my face. "I remember you too, although the last time I saw you, you were barely visible to the naked eye."

He takes my hand in both of his. He lets go, but his eyes hold on to me for another moment.

"Come in. Come in," he says, his gaze finally breaking away. He smiles and nods at Cami. "I don't believe I know you, but welcome. My wife made some lemonade before she went out. It's horribly hot today. Looks like we're in for another scorching summer."

"Do you know what's going on?" I ask as we step into a spacious living room. "Do you know why my brother died?"

He shakes his head. "I don't know," he says. "Let's sit down, shall we? See what we can sort out."

There is a silver tray on the coffee table with a glass pitcher of lemonade encircled by several glasses of ice. Dr. Hodges starts pouring, but I don't want to sit down on his expensive sofa, and I don't want to drink lemonade. I want answers.

"What exactly did Dr. Preston tell you?" I ask.

He stops midpour. "He said that you and your brother were both conceived at the clinic and that your brother recently died. I'm very sorry," he says, looking at Dad, then back at me. "He told me about Alexis Warren. He told me that they both died on or near their eighteenth birthdays."

"And there's another one." I look at Dad, trying to gauge if he already knows about Triagon. He doesn't. It's obvious from the way his back stiffens in an effort to hold himself together. "His name was Triagon Summers. He lived in Nebraska. He died on his birthday, just like Connor, and he was conceived at Genesis."

Dr. Hodges leans back against the thick cushions of his sofa. "And there's Hannah Welch," he says with a heavy voice. "After Dr. Preston called me, we discussed what information we have about Dr. Mueller's patients, and I made some calls."

"Four Mueller babies have died?" The stiffness in Dad's spine slackens, like he's overwhelmed. Three dead kids were bad enough, but four is just too many. "Why? What's wrong with them? How many are there? How do we fix them?"

"Dr. Mueller disappeared almost eighteen years ago. He took all the files with him. I can't tell you how relieved I was, Mr. McAdams, when you and your wife called about having your twin implanted. There was only one frozen embryo in the lab, which was odd enough for a fertility clinic, but Dr. Mueller hadn't bothered to write your name anywhere. There was just a Post-it note on the outside of the cryopreservation unit. 'Twin,' it said. And the date it was created."

"What are you talking about?" Dad asks. "What about the other people who worked there?"

"Dr. Mueller started Genesis, and he was its only doctor until I came along. I met him twice before he hired me to be his partner. He seemed to be very involved with every aspect of running the clinic. Controlling, you might say." Dr. Hodges smirks as though, in hindsight, he realizes he should have known something wasn't right. "At the time, he said he'd just fired his nurse for being incompetent and had a retired woman working part-time as a receptionist. He said there was a private agency he'd hired to take care of billing and insurance. To be honest, I was concerned about what I was getting myself into. But I saw it as a great opportunity. Being part of Genesis was like a dream coming true. As a gynecologist, seeing so many couples struggling to conceive, I felt this was an opportunity to really help individuals achieve parenthood. But my dream job started off as a nightmare. Dr. Mueller disappeared the same day I started working there."

Dad shakes his head in disbelief. "When we came to have Kyle implanted, my wife and I were told he'd left, but no one said anything about him disappearing."

"As you can imagine, the clinic—which consisted of me, no records, and an unidentified embryo—was in complete turmoil. When you called about having your twin implanted, I thought about telling you, but you were so happy. So excited about having your second child. Genesis was finally starting to function like a normal clinic, and I guess I just didn't want to worry you when there seemed no point. The police had all but ended their search. Dr. Mueller had vanished quite thoroughly."

Dad stands, outraged. It looks like he's about to punch someone, but there's no one to hit. "So there are no records of what he did to our children? To any of them?"

"I'm afraid not," Dr. Hodges says. "The police asked for help after his disappearance. They ran a story on the local news asking anyone with ties to Genesis to notify them. Two families came forward. I had Dr. Preston pull their information. One of them lives here in Wichita. I called their number and told the mother that the clinic was updating old files. Her daughter is fine, but her birthday isn't for three weeks."

"And the other one, Hannah," I urge. "When did she die?"

"Her father answered the number I called. He and Hannah's mother divorced a few years ago. Hannah'd been living with her mother in Denver. She would have turned eighteen three months ago, but she died the week before her birthday. Heart failure, though there seems to be no apparent cause."

I feel sick. I feel like I've just stumbled off one of those cheap carnival rides manned by a sadistic chain-smoker who makes the ride spin faster and faster the greener the occupants get. I grab hold of a high-backed chair and try not to pass out or throw up. "You don't know how many there are? How many might have already died? How many are about to die?"

Dr. Hodges shakes his head.

"And after all these years, Dr. Mueller still hasn't been found?" Dad asks.

Dr. Hodges pours some lemonade into an iceless glass and downs it like it's a shot of hard liquor. "No, he hasn't. Of course the search would be easier if Dr. Mueller were his real name. The police discovered pretty early on that the name was an alias. His true identity was never discovered."

"Let me get this right," I say. "The doctor disappears, the files disappear, then it turns out he wasn't even who he was supposed to be?"

"It doesn't make sense. None of it. I know." Hodges looks up at us, his expression one of shared confusion. Then his eyes narrow. He looks at me, then at Dad. He starts to say something, then stands and comes closer.

"I read the article in the paper about your son, Mr. McAdams. And I saw the news report about Alexis Warren. When I talked to Hannah's father, I asked him about her academic and other achievements. It turns out that while she tested as extremely gifted, Hannah did poorly in school. Her father attributed this to her general dislike of conformity and organized education. He said she was an avid reader and writer, and that their mother moved them to Denver to pursue her talents in modern dance. He also said she was a very beautiful girl." Dr. Hodges looks at Dad. "No offense, Mr. McAdams, but you are a rather average-looking man. And Kyle is exceptionally handsome." He turns to Cami. "Would you agree?"

She bites her lips, and I know she wants to say that I'm exceptionally annoying. She meets my eyes for just a second. "I guess," she says.

Dr. Hodges sighs, no doubt frustrated by the lack of conviction in Cami's voice. It's not like she's a sheet of paper with lab results typed on it. She can't, or won't, confirm or deny his diagnosis about my looks.

"How tall is your mother?" Dr. Hodges asks.

"I don't know. Around five foot five."

"And you, Mr. McAdams. You can't be more than . . . five foot seven?"

Dad nods.

"It's odd, not impossible, but odd, for a boy to be—what, six two?—when his parents are well below that. And your hair. You and I, Mr. McAdams, seem to share a genetic predisposition for male pattern balding. But you." He brushes my hair from my forehead to better see my hairline. "Your hairline would seem to suggest that you will always have a nice full head of blond hair. And you have blue eyes, brilliant blue eyes, while your father's are brown. Could be that you inherited recessive genes from both your mother and your father, but if her eyes are brown, there would only be about a twenty-five percent chance of that happening. Does your mother have blue eyes?"

"Hers are brown too," I say. "But we all have blue eyes—at least Connor, Alexis, and Triagon did."

Dr. Hodges looks at my dad. "Did Mueller, or whoever he really was, did he ask you what color you wanted your child's eyes to be?"

A shadow crosses my father's face, making him look guilty.

"What about how tall you wanted your child to be? How intelligent? How about athleticism?"

"He asked us a lot of questions," Dad snaps. "But all we wanted was a healthy baby. My wife had already had *six* miscarriages. Then when we thought we had a healthy baby, we were told we both carried the gene for a type of muscular atrophy. We watched our son, our baby, die a slow, horrible death. We just wanted a healthy child. We didn't care if it was a boy or a girl. We didn't care about height or eye color. We wanted a child who would live. Is that so much to ask?" His voice cracks. "Dr. Mueller started asking us all of these questions.

We kept saying that none of those things mattered. We just wanted him to take out the gene that could kill our child and let nature take care of the rest. But I'll never forget what he said." Dad looks at me as if he's trying to explain why he did something wrong, like he's about to offer an excuse, a defense. "He said that nature had killed our first son, and there was a one-in-four chance that nature would kill any child we ever had. He said we didn't owe *nature* anything, so why not take advantage of his skills and show nature what science could do. With all we'd been through, why not give our new child all the advantages we could? Yes, we said we'd prefer a boy, but I swear, we were just hoping and praying he could get rid of the gene that might kill our child. We didn't believe Dr. Mueller could really do all those other things."

"Things like making your child tall and handsome and intelligent?" Dr. Hodges asks.

Dad looks at me, and suddenly he doesn't seem so ordinary, so average anymore. He'd hired a doctor to not only make his son healthy, but to make him superior. And Connor had been. So had Alexis and Triagon and Hannah. But Hannah sucked at school. Not because she wasn't smart—she just didn't try because she didn't like it. What about me? Could I get the highest GPA in my class like Connor had? Could I break records and win games? I'm superior at video games. What else could I be superior at?

"Dr. Mueller was manipulating genes," Dr. Hodges says. "Do you know how certain traits are selected today? Traits like having blue eyes or having a boy or a girl?"

No one answers.

"Fertilization takes place in the lab. Once the cells in the fertilized eggs begin to divide, cells are taken out and tested. The embryos with the undesired traits are discarded, and the ones with the desired traits are implanted or frozen. As you can imagine, some have thought this to be an unethical use of the genetic mapping of human traits. But what Mueller was doing . . . actually changing the genetic map of a human . . . it's . . . beyond what science could do back then. Science is still struggling with this technology today. Our mystery doctor must have been, and still possibly is, quite brilliant."

"He, Mueller, said he'd developed a way to get rid of certain genes," Dad says. "He assured us that it was safe and that we'd have a healthy baby. That was all we cared about. You want to talk about ethics? Bringing a child into this world who will suffer and die, that's unethical. That's wrong. He gave us not one, but two healthy children." His eyes fill with pain and tears. Dad looks at me, and I've never seen him so helpless. "He didn't give us healthy children, though, did he? Something's wrong with them."

"It could be that manipulating so many genes caused some type of unintended mutation. Where Kyle's concerned, we have to take into consideration that even though the others died on or near their eighteenth birthdays, Kyle was frozen for two years. This may or may not have an impact on how his body will react to any mutation."

"What are you saying?" Dad demands, but I know what he's saying. Being frozen may have done something to me, something that might make me live longer than the others or make me die sooner.

"We need to get the two Mueller babies that we know about, you and the girl, in for testing," Dr. Hodges says. "We need a full genetic screen for comparison. There's a hospital in Dallas that specializes in cardiac care. It's one of the best in the world. I'd like to send you there. I'm sure Dr. Preston will agree that the clinic should pay for your traveling expenses. I'll start making the arrangements. We can start the genetic panels right away. "Hopefully"—he puts a heavy hand against my shoulder—"we've got more time to sort this out for you. She doesn't have much time."

"There's at least one more," I say. "Triagon had a blog and this guy James M. posted a response to it. I'm pretty sure he's a Genesis baby, but I don't know his full name. I put my information on the blog, hoping he'll contact me, but he hasn't yet."

"We can put it on Facebook," Cami says. "Have all of our friends put it on too. It's a long shot, but you know how crazy the connections are. We get enough people posting that we're looking for him, he might see it."

"What about Emma?" I say, and mentally, I'm not in Dr. Hodges's living room. I'm on the playground outside the church where Connor's funeral took place. Emma is looking at me with those tear-filled eyes. Deep endless tears, like she'll never stop crying. Ten years from now, twenty, when someone tells her a joke and she laughs, those tears will still be in her eyes because she'll never stop missing him, just like I'll never stop wishing we'd had more time together, time to be what we should have been. "I don't want her to know about any of this. She'll see it on our posts, and she'll ask questions."

Cami nods. "We'll come up with something."

"We need to find whoever is left," Dr. Hodges says. "We need to get the genetic screens, then get all of you to Dallas. If you find out who this James is, let me know. I'll make the arrangements for everything else."

I couldn't save Triagon or Alexis or, now, Hannah Welch. I couldn't save Connor. But I want to save James, almost as much as I want to save myself. "I wish we could use Facebook to find Dr. Mueller," I say. "We still don't know *why* he disappeared."

"Maybe he knew something was wrong," Cami says.

"Or maybe," Dr. Hodges says, "he was done with that stage of his experiment. Maybe he just wanted to see if he could do it, if he could manipulate genes."

"But he wouldn't know if he was successful, not back then. Not when he disappeared." An icy feeling inches up my spine. "He wouldn't know if we were athletic or smart or good-looking back when we were babies. He'd have to watch us grow up to know if it worked."

Dr. Hodges nods. "And if he's alive and watching, he knows what's happening."

"Then why doesn't he *do* something?" I nearly shout, because he *should* do something. Like it or not, I wouldn't be alive if Dr. Mueller hadn't made me. Mom and Dad might have conceived me and Connor naturally, and we probably would have died like our brother, our lungs ever so slowly refusing to take in air, our hearts becoming as immobile as stone. Dr. Mueller, or whoever he is, created us. All of us. But he must not be alive, because if he was, he'd be watching, and if he was watching, he'd care.

Cami came up with a brilliant idea. She'd seen a post on Facebook about a stray dog someone found. That person posted a picture of the dog and the information from its collar. So we posted that I'd found a dog with a tag that said its name was Triagon, and the owner's name was James M. "The dog is old, maybe even close to eighteen, so we really need to find his owner. If you are James M. and care about Triagon, contact Kyle McAdams." I also posted Dr. Hodges's information on Triagon's blog site, just in case James M. checked it again.

It's been two says since I posted about the dog on Facebook. To be honest, I don't have that many friends. But Cami does, and so do her friends and their friends and their friends. It's crazy how the fingers of Facebook reach out through the borders of counties and cities and even states and countries. But nothing yet. If we've ignited any type of a fire, James M. isn't seeing the smoke.

I got up this morning, checked Facebook, and when there were no friend requests, I put on my tennis shoes and headed out the door. I never understood why Connor liked to run.

I've always hated PE, especially the part where we'd have to either run laps around the gym or go outside and run around the track. But I'm not sure why I hated it. It's not like I got out of breath or got that killer pain in my side people complain about. I think it was because I felt like people were watching me, wanting to see if I'd sprint my way to the front of the pack. They wanted to see if I was another Connor. So I didn't sprint. I stopped to tie my shoes a lot. Occasionally, I stopped to look at a cute ass. I didn't want anyone to think I couldn't run. I just wanted them to think that I didn't want to.

But now I'm curious. I want to run. I want to run fast. I want to see what I can do.

In the middle of town, there's a road that goes over a highway. The road slants gradually at first, then keeps climbing until it finally levels out for several yards, then slants down again. There's a sidewalk alongside the road. I jogged the three blocks to the center of town, and now I wait for the imaginary gun to sound in my head. Then I run.

I want to run fast. I want to feel my heart pounding. I want to feel it screaming in my chest. I want to feel blood pushing through my veins, forcing its way through the narrow channels like bulls forcing their way down the streets of Pamplona. I want to feel hot and sweaty, and if I'm going to die, I want to be the one to make it happen.

I push myself as hard as I can, willing my legs to go as fast as they can. My thighs start to burn as I near the top of the overpass. I fly across the sidewalk, oblivious to the cars moving beneath me, and when the road starts to slant, it's all I can do to put the brakes on before I sail past the stop sign and into traffic.

Shit! And I can't help but smile. That felt incredible. No wonder Connor loved it. I turn around, and without giving myself any time to catch my breath, I take off again. I wish there was someone, some coach waiting with a stopwatch on the other side. I know I'm not breaking a record. No one's ever kept track of how long it takes to run the overpass. But it feels like I'm flying.

I'm not tired. I'm barely winded, but I collapse in the grass along the sidewalk and stare up at the cloudless sky. I remember a day like this once. It was last summer. I'd been mowing the lawn, and halfway through, I stopped and just lay down in the grass in our backyard. I was watching a plane flying so high it seemed motionless against the clear blue, and then Connor's face was looking down at me.

"Come run with me," he said.

"I'm mowing," I said back to him.

"Yeah, it looks like it." Connor kicked my foot. "Come on. You'll like it. Hell, you'll love it. Just come with me."

"I'm too out of shape."

Connor scoffed. "If you get too tired to make it back, I'll carry you, okay? But you won't get tired. Come on." He grabbed my hand and tried to pull me up.

"I hate running," I said, and a little voice wanted me to add, *and I hate you.* God, I came so close to saying it. Really close. I mean, he wanted me to go running with him? Seriously? Yeah, right, take me out in public and show everyone how much better you are than me. Let them see me struggling to keep up with you.

"You've never tried," he said. "I'm telling you, you'll love it."

I jumped up then. I was hot from mowing, pissed that he seriously wanted to humiliate me in front of the whole town. Pissed that he was telling me what I'd love. Who was he to tell me anything? Mr. Perfect. Mr. Mascot for the whole fucking town. "You want to run, go run. Have a blast. But leave me the fuck alone." I pushed him away, literally. I put my hands on him, and I pushed him.

Connor didn't push me back. He looked at me. His eyes, those fucking blue eyes, trying to say what words couldn't. But I didn't listen. Why didn't I listen?

I stare up at the sky, the same blue sky. Connor knew I'd love running. He knew because he saw something in me that I couldn't see in myself. He saw that I was like him. And I pushed him away.

I feel tears slipping from my eyes, sliding down my temples. Then I hear a voice.

"Need an ambulance?" someone hollers from the window of a car that's pulled up to the curb. Teddy Eskew, school bully and X-Man wannabe, is getting out. "You in training or something?" he asks as I get back onto my feet.

"Leave me alone, Teddy," I warn.

"Leave you alone?" Teddy's wearing a T-shirt with the arms cut off to show off his steroid-enhanced muscles. He looks like he's been hitting the weights and the 'roids pretty hard. Large veins run along his inflated biceps. God, he's such an idiot.

He's going to have big muscles, testicles like raisins, and a liver more effed up than an alcoholic's.

"Come on, Teddy," a guy says. I recognize the voice. It's Byron Holt. He's a scrawny little math geek. He and Teddy had an arrangement. Byron would do Teddy's geometry homework, and Teddy would quit giving him bloody noses. Now it's summer, and they're hanging out? Maybe they bonded over isosceles triangles and bloody tissues.

"Teddy," he hollers from the window, "you'll mess up your probation."

"So what are you training for?" Teddy asks, ignoring him. "Are you trying out to be the next Connor McAdams?"

"I'm not telling you again, Teddy. Leave. Me. Alone."

He smiles, like I knew he would. And I ram my head as hard as I can into his gut. Unlucky for me, there's a stop sign a few feet behind Teddy, and between my head ramming into his stomach and the metal post of the sign ramming against his back, the contents of his stomach are cannoned right out of him and onto my back. I strip my T-shirt off and, without giving him time to recover, punch Teddy as hard as I can in the face. He staggers, avoiding the stop sign this time. He raises his fists like he's going to punch me back, but I nail him again in the chin.

"Stop!" It's a girl's voice. I hear it gradually drawing closer, but I don't care. It feels so good to hit someone, to hit the prick who's slammed my locker door shut and nearly severed my fingers at least a dozen times since freshman year. Teddy bends forward, and I'm about to knee him right in his face when someone catches me by the arm. Instinctively, I push the person off. When I turn, I see Emma fall to the sidewalk.

"Shit! Are you all right?" I offer her my hand.

She's wearing short shorts and a T-shirt identifying her as a member of the high school yearbook staff. I don't see any blood on her knees or her elbows, but I know I pushed her hard.

"What the hell is wrong with you?" she yells, slapping at my hand and getting to her feet. "Look at him!"

I do as instructed. Byron is helping Teddy toward the car. There's blood streaming down his face, hopefully not from a broken nose. The blow to his stomach has left him unable to straighten his spine. I think of all the times that he's shoved me against the wall or come up behind me and pushed my face into the water fountain when I was getting a drink. I've never gotten to defend myself against him, not without some teacher intervening first, and it feels good.

I watch Byron get behind the wheel and drive away, then look at Emma. The disgust in her beautiful eyes tells me that she sees what I feel: no remorse.

She starts back toward the clown car she abandoned by the curb, then stops and turns. "You have to grow up sometime, Kyle. I know you're dealing with a lot, but that's no excuse."

I know it doesn't make any sense, but I start laughing. I've never been in a serious relationship, but it doesn't take a genius to know that laughing at a pissed-off girl just makes her more pissed off. Still I can't help it. "Me—dealing with a lot! You have no idea."

She stops mid flip-flop stomp and stares at me. "Is something else going on?" she asks. "Something I don't know about?"

Her hair is divided into pigtails, and on her, it's actually a good look. But I hate the glistening of her blue eyes. I hate those ever-present tears.

"I'm fine," I say. "Everything's fine." I glance toward my barfed-on T-shirt and debate whether to pick it up or not.

"I'm glad," Emma says. "I saw your Facebook post about the dog, the one with the strange name? You find his owner yet?"

"Not yet." I don't have to fake a look of concern or disappointment at this. It's totally genuine.

"How is he? Such a weird name for a dog."

"Yeah, I'm guessing James M. is a science fiction buff."

She purses her lips in agreement. "What kind of dog is he?"

"Mutt," I say without pausing to give it any thought, then thinking better of it, "Might be part beagle. That's what the vet said."

"Eighteen, that's really old."

I want to say, "That depends," but I don't.

"There's something I need to tell you," she says. She takes a step closer, then steps back again when she notices that I'm not wearing a shirt. I know my physique is nothing like Connor's. I don't have his rounded pectoral muscles, and I sure as hell don't have his six-pack abs. But she stares at my skin, stares at the flatness of my stomach, and I can almost feel the ache in her fingers because they want so much to reach out and touch me.

I bend down to pick up my shirt but decide that anything with Teddy's puke on it is not worth taking home.

"That's littering," Emma says.

"So you want to lecture me about environmental issues?" I ask. "Don't worry; I'll eventually do my part to help the Earth."

Let me count the ways. If we don't find Dr. Mueller and figure out how to keep me from dying on my eighteenth birthday, I won't eat any more food, consume any more water, breathe any more air, or leave any more puked-on T-shirts or fast food wrappers where they don't belong. Oh, and I can't forget the whole feeding-the-worms thing. That really helps out the good old Earth. I'll become human compost.

"I'm moving," she blurts out. "I've got an aunt and uncle who live in Duluth, so . . . I'm moving up there." Emma looks at me, her eyes piercing mine as she waits for my response.

"When?"

"Tomorrow morning," she says.

My breath is gone, like an invisible Teddy just landed a lung-crushing blow. "Tomorrow? For how long?"

"I'm *moving*," she says. "Taking all of my stuff and moving to Duluth."

"No way. You can't move to Duluth. Nobody moves to Duluth. The people who *live* there never even moved there. They were born there and haven't realized they can leave. And tomorrow's the third. You're going to leave the day before July Fourth?"

"I can't be here anymore," she says. "I need a new start. I need to go somewhere different. Everywhere I go, people look at me like they're surprised I haven't fallen completely apart. The truth is, I don't know how I'm holding together. It's just too hard here. There're too many memories. Too many reminders."

I want to drop down on my knees and beg her not to go. I want to promise her that I'll take care of her. I can be Connor now. Really *be* him because we are the same. We're both "superior" beings. But I don't know where Dr. Mueller is. I could spend the next two years of my life running and studying and becoming Connor, and then once Emma loves me, loves me like she loved him, I could die too.

But I don't plan on dying. The arrangements are being made for our trip to the cardiac hospital in Dallas. The doctors *have* to come up with something. They have to. But if they don't, I don't want Emma to see Connor dead twice. I don't want her to go through it again.

I nod my head. "Okay," I say. "I understand."

She looks stunned and a little relieved. "I thought you would fight for me a little harder," she says, her cheeks and her eyes reddening.

Fight for her? Is that what she wants? It's what I want, goddamn it! But I can't. Not now.

"I just want you to be happy, Emma. That's all I want. So you're leaving tomorrow?"

"Tomorrow morning."

"What about your friends? How's Cami taking it? You guys have been best friends forever."

"She doesn't want me to go, but people don't always get what they want," she says in a hard voice I barely recognize.

"You're not taking the clown car, are you?"

Emma sighs. "Yes, Kyle. I'm going to drive all the way to Duluth on only one tank of gas, leaving little to no carbon footprint."

I've been to Duluth. My mom's uncle lives up there, and we went for a visit one Thanksgiving. There was a blizzard, and we ended up stuck there for a whole week. And Emma's taking the Smart car?

"Can I come by in the morning and say good-bye?"

She hesitates. "Will you wear a shirt?" Emma's eyes try to stay focused on mine, but they fail, falling for a second to my bare torso.

"Sure." I smile, or do my best imitation of one.

Emma tries to smile back, and I watch her walk toward her car, expecting that, any second, she'll turn to glance at me. But she doesn't. She just drives away.

It's only a few blocks to Emma's house. In a small town, every place is basically a few blocks away. I roll down the window and take in the smell of cut grass and the early morning dampness that skirts the front porches of old houses. Emma's parents are talking and glancing at their watches as I pull up behind her father's SUV. I take one last glance around the Jeep, and then grab the title out of the glove compartment. Emma is sitting on their front porch, holding a yellow tabby in her arms, telling him good-bye. She hugs the cat, kisses it on the head, opens the front door, and lets the cat tumble into the house.

She's smiling as she walks toward me in her comfortable traveling clothes—cutoff sweat pants and a T-shirt. Her eyes are puffy and red. She looks at her parents and nods toward the house. Her dad points at his watch, then follows his wife through the front door.

"Up bright and early," Emma says.

"I thought Cami would be here," I say, swallowing my emotions deep down into the pit of my stomach. Be strong. Be strong, but it's hard.

"Cami was over last night. We said our good-byes then. And it's not like I'm falling off the planet. I still have a phone and Facebook. No way you guys are totally getting rid of me."

I can smell the sweet scent of Emma's shampoo. God, I want so much to place a hand under her chin and lift her face to mine. I want to kiss her hello, not good-bye.

I hand Emma the title to Connor's Jeep along with a notarized bill of sale saying that my dad sold her the Jeep for a dollar.

She opens the piece of paper. "What's this?" she asks. She lifts her hands questioningly, so I drop the key into her outstretched palm.

"It's yours now. You just take that to the DMV in Minnesota, and they'll give you a new title. But that's legal, so if you get stopped for speeding, you can prove you own the car. And you might get stopped, because the Jeep goes more than thirty miles an hour."

"My car goes more than thirty. I'm not taking Connor's Jeep. Your Jeep." She tries to hand the keys and title back to me.

"This is what Connor would want. There's no way in hell he'd let you drive that . . . car . . . all the way to Minnesota, let alone drive it around *in* Minnesota. The average snow drift is three times as tall as that car. I doubt it could get through two inches of snow, let alone two feet."

"They have snow plows. They salt the streets. They know how to handle winter up north."

"And everybody owns a four-wheel-drive pickup. I mean, could you imagine trying to strap a deer onto that?" I motion toward the Smart car. "Connor would want you to be safe. That's all he'd care about, and you know it. This is what he would want. So, let me do this—for him." I say the words that will convince her, because even though I'd do anything for her, first and foremost, I owe it to Connor. I owe it to him to look after her.

"But what about you? What are you supposed to drive?"

I walk toward the Smart car and pretend to wipe a smudge off the hood. "While you're polluting the ozone, me and my superhero vehicle will be doing our part to save the planet."

"And what if there's a blizzard in Kansas?" she asks.

"First off," I point out, "if there's three inches of snow, school will get cancelled. And even if it isn't, I can walk. If I think there's any chance the snow will melt during the day, which it usually does, I'll just throw . . . Betsy here," I pat the hood, "into my backpack before I leave for school, then take her out and drive her home afterward."

"You hate that car. I can't trade with you."

I put my hands on her shoulders. "I don't hate the car. I love it. Really, really, love it. Every time I get behind the wheel, I'll know you're safe in the Jeep. So I'll help you unload the two shoe boxes you managed to fit into your old car and help you load up the Jeep."

Emma laughs and sobs at the same time. She wraps her arms around me, and I wrap mine around her. I hug her tightly because I don't want to let go of the girl who always looks back and smiles at me. She's so beautiful everyone notices her, but she notices me. Even being Connor's girlfriend, her eyes still kind of lit whenever she was around me, like I mattered. But they blazed when she was with Connor. I tighten my arms even more for Connor, because he can't hold her. His arms are pressed against his sides, or maybe they're crossed over his chest. I don't know because I never saw him in the coffin.

I feel her body trembling, and then she lifts her tear-streaked face and rises onto her tiptoes. I know what's coming, and I close my eyes. Her lips are soft. At first, they barely touch mine, but then she starts to press her mouth hard against mine. My lips give way to hers, and she tastes like mint toothpaste and salt. I want to let her kiss me, to let her pretend she's kissing Connor good-bye. After all, she is kissing his DNA, but the taste of tears is too much, and I pull away. She doesn't look at me as she wipes her face against her sleeve.

Her parents emerge from the garage, where I'm pretty sure they've been eavesdropping.

Her dad slaps his hands together and smiles like she's heading off to college instead of running away. "We've got a tight schedule," he says.

Together, Emma and I move boxes from one car to the other. Then I leave. I don't want to see her driving away.

Don's Diner has one specialty on the menu: grease. Breakfast is probably the worst. Greasy eggs, greasy bacon, greasy hash browns. Plates glisten with the stuff, and I'm pretty sure that the bottoms of the tables have drips of solidified grease growing like stalactites on cave ceilings. It's heaven.

Mom doesn't want me eating unhealthy shit. It's all vegetables and fiber and fish rich in omega-3's at home. But what else am I supposed to do? It's 7:48 A.M. The girl of my dreams is getting farther away by the minute. No bar is open, and they wouldn't serve me if they were. In two days, I'm going to be in Dallas eating nothing but cholesterol-free powdered eggs, and I still haven't gotten a friend request from James M.

If I can't drown my sorrows in bourbon, I'll drown them in bacon. And it's damn good too.

Mom will smell it on me, and the smell of grease will rile her up more than a shirt reeking of marijuana smoke would. I could lie, tell her I stopped at Don's for an unbuttered slice of whole wheat toast, but I won't do that. I won't lie to her.

It's just that I've come to the conclusion that what I eat

probably doesn't matter. Connor was a health freak. He ate flaxseed and tofu, and he died anyway. If by some chance my DNA is messed up and I'm going to die, I might as well eat what I want. I need something, something bad for me. Something to fill the hole in my soul, the hole that's growing wider and deeper with every passing minute.

I stab the center of an over-easy egg and watch the orange slime spread like lava over the glistening whites. I'm about to dip my buttered white toast into it when the door opens, and Cami walks in. She scans the tables and booths, a hopeful smile on her face that slowly turns to disappointment.

I take a drink of orange juice and wave her over.

"Have you seen Emma?" Cami asks. "She was supposed to leave this morning, but her car's right there." She points to the metallic green car that looks like a bloated package of spearmint gum.

"My car," I correct her. "We traded this morning. She definitely got the better deal."

"You gave her Connor's Jeep?"

"My Jeep." I say the words, but I don't believe them. It was never mine. It was always Connor and Emma's, and now it's just Emma's.

Cami sits on the other side of the table and stares at me. "You hate that car."

"I hated Emma driving it. It's not that bad, as long as I remember to feed the hamster that runs on that little wheel in the engine."

"Did you tell her about—"

"Hell no." My voice is casual, like we're talking about something trivial, something normal.

I offer her a slice of toast, and she takes it. She tears off a small piece but doesn't put it in her mouth. "It would have never worked with you and her. You've got to know that."

There is still a small mound of grease-glistening hash browns on my plate, but my stomach has put out the NO ENTRY sign. "Why? You didn't care that I had a crush on her when Connor was alive. So now that he's . . . gone, I'm just supposed to turn my feelings off? We could work. I mean, besides the whole 'your heart may have an expiration date stamped on it' thing. What did Connor have that I can't get?"

"Emma," she says, putting the toast down like she's lost her appetite too. "You'd never know if she was with you because of you or because you remind her of Connor. Every time she kissed you, you'd be wondering who she was thinking about. Every time she told you she loved you, you wouldn't know if she really meant you, or if she thought in some weird way, Connor's spirit could share your body."

I think back to this morning, to less than an hour ago, when she'd kissed me. "Sometimes you have to take what you can get."

Cami scoffs. "Do you know why I used to call you Connor?"

"To piss me off."

"No, but that's not a bad reason. I did it because every time you flipped me off, you'd smile. Not a big one. Barely noticeable, as a matter of fact, but still there. You never smile. It's like you're always beating yourself up because you don't measure up to Connor, but you're not Connor. The world never needed two Connors. It needed one Connor and one Kyle."

The waitress comes with the ticket. I reach for it, but Cami snatches it up. She shakes her head, her soft brown curls shifting against her forehead. "This one's on me," she says, digging in her purse for her wallet.

"Give that back." I reach again, but she stands and holds the ticket close to her chest.

"You're unemployed, remember. Besides, what you did for Emma, giving her the Jeep . . . And now you're driving that." She motions toward the car that only takes up half of a parking space. "That was an awesome thing to do. You're . . ." She looks away, concentrating on counting out the right number of bills. "Connor would be proud." Cami tucks an s-shaped curl behind her ear. "Feel free to flip me off whenever you want."

I don't feel like flipping her off. "Thanks. You ever run out of gas money for your truck and need a ride to work, let me know," I offer.

She leaves the money with the cashier and comes back to the table. "You know, I heard that boys who drive big cars are compensating for small penises. I wonder what that says about a guy who drives a tiny car."

I can't help but smile, and she gives me a "gotcha" look, like getting me to smile is her mission in life.

"So . . . I get off at eight," Cami says. "How about I come over after that? I know something we can do to get your mind off of things."

"I may be vulnerable, but I do have some self-respect."

"You wish," she says.

I start to say something, but then I see a man sitting at a corner table. He's drinking coffee and reading the newspaper.

Cami follows my gaze. "Who's he?"

"I don't know, but I saw him at Connor's track meet. He was taking pictures of Connor right before Connor jumped. I figured he was a scout from a university. But why would he be here now?"

"I've seen him at the Sak & Save a few times. Never buys much. Gum mostly. Occasionally milk."

"So he's from around here?" I stare at his down-turned face, at the dark hair that hangs over his forehead. His phone is sitting next to a plate of half-eaten pancakes.

"He must be. Why so interested?"

"I don't know," I say, wishing he'd look up from his paper and meet my eyes. There was something about how he'd looked at me that day.

"Maybe he works for the *Gazette*. You know how much they loved running stories about Connor. Or he could have been a fan wanting to remember Connor's last meet."

She's right. I know she is, but I keep thinking about Dr. Mueller—about how, if he is alive, he'd want to know if his genetic manipulations were a success. But there were so many people at the track meet. So many people were always watching Connor. And I wonder how many people went to watch Alexis Warren's soccer games or her performance in her school's production of *Godspell*. I wonder how many people went to hear Triagon play the piano or to see Hannah Welch dance.

"So I'll see you around eight?" Cami asks.

I nod, but I can't take my eyes off the man who doesn't lift his head to look at me.

I've spent the last three hours scanning websites for anyone at fertility or genetics conferences who resembles Dr. Mueller. He's probably dead. He was already middle-aged when he created Connor and me. But he might be alive. He might be out there somewhere, lecturing at conferences all over the world about genetics and what can go wrong if you try to tweak too many genes at once.

Between looking at sites for Dr. Mueller, I go back and forth to Facebook, hoping desperately the little person icon will have a tiny 1 over it. Then I check Triagon's blog. I look at his picture, then at Alexis Warren's profile picture, then Hannah's.

Hannah Welch was a beautiful girl. Of course she was. Dr. Mueller would have designed her that way. I can't tell from her profile picture if her eyes are blue or not, but I bet they are. She's sitting on a stage in a sleek black costume. One leg is crossed over the other and her arms are wrapped around her bent knee. Her pink-tinted hair is cut short. There is a diamond stud in her right nostril, and I can just make out a tattoo on her wrist: a small red rosebud.

I wish I could get past her profile picture, but there's no sense in sending her a friend request. I wish they had Facebook in heaven. I could message Connor, tell him I might be coming to see him before too long. He could tell me about the place, things that everyone wants to know, like do people eat in heaven, and if so, what's the food like? Are we required to spend a certain number of hours a day singing God's praises with the angels, or is God more laid-back? What is He like, anyway? Does He intervene in our lives? Does He give a shit? Does He just sit back and watch us like we're ants in an ant farm?

"She's pretty," Cami says, scaring the shit out of me.

"Fuck eighteen," I say, grasping my chest. "You're gonna kill me now. Ever hear of knocking?"

"Your bedroom door was open," she says, sitting down on the edge of my bed. "Is that Hannah?"

I nod and click to close the tab, but the obituary I'd been reading pops up. I move the mouse to close that tab, but Cami grabs my hand.

She leans forward and starts reading. "She had a scholarship to study at Juilliard. She danced in Paris last year. In Italy the year before that. Think what her life was going to be like. What all their lives . . ." She stops herself and forces a smile. "So, are you ready for a distraction?"

I close the Internet page. "Hell yeah."

I look through the window into the bed of Cami's small pickup truck. She's raided her uncle's firework stash, and I can't imagine there's much she didn't take.

"There must be two hundred dollars' worth of stuff back there," I say. "Is he going to be pissed that you took all that?"

"No," she says, pulling onto one of the roads that leads out of town. "Uncle Jimmy has tons more. He has connections, so he gets a great discount. And now that he's living with us, his disability check goes a lot further."

"Disability?"

"He was injured in Afghanistan. He's a marine. He got hit by an IED. Shrapnel went into his head and one of his kidneys. He lost his kidney, but they managed to save most of his brain."

"Most of it?"

Cami shrugs. "Okay, all of it, but he's a little different now. Sucks too, because the whole reason he went into the military was so they'd pay for his college. He didn't get the best grades in school. It wasn't until seventh grade that a teacher finally realized he was dyslexic. He got help, but by then it was hard to catch up. He wanted to be a teacher, one that wouldn't just assume somebody was dumb or lazy. He wanted to make a difference, but now . . . his mind kind of wanders, and he can be very animated when he's excited. Plus, he's got the standard PTSD."

I look back at the cardboard box filled with Blackcat M80's and odd-shaped containers labeled *Neighbor-Hater*, *Night-Fire*, and *TNT*. "Why would somebody with PTSD want stuff like this? Don't noises freak him out?"

"Jimmy did one tour in Iraq and three in Afghanistan. Tomorrow night, when the sky starts to darken and everyone starts shooting off fireworks, Jimmy will be out here somewhere. He'll be setting off his own miniature explosions. That way he'll be in control of the noise."

"You're sure he's not going to be pissed?"

"He's medicated now, so we don't have to worry. Besides, he hasn't killed anybody since that barroom brawl in Colorado last year."

I stare at her, waiting for her to tell me that she's joking, but she drives on for almost a mile before she looks at me and smiles.

"He's living with you now?"

Cami turns down a dirt road. "Yeah. He's been in and out of the VA hospital. He tried living on his own for a while, but it didn't work out so well. He's my dad's little brother, so we're helping him out. It's going okay. We just have to keep an eye on him. He doesn't always take his meds, and sometimes when he does take them, he takes them with beer. And occasionally he goes outside and smokes a joint and thinks that we can't smell it when he comes back in. But he's family, so . . ." She shrugs and smiles again.

We keep driving. Evening is falling fast, but I don't want it to. I want the sun to hover a little longer, to dig its rays like claws into the approaching shades of night and stay a while. I want to be able to see Cami's face, the strength in her brown eyes and her unwavering smile. She's already been saddled with taking care of her little brother, and now she's got her uncle to worry about too. And she's babysitting me, distracting me from the countdown hanging over my head.

"This is the place," Cami says, pulling the truck over onto

the side of Tornado Road. They call it that because of the 1999 tornado that took out half of the nearest town and a couple of farms. It's creepy as hell. The tornado was an F4. The trees still haven't recovered. In the winter, they look like deformed skeletons with various bones snapped and hanging. In the dark, with their branches clothed in thick leaves, they look like slumped, aging giants.

We start with the little stuff: firecrackers, fountains, and Roman candles. I love holding the Roman candles in my hand and seeing the baby fireballs fly out. Cami was so right. This is exactly the distraction I need. We light some rockets, lame ones that shoot out parachutes we can't see in the dark and others that zoom away so fast we have no idea where the hell they've gone. We find a package of sparklers that he must have bought for Josh. We light them and run around in the dark like we're five. We even try to write our names in light across the black air, but by the time the last letters form, the first letters are gone.

Eventually, we run out of the little stuff. We set up the hard paper tubes and start lighting fuses. Cami keeps yelling for me to run every time I light a fuse, as if she's afraid I'm going to do something stupid like stick my head over the tube to make certain the fuse really lit. But I do what she wants. I light the fuse, then run, and together we wait for the initial heavy sound as the explosive ball rockets high into the sky. We hold our breath and wait for the second explosion, the one that sends showers of blue or red or silver cascading over the black canvas. And together, we gasp.

We save the best and the biggest for last. It's slightly larger than a shoebox, and on top of it, there's a picture of a blonde with big tits and tight red shorts. Her legs are straddling the fuse. I know this one will be amazing. It's probably the biggest explosive a person can buy without being reported to the CIA as a possible terrorist. It will blast explosive ball after explosive ball into the air, and the force from the explosions will make our stomachs vibrate.

"Be careful," Cami says again as I bend over to light the fuse. It's a long fuse, to give the sucker lighting it plenty of time to back away.

The fuse ignites, and tiny, almost microscopic, sparks leap away from it. I run to the blanket Cami has spread out across the road and we lie down, our shoulders touching as we watch bursts of fire launch into the sky. It's so loud, but I don't care. We watch as brilliant lights spit and crackle against the darkness. They fall and melt away and are replaced by another barrage of sounds and lights.

Tomorrow is July Fourth. Connor loved fireworks and Dad's homemade ice cream and going to the park to watch the town's budget being blown into the sky to the sounds of Aaron Copeland music.

Dad won't make ice cream tomorrow. We won't go to the park for the fireworks show or comment on how much money the neighbors must have blown—literally—on fireworks. We'll pack our bags for our early morning flight to the cardiac hospital in Dallas and then try to sleep with our pillows pressed on top of our heads to block out the sounds of celebrations.

July Fourth will never be the same again. Neither will Thanksgiving or Christmas.

I stare at the black sky and the explosions of color, and suddenly every spark seems to represent a way our lives will be different, will be empty, because Connor's gone and he's never coming back.

My shoulder trembles against Cami's because I want Connor to be here. My chest aches, it burns like the tears in my eyes because I want him back. I want to see him and hear his voice. I want to let him drag me to the fireworks show with our parents because it's a tradition.

Flecks of sparkling gold fill the night sky and for a second, I think I can almost see his face. My shoulders tremble even more.

Cami doesn't say anything. She just slips her hand into mine, and we watch until the sounds and the colors stop.

"**C**an I get a few more towels?" I ask the man at the front desk of our hotel in Dallas.

"Sure." He smiles, then disappears through a door marked STAFF ONLY.

Usually when we travel, Mom and Dad get one room and Connor and I share another. Last year, traveling meant my folks and Connor going somewhere for the weekend because of a meet or a tournament. They didn't like me staying home by myself, but if it was only for one night, they'd let me. They weren't worried about me inviting all my buddies over for a beer-drinking potfest. I didn't really have any buddies to invite over.

With Mom, Dad, and I sharing a room, we need more than the standard two towels, and I am more than happy to volunteer to run down to the front desk. I love my parents, but too much of a good thing is still too much. We were at the airport two hours before our flight, which got delayed for another two hours. Then we were crammed together for an hour-and-a-half flight followed by a fifteen-minute cab ride. I'm so ready to breathe some parent-free air.

The phone rings, and the desk clerk appears again, two towels in his hand, but instead of handing them to me, he sets them down and answers the phone.

I turn and look around the lobby. There's a small area with four round tables where patrons, earlier, consumed their continental breakfasts. A flat screen hangs on the wall broadcasting the noon news. There's another closetlike room with a computer and free Wi-Fi. Next to the large window and the sliding glass door are three chairs. Only one is occupied. There's a woman sitting with her long, tan legs crossed at the ankles. They're nice legs, but I can't see what the woman they belong to looks like because she's holding up a *USA Today,* and it covers her face and most of her torso. I don't know why she doesn't put the paper down and *watch* the news on the television. She turns pages, and the charm bracelet on her wrist rattles. I catch a glimpse of blond hair.

The desk clerk hangs up the phone, then apologizing, hands me the towels. I take them and feel the hairs on the back of my neck stand on end. Someone is staring at me. I can feel their eyes, but when I turn around, the only new person I see is a tall girl wearing sweatpants and an oversized T-shirt. She's standing in front of a complimentary basket of fruit. She's holding an apple in her hand, shifting it from her right to her left to her right again as she stares at the apples, oranges, and bananas. I'd wager anything she's not thinking about fruit.

She's beautiful. Her skin is the oddest color. It's pale but warm at the same time, and I doubt any amount of time in the sun or under a tanning lamp would change it because this is the color Dr. Mueller had painted in her DNA. This is how he'd envisioned her—tall with a long neck, large, deep eyes that aren't blue, but are so gray they hardly seem real. Her nose has a perfect, level slope to it, and her hair, held against her head in a bun, is almost as red as the apple she's cradling in her long, slender fingers.

I can't help but think of her as Snow White's evil, beautiful stepmother. She doesn't look like a sadistic person who murders with fruit, but she doesn't look natural either. She looks like the product of some witch's spell. Her eyes turn to me, and she smiles. I can tell she knows instantly, like we're separated siblings, that there's a connection between us.

She tilts her head toward the hallway leading away from the lobby, and I follow her.

"So you're the boy from that little town outside of Wichita," she says once we're standing alone in front of a row of numbered doors.

"Rose Hill," I say. "Ever been there?"

"Sorry, I can't say that I have."

"Don't be sorry. It's not like you missed anything. The hot spot's the convenience store. As of June first, there's a do-it-yourself sundae bar. Hot fudge, caramel, nuts—the works. It's pretty awesome."

"Well." She smiles. "Ever since Dr. Hodges called my parents and told them I'm about to have a heart attack, they've had me on a strict no-hot-fudge-sundae diet. That's why I came down here where they have a wonderful assortment of healthy fruit. But . . ." She looks around like she's afraid her parents are going to come popping out of the elevator. "Can I tell you a secret?"

"Sure."

The girl, the Mueller baby from Wichita, comes close enough to whisper in my ear. Her warm breath tickles against my neck, but just when I think the words are about to come, she moves her face in front of mine and kisses me. Really kisses me, tongue and all. Then just as abruptly, she backs away.

"Can you taste it?" she asks.

"Yeah," I say, my mouth wanting more, and I'm not sure if it wants more of the flavor of chocolate or more of her. She's a damn good kisser, not that I'd probably know the difference, since I've never been kissed like that. Actually, besides Emma's good-bye kiss, the only other time I've kissed a girl was at Samantha Pritchard's twelfth birthday party during a game of laser tag.

"Besides a basket of healthy fruit, there's a vending machine. I crammed a whole Hershey's bar in my mouth and just let it melt there." She closes her eyes, savoring the memory.

Her gray eyes glint with tears, but she refuses to cry, and not a single tear escapes onto her cheek.

"This whole thing sucks," she says.

"What's your name?" I ask, feeling like I should know the name of the girl who just left a hint of Hershey on my tongue.

"I'm Amber. And you?"

"Kyle."

She looks toward the elevator. "Are you scared, Kyle?"

I nod. I am scared, I'm scared shitless. But hopefully if the freezing thing didn't mess me up, I've got some time for the doctors to figure things out—to find a way to save me. Right now, what I'm most afraid of is Amber. I don't want her to die. I don't want her parents to lose her and have to bury her. I don't want her dad to lie about having allergies and her mom to quit her job because she can't keep herself together. Mostly, I just want Amber to live. To have a chance to kiss lots of guys or, more importantly, the right guy.

She stares down at the apple, turning it over and over in her hands. "My friends were supposed to take me to Club Rodeo for my birthday. I still can't drink or anything, but . . . it would have been fun, you know? Do some dancing. Meet a cute guy. Do you have a girlfriend? I bet you do—I mean, you're gorgeous, but then again, you probably would have thought I've had lots of boyfriends, but . . . My friends say it's because I'm *too* beautiful. Boys are intimidated by me, or they assume I'm a conceited bitch, which I'm not." She bites on her lower lip in an attempt to keep it from quivering.

I get it now, the sweatpants and hair pulled in a mess against her head. This isn't just because she's lounging around her hotel room with her parents; this is how she always dresses. But it's no use. There's nothing she can do to make herself less beautiful. I can't imagine what she'd look like if she put on a prom dress, makeup, and had one of those fancy upswept hairstyles. Guys would worship her. They'd have no choice.

"Do you have a girlfriend?"

"Not exactly," I say.

She tilts her head back, shaking it at the injustice of

everything. "I finally meet a guy who doesn't have a girlfriend and who wouldn't be totally intimated by me, and I'm probably going to be dead in a few weeks."

"They'll figure something out," I say. "This is one of the best hospitals in the world. They'll find a way to save us."

She nods, but this time the tears come too quickly; she can't stop them. "Well, Kyle from Rose Hill, will you promise me something?"

"Sure."

"If I'm alive on my birthday, promise you'll sneak into Club Rodeo and dance with me. Be my boyfriend, even if it's only for a night."

I nod because I don't trust my voice right now. I have this growing cemetery in my head. Connor and Alexis Warren, Hannah Welch and Triagon Summers. I don't want Amber to join them.

She wipes the tears away with her sleeve, then takes the apple and tosses it into the garbage can next to the elevator. Then she takes my face in both of her hands and kisses me like she's Sleeping Beauty or Snow White and this kiss isn't just a kiss but a spell, a bridge between the living and those afraid to slip into that eternal sleep.

She goes to the elevator and pushes the button. As she waits, she wipes her eyes again. She has a huge smile on her face when the door opens, like her parents might be in the elevator, coming to look for her, and she wants them to see her being strong. I wonder if Dr. Mueller gave us a gene for bravery. I don't know if there is such a thing, but I hope there is.

I hate hospitals. It's only been three days, but we've already sunk into a routine of eating breakfast at the hospital cafeteria after I've had my blood drawn—no food or drink after midnight so they can get an accurate read on my blood sugar and triglycerides. Then we sit around the fourth floor waiting room, where we have a wonderful view of families coming and going in the parking lot.

Occasionally a nurse will come in and call my name. Then I'll have an EKG or run on a treadmill and get a CT scan. Then it's back to the waiting room. Down to the cafeteria for lunch, back to the waiting room to watch some horrible daytime television while we wait to see if my name will be called again.

I don't want to be poked or prodded or X-rayed or injected, but I'm almost happy when my name is called, because at least then the scenery changes a little.

I keep a look out for Amber, and I can't help but wonder if she's being held in a waiting room on another floor. Chances are she's having more tests than I am. After Connor died, our family doctor ran me through the cardiac wringer. This is all new to Amber. Last week she was planning her birthday, and now . . .

Mom's pretending to read a novel she picked up at the hospital's gift shop, but I've noticed that she never turns the page. She's not wearing makeup either. I remember when I was little, she'd never go anywhere without 'her face,' as she put it. But over the past month and a half since Connor's death, she's stopped wearing makeup. What's the point if she's just going to cry it off? Dad's holding a newspaper, but he's not reading it either. He remembers to flip the pages every once in a while, even makes a show of shaking out the creases, but I know he's not reading. If he were, he'd be making comments about this story or that.

"I'm going to take a walk," I say, because I can't stand it anymore. I can't stand the endless talk shows about food and swimwear and how to know if your husband is cheating on you and *who is* the father of the baby.

"We should get some playing cards," Mom says, putting her book down. "We can go down to the gift shop and see if they have any. Maybe they have board games."

"It's okay, Mom." I stand and stretch my legs. "I just want to walk around a little. I won't go far."

"What if they need you?" Dad says.

"Text me," I say, "or have them page me." That's something else I'm sick of—the constant overhead voice telling Dr. So and So that he has a call on extension twelve, and can Dr. So and So come to room 489, and Dr. So and So is needed in exam room seven.

I open the door to the hallway and choose, for no particular reason, to turn right. There's a drinking fountain, and I stop, even though I'm not really thirsty. At the very end of the hall are double doors labeled OPERATING ROOM FOUR. There's another waiting room on the left, where a large family is huddled together in prayer. I continue walking past patient rooms until a familiar sound makes me stop. It's the sound of a can of pop falling from a vending machine. I check my pocket for change and bingo! A can of sugary caffeine is just what I need. Maybe I'll see Amber there, sneaking another candy bar. Maybe she'll want to share the flavor with me again.

I follow the sound down a long hallway. At the end of it is a square room. The walls are a pale yellow, and there are no framed pictures or inspiring photographs hung on them. There is a long table draped with a white plastic cloth covered with a variety of donuts and a sign reading HELP YOURSELF. On another table is a row of coffee makers, two labeled regular, one labeled decaf.

I go to the freebie table first and pick up a cinnamon-and-sugar-covered cake donut. Then I go to the vending machine, put in my change, and wait for my can of Mountain Dew to fall like manna from heaven.

"Shit's bad for you," a deep voice says, and I nearly jump out of my shoes.

"Fuck." I grab my chest because I swear my heart has literally skipped a beat.

"Sorry. You okay?" An African American boy, close to seven feet tall, is standing in the doorway. He comes forward and puts a hand on my shoulder. "Last thing any of us needs is a premature heart attack. Premature being before our eighteenth birthdays."

"James M.?"

He offers his hand. "In the flesh."

I don't take his hand. He's close to a foot taller than me, but I go up on the balls of my feet and throw my arms around his neck. At first, he seems startled, then he hugs me back, even lifting my feet off the floor before letting me down.

"James M.," I say, giving his firm shoulder a pat. "I'm so glad to see you."

"So I gather," he says, flashing me the biggest, broadest, best smile I've ever seen. He leans over the freebie table and picks up a glazed donut.

"I thought you said this stuff's bad for you," I say.

He puts a finger to his lips. "I won't tell if you won't."

He's beyond handsome. His face is ridiculously chiseled. His jaw, his nose, his prominent cheekbones look like they were either formed by a skilled artist's hand or by God himself on an exceptionally good day.

"Sucks they're keeping us apart. Well, I guess they're doing it on purpose. Trying to protect our emotional states, I assume. They don't want us getting too close in case . . ." His eyebrows lift, and he sighs. "Have you met the other one, Amber?" he asks.

"Yeah."

"She kiss you?" he asks, his dark eyes narrowing.

I laugh. "You too?"

His laugh is deep. It makes the air vibrate, and when he stops, there is an eerie stillness because we know why she kissed us. Because there is a fuse two weeks in length burning toward a bomb that will explode and kill her. But there're people who know about the bomb—people who are trying to douse the fuse with water while others work to defuse it.

"I'm sorry I didn't send you a friend request," James says.

"That's okay."

"I was kind of scared to. Dumb, I know. It's just that I sent Triagon a friend request, and he died. And there was this girl I met at a scholar's competition. It was a daylong event, invitation only, and the person who most impressed the panel of judges won a full-ride scholarship to the University of Missouri. This girl, she was smart. Genius kind of smart. She got a perfect score on her ACT, but she said she basically cheated, because she had an eidetic memory. You know, where you remember every single thing you read."

"That could come in handy," I say. "Especially in world history."

James grimaces like history isn't his favorite subject either.

"So the girl?"

"We ended up spending most of the day together. Kind of skipped some of the competitions, but we both had our sights on other universities, so what the hell."

"She was one of us?"

He nods. "I wanted to ask her out, but I was kind of chicken, so I told her I'd send her a friend request. She accepted it . . . and then she died." James goes to sit down in one of the chairs, and I can't help but think of the story of Goldilocks and the three bears, because with his stature, there is no chair in this room, in this hospital, that will fit him just right. "I know Facebook isn't cursed, but guess I was still afraid that if I sent you one, you'd die too."

I open my can of pop and sit down next to him. With our legs out straight, his legs dwarf mine.

"I guess Dr. Mueller thought my parents wanted me to be a basketball star," he says. "My parents would have been fine with that. They put me in leagues as soon as I could walk, but I was more interested in angles and velocity. The aerodynamics of the ball and the force that propels it in any certain direction. Physics. That's my thing. Love the stuff. Got a scholarship to MIT."

"That's awesome," I say and hope to hell he'll get to use it.

"So I'm curious." He looks at me. "Is there something wrong with your parents—their DNA, I mean? That girl I was telling you about, Maci, Huntington's runs in her family. Her dad and her aunt both have it. I've got three brothers with sickle cell anemia. So what disease were your parents trying to avoid by trusting the good doctor?"

"Spinal muscular atrophy," I say, sinking into my chair. "Do you think it's the same way with everyone? Every family had something in their genetics they were afraid of, so they went to Mueller?"

"I bet so. Question is, how many families went to him?" James asks. "How many of us are there, and why are we dying?"

"What do you think?"

James bends his knees and props his elbows on them. "Best I can figure, he went too far. Maybe all the energy, the life force it takes to make us this way—superior, as Triagon put it—is too much. Maybe us Mueller babies are all born with a certain amount of life force, and around the time we turn eighteen, we run out, like a battery going dead."

The whites of James's eyes, and even their black centers, are illuminated. Maybe he's right. Maybe we're like lightbulbs, destined to shine brightly until we go out.

I hear a strange humming sound, and James pulls his phone from his pocket. He reads the text, then puts it back in his pocket. "Time for my treadmill," he says, standing and jumping from side to side like he needs to warm up. "Good thing I've got my running shoes on."

I stand too. "I guess I'll see you around."

He extends his hand. I take it, my hand disappearing in his large grasp. "Thanks for looking for me, for putting Dr. Hodges's info on Triagon's blog. If you hadn't done that, I wouldn't be here. If you hadn't connected the dots, none of us would be here. Thanks to you, we might have a chance." He walks to the door and stops. "And just because you're too polite to ask, I'll tell you. I'm seventeen years and eleven months old. Amber's birthday is in two weeks; mine's in four."

Four weeks. On one hand, a month seems like a long time for the doctors to figure out how to save us. On the other hand, I can't help but think that if Amber and James are the only two remaining Mueller babies, in four weeks, I might be the only one left.

I'm almost back to the waiting room where Mom and Dad are. A door to the left opens, and Amber steps out. She's dressed in a green hospital gown and the same sweatpants she was wearing at the hotel. She's headed toward another room, where her clothes are waiting in a locker or maybe on a plastic chair.

She starts to open the door but must feel my eyes on her, because she turns. "Hey." She smiles. Her hair is in a ponytail. There's a hint of gloss on her lips, probably ChapStick. "Come here." She waves me toward her. "How are you?"

"Okay," I say. "I just met James."

Her eyes widen. "He's something, isn't he? I don't think I've ever seen a boy so . . . statuesque. Or beautiful. But . . ." She puts both hands on my chest and pushes me against the wall, next to a sign that says CAUTION: OXYGEN MAY BE IN USE.

Before I know it, her tongue is on mine again, but this kiss is different—not as urgent. She's not forcing me to experience a flavor. She's forcing me to experience . . . an experience. This kiss is sacred, like the kiss given to a soldier before he heads off to battle, or the kiss of lovers clinging to each other as the plane starts to plunge. It's the kiss of desperation and longing and hope and death. I kiss her back as intensely as I can because this kind of kiss deserves this intensity, and because only a few select people in life ever get to experience such sweet bitterness.

When the kiss ends, she doesn't move away. Instead, she lays her head against my chest.

"I can hear your heart beating," she says. "I just saw mine on a little screen. It was pumping away."

I remember the echocardiogram I had back in Wichita after Connor died. "Did your heart look like an alien?"

Amber gives a slight laugh and steps back, her hands lingering for a moment on my chest. "It did. And not the nice kind of alien either."

"No E.T., huh?"

"No." She shakes her head like the creature from *Alien* had reared its ugly head on the sonogram screen.

"Getting tired of being a guinea pig?"

"I don't mind. I just wish we'd move from the diagnosing stage to the actual fixing stage. Maybe they'll tell us something in our big meeting tomorrow."

"I hope so."

Amber puts her hand on the door. "My clothes are in here," she says, matter-of-factly.

"Are they?"

"They are." She turns the knob and opens the door a few inches. "Ever have sex in a hospital?" she asks, and I know she doesn't want to have sex in a hospital. She just doesn't want to die a virgin.

"You're in a heart hospital, Amber. You're going to be okay. And a girl's first time shouldn't be in some cold, sterile hospital. It should be someplace romantic. Like the backseat of a car."

She laughs. "I don't suppose you have some roomy four-door parked outside do you?"

"My mom drives a minivan, but we flew down and took a taxi from the airport."

"Bummer," she says. "A minivan would have done nicely."

"You deserve better than a minivan," I say. I want to tell her that she deserves to be in love. She deserves a future, but it doesn't matter because Connor deserved a future, and so did Alexis and Triagon. What any of us deserves doesn't seem to matter.

I hear a sound behind me and turn. A woman is bent over, picking her cell phone off the tile floor. On her wrist is a charm bracelet—the same one the woman in the hotel was wearing. She looks up at me, gives me a slight smile, then casually stands and starts walking away.

"Hey," Amber calls after me as I rush toward the woman and take hold of her arm.

"Who are you?" I ask.

"Excuse me?"

"Who are you?" I ask again. "You were at our hotel. I saw you in the lobby."

"I don't know who or what you thought you saw, but it

wasn't me," she says. Her waist is thin, her hips narrow. She's wearing high-heeled shoes that make her body look even taller and sleeker than it is. Her blond hair is cut short. She looks like a character in a video game, like she should be holding a sniper rifle, and if I had a gun and could shoot her, her body would disappear and come back somewhere else in the video game arena.

"So you work for the hospital?" I ask.

Her red lips curve in a smile, but it's not a pleasant one. "I'd say that's obvious."

"Then you won't mind showing me your hospital ID."

She scoffs. "I don't have to show you anything. Now, would you mind letting me get back to work?" She starts walking away.

"I suppose hospital security can tell me who you are."

"Wow." She stops. "Maybe I should call security and tell them that a patient with an obvious paranoia problem is running around the hospital, making wild accusations."

It's time for my eyes to narrow. "What makes you think I'm a patient?" I lift my wrists to show that I'm not wearing a hospital bracelet; we only get issued those when we're about to have a test of some sort, and so far today, I'm test free. "Do I look like a patient? I mean, this is a heart hospital. How do you know I'm not visiting my grandfather or something?"

Our heads both turn at the same time. There wasn't any noise. No cry for help, no gasping for air. It was the movement, the way Amber had been standing there one minute, watching us, and falling to the floor the next that caught our attention.

"Amber!" I scream, running toward her. "Help! Somebody, help!"

Almost instantly there are people everywhere, pushing me out of the way and yelling for help. They pick her up and carry her into the room she'd just come from, and more people arrive pushing carts with machines on them.

A middle-aged couple comes running down the hall, the man's arms wrapped around the woman, like he's holding her up or he's using her stout figure to steady himself. The woman has red hair, not the same brilliant red as her daughter's, but red. That's the only similarity. Neither of Amber's parents is tall. Neither gives any hint of having been beautiful or handsome in their youth. But of course right now, they don't look their best. How could they when they know their daughter is dying or is already dead?

I look down the hall, toward the woman with the bracelet who had known I was a patient. She's on her phone, talking to someone as she steps into the elevator and disappears.

They have us assembled in a meeting room with several round tables and a podium near a projector screen at the front of the room. I recognize Dr. Preston from the fertility clinic and one of the cardiologists who's examined me a couple of times since I got here. His name is . . . I can't remember, but I'm sure once things get rolling, he'll introduce himself.

James walks in with his parents. He and I look at each other, but not for long; it's too hard. We both kissed the same girl, the girl who died two weeks before her eighteenth birthday. It's so unfair. She was supposed to have two weeks left. At least that! Maybe it has to do with how brightly we burn, like James said. Amber was so beautiful, so exceptional that her energy, her light, went out faster than everyone else's. And if that's true, James can't live much longer. Unless they've come up with a cure.

Dr. Preston stands. "I know you've been patiently waiting for answers, so I won't draw this out. You've all met Dr. Fabos."

Dr. Fabos. That's right. I remember thinking that his name

seemed like a nickname, short for Fabulous, and I'd hoped he was fabulous. But with Amber gone, now I'm thinking he's not.

The middle-aged man with silver hair and black-framed glasses stands in front of us. "Let me start by saying how pained we are that we were unable to save our other patient. My staff and I didn't have the pleasure of knowing her for very long, but in that short period, she touched all of us." He pauses respectfully for a moment. "Her autopsy results show no abnormalities of the heart, no blockage in the arteries. These findings are consistent with the other autopsy reports we've studied." His voice is so mechanical, like he's reading off data to a group of investors. But then he catches himself. He isn't reading numbers or random lab results. One of the autopsies he's referring to is my brother's, and one report is from the patient he regrets not being able to save. Dr. Fabos looks at my parents, at James's, and I see a hint of an apology in his expression.

"Couldn't you have done something?" James asks. "For Christ's sake, she was here at the hospital! And you couldn't save her?" His large hands curl into fists.

Dr. Fabos looks at James. "We tried everything we could: CPR, defibrillation. We even placed her on a ventilator, but . . . Let me introduce Dr. Lee. He's an expert on genetics. He can tell you more."

The medium-sized Asian man with glossy black hair stands and stares first at James, then at me, his expression a mixture of grief and fascination. He straightens his white coat and inhales deeply, as if readying himself to give a long speech.

"We completed mapping out the genetic sequences for each of the known children conceived during the period of time when Dr. Mueller was at the clinic. We were looking for a similar trait, a genetic sequence that you all have. Something that could explain why hearts that seem to be functioning normally just stop. And we think we found it."

"Can you fix them?" Dad demands. "If you know where the mutations are, can you fix them?"

We all stare, breaths held.

"You have to understand—"

"Can you fix them?" Dad says again. His words are hard and exact, but no one could fail to hear the fragility in his voice.

"Not exactly," Dr. Lee says.

"Please." It's Mrs. Monroe, James's mother. She's a small woman. Her delicate features seem even more delicate for the word she's saying. She seems hollow somehow, and if the doctors can't fix her son, her one healthy son, she'll collapse into something small enough for the wind to carry away. "Can't you just . . . manipulate them back?"

"Genes are made up of DNA. DNA is made up of sequences of chemicals. It's these chemicals that have somehow mutated into something I've never seen before. Science has mapped out the entire human genome. We've identified sequences for left-handedness, depression, certain types of cancer. There's even a genetic sequence associated with being a serial killer, but *this* is something we've never seen before. We think that for some reason, this particular strand of DNA causes sudden and catastrophic heart failure at approximately the age of eighteen."

"Then take it out." This time it's my mom pleading for a solution.

"I'm afraid it's not possible, Mrs. McAdams."

"But Dr. Mueller took out the bad genes," she says. "Take out this one."

Dr. Lee smiles sympathetically. "When Dr. Mueller modified your son's genetic makeup, he was a fertilized egg—a zygote—consisting of a few cells. As a fully-formed human, he consists of approximately forty trillion cells. Every cell, except certain blood cells, carries a person's genetic makeup, their DNA. To get rid of this sequence means changing the DNA of every cell in the body. I'm afraid that's impossible. If we had Dr. Mueller's notes, if we knew exactly what he'd done to manipulate so many genes, we might be able to find a way to 'turn off' the sequence. But we don't."

"Dr. Lee," James says, "where did this sequence come from? And if you can't change it or turn it off, can you save us?"

"Yes," Dr. Lee says. "I'll let Dr. Fabos explain that in a moment, but as far as knowing where the sequence came from, our best hypothesis is that it's some form of a mutation caused by the number of genetic manipulations Dr. Mueller performed on each of you. Simply removing a gene for sickle cell anemia or cystic fibrosis would most likely not have caused such a mutation, but he wasn't merely removing genes, he was manipulating them, designing all of you to have specific traits."

"However," Dr. Fabos says, stepping forward, "just because we can't change the genetic structure doesn't mean we can't do *something*."

"What?" James's father stands now. "What are you going to do?"

Dr. Fabos lifts his hands in what is meant to be a calming gesture. "We insert a pacemaker. It will regulate the heart's electrical system, and when this genetic sequence tells the heart to stop, the pacemaker will send a precise electrical signal to the heart to keep it going."

"How dangerous is it?" Mom asks.

"It's a minimally invasive surgery, just local anesthesia. It takes less than an hour to perform, and believe me, dozens of these operations are performed every day here at the hospital. A small incision is made next to the collarbone. Using an X-ray, a wire is inserted through a vein and guided into the heart. The wire is attached to a small computer called a generator. We use the incision to form a pocket that holds the generator. Close up the incision, and it's done. Once the"—he stumbles for the right word—"critical period is over, we can decide whether or not the pacemaker needs to remain, based on monitoring the information from the device. This can be done at your cardiologist's office, or even using a phone that has a special transmitter attached to it. You just hold the phone up to the generator, and it will transfer information using the internet."

"So it will keep my heart from stopping or get it going again if it does stop?" James asks.

"That's the idea," Dr. Fabos says.

James's back stiffens. He looks at his parents, at the petite woman who gave birth to him. Then he looks at his father, who by normal standards is tall and broad and handsome for his age. But next to his extraordinary son, Mr. Monroe is unimpressive.

"And if it doesn't work?" James asks.

I'm the only one looking at James. No one else will meet his eyes, not even his parents. We all know the answer to his question. If this doesn't work, if the generator doesn't provide enough electricity or doesn't provide it at the exact moment when it's needed, he'll die.

I come out of the hotel bathroom, and Dad shoots me a look like he's wondering if the super-healthy diet I'm on is making me constipated. I don't want to tell him that I'm texting Cami and that together, we're scouring the internet for anyone who might be our mysterious Dr. Mueller.

"You okay?" Dad asks. Mom stops, a white hotel towel in her hand. Her face floods with concern.

"I'm fine." I pat my stomach. "Too much whole wheat toast."

They give each other a reassuring nod, and Mom resumes shaking out towels and peeking under the beds to make sure we don't leave anything behind.

"You want to go keep an eye out for the taxi?" Dad asks as he tries to get the zipper to close around the suitcase. "We'll be down in a few minutes."

"Sure," I say, happy to have a minute by myself somewhere other than the bathroom. We've pretty much been glued together since we got here. It wouldn't be so bad, might have even been kind of nice, if it weren't for the strangeness of it all. They keep smiling, being positive. Their son, their last son, is not going to die like their other two. God, wouldn't be that cruel—but then again, what's God got to do with me?

The humidity is awful. The air is thick, and moisture clings to my skin as soon as I step outside. Dark, heavy clouds from a late-night storm linger indecisively in the sky. A jackass father yells at his kids to hurry up as they drag animal-shaped pillows across the parking lot. He looks like he might pop them one if they don't hurry up, and the little boy and girl look like they know it, like they've felt the sting of the back of his hand before. He drops his suitcase next to an SUV and grabs the little girl by her arm, yanking her. A woman comes out of the lobby holding two paper plates with donuts on them in one hand and a bottle of apple juice in the other. Evidently, the asshole is in too big of a hurry to let his kids finish their free continental breakfast.

I shake my head and exhale deeply, as if my breath is steam and if I don't let it out, I'll explode. I take my phone, ready to video this jerk if he decides to backhand one of his kids or his wife. Then I'll call 911 and with a shot of his license plate, his stay in the great state of Texas might be extended for a day or two or a month. I lift my phone, then he looks at me. I act like I'm checking for a signal and turn away. That's when the image of a different man, a man taking pictures of me from less than twenty feet away, fills my screen—the same guy who was taking pictures of Connor at the track meet.

"Hey," I yell after the guy. "Hey." I move toward him, and he takes off running. I don't think; I just run. I'm going to catch him and take his phone. How many pictures of me has he taken? When did he start? Was it right after Connor died? Take pictures of Connor and then once he's gone, move on to his brother? Why? Because Dr. Mueller is paying him to? Making sure his experiments have turned out the way they're supposed to?

There's a steep ditch between the hotel parking lot and a busy intersection. He stumbles a little in the mud, but I manage to keep my footing. He's just a few feet ahead of me, and with a slight break in traffic, he dashes across the two lanes of vehicles heading west. He stays in the median for a second, wondering, no doubt, if I have the balls to keep chasing. I do. I wait for a metro bus, a black pickup truck, and a Mustang to pass before I make a move. The man checks the eastbound traffic and starts across the next two lanes. He makes it and pauses in the far lane to look back at me.

A car honks, and I jump back onto the grass shoulder. Damn it! I wait for a break in traffic and run to the median. There's a string of cars, and I'm watching as he runs in front of a row of two-story industrial buildings. I get across the first lane, wait for a UPS truck, then cross the last lane and start after him. He's maybe a quarter of a block in front of me, and he's so fucking fast! But I'm going to catch him. I'm going to find out who he is, and if he works for Dr. Mueller, I'm going to—

He turns down an alley between buildings but then I see him again, only this time, he's not running, he's flying, then falling onto the wet pavement in the center of the street. The brakes of the delivery truck that hit him are making a horrible screeching sound. Then I hear more brakes as a car tries to stop, the driver wrenching the wheel. She's trying not to hit the man who has already been hit, but she can't stop in time. The car pitches sideways, the rear tires running over his midsection. So much movement. So much chaos, and then time just stops. The woman in the car, the man in the truck, we're all motionless until some inaudible buzzer sounds, and we move, each of us running toward the man in the street.

"Oh my God!" the woman says. "Oh my God!"

"Call 911!" the truck driver tells her as he leans over the man, and the woman runs back to her car for her phone. "What was he doing? He just ran in front of me. Did you see it?" he asks as I kneel down.

I nod, staring at the man with dark hair and an athletic build who'd looked at me at the track meet, who'd been eating breakfast in the diner back home. "Help's coming," I tell him, but I don't think it matters. Blood is pooling underneath his head, and one side of his chest is lower than the other, like his ribs have been crushed against his lungs. He's struggling to breathe, and a strange whistling sound comes with each attempt.

"My pocket," he wheezes. "Take it."

A horn honks as more tires squeal. The truck driver rushes toward the approaching traffic, yelling for people to stop, yelling that there's been an accident, because people are too goddamned blind to notice.

I reach into the pocket of the man's jeans and take out his cell phone. He knows he's dying. "Help will be here soon," I say, because I've had enough of death. I'm sick of death. I'm so fucking sick of it! "You have to hold on, okay? Just hold on."

His hand grips my arm. "He needs to know where they die. Where the body is taken. Needs to access the autopsy reports." The man coughs, spraying droplets of blood into the air.

"You're watching me so you'll know where I die? So Mueller knows where the autopsy will be done?"

He doesn't nod, but he doesn't have to.

"But I'm only sixteen. I've got two years left."

He coughs again, tries to shake his head, then moans. "You don't," he says. "He made you different. You won't make it to seventeen."

Blood starts to pool in his mouth. He coughs, chokes. He looks at me, and it's so strange, because I see sympathy in his brown eyes, because even though he's dying, he's made it into his twenties, maybe even his early thirties, but I won't. I won't make it to seventeen. That's what he said. Those were his last words; now he's not looking at me anymore. He's not looking at anything, and the harsh whistling sound coming from his chest has stopped.

I told the police the truth, most of it anyway. I told them that I'd seen the guy—Scott Stiles, according to his driver's license—in the parking lot. I left out the part about him taking my picture, because I also left out the part about me taking his phone. I've seen enough cop shows to know that everything ends up in evidence, and luckily, the delivery truck driver was so concerned with not being blamed for the accident, he didn't seem to remember anything after hitting the guy, and the lady, in shock, hadn't been able to find her cell phone and ended up calling 911 from inside one of the buildings. I doubt she told the police much of anything.

I told them that I was concerned because I'd seen this man back in Kansas at my brother's meet and at the restaurant, and considering everything going on with our missing Dr. Mueller, I wanted to talk to him, to see if it was just a coincidence that he was in Dallas. But when I approached him, he started running so I followed. The detective showed Mom and Dad his driver's license, and Dad remembered seeing him at the meet.

We missed our flight back home, and the police took our

information in case more questions came up. They seemed satisfied, and we took a later flight. By plane, it's not far from Dallas to Wichita. I managed to hide out in the restroom for a few minutes to look at the pictures on Scott Stiles's phone. Almost everything on the phone required a passcode to access, but the last pictures he'd taken hadn't been saved to a file yet.

There are five pictures. One is of me walking through the hotel lobby. Then there's me walking through the lobby door, then standing in the parking lot. Next, I'm looking totally pissed off at the guy being an ass to his family. And the last picture Scott Stiles ever took was of me looking at him through my phone.

Everything else is locked away. I can't even access his contact page or text messages. It sucks because I know he was working for Mueller. His contact information must be on the phone, but I can't get to it. And then there's that thing he said, the thing I didn't share with my parents.

He made you different. You won't make it to seventeen.

What exactly does that mean? The doctors did a complete genetic panel. They'd found the sequence—the death sequence—but mine was the same as everyone else's, and they lived past seventeen. How am I different? And what did he mean by *made*? The doctors think the sequence is a mutation—an accident. But Scott Stiles said I was *made* differently. Did Mueller intend for us to die? He couldn't. Maybe he needs the autopsy reports to help him figure out *why* we're dying. But Stiles said "made." Maybe Mueller knows exactly why we're dying. Maybe he just wants the autopsy reports to verify it.

Dr. Lee said that if they had Dr. Mueller's records, there might be a way to save us. I have the phone. Maybe it can help me find Dr. Mueller and his records. It has to, because I don't want to die, and because I have to know what he did to us.

Before I go to bed, I search through my high school yearbook, looking for anyone voted most likely to hack into a government agency's database or maybe a huge bank's vault. We have a few geeks at our school, but being in rural Kansas, I'd have a lot more luck finding someone with an expertise in barrel racing or bull riding.

There has to be someone who can hack into a phone, and I need to find whoever it is fast. My seventeenth birthday is in less than six months . . . *You won't make it to seventeen.*

I close my eyes and try to replace the bloodied face of Scott Stiles with thoughts of James. Tomorrow he'll get his pacemaker. It'll work. James will make it past eighteen, and I'll make it past seventeen.

Cami's truck is parked in the driveway. Her house is a nice, standard ranch, like almost every other house in town. There's a flower bed trimmed in brick out front, but from the way the weeds look right at home, I don't think flowers have been planted in front of the yellow house for a long time.

As I walk up the drive, I notice feet sticking out from under the truck. Her dad must be changing the oil. I've never met him. I've seen him mowing the lawn a few times over the years when Connor and Emma would drag me and Cami along to a movie and we'd swing by to pick her up. But he and I have never been introduced.

The feet are wearing worn-out tennis shoes. The cuffs of his jeans are frayed and dirty. I clear my throat to get his attention and hear a thud followed by a "shit."

He slides, or rather scoots, out from beneath the truck, and I realize right away that this man is not Cami's father.

"Hey." He nods and then wipes his grease-covered hands on his grease-covered jeans. "I've never met you before. Name's Jimmy." He offers his hand.

I want to shake it lightly. Actually, I don't want to shake it at all, but he latches on to my hand with a killer grip.

"I'm Kyle," I say.

"You a friend of Cami's?" he asks, still clenching my hand. His dark brown eyes burn into mine. "You're not selling something, are you? Not one of those Jehovah's people?" His eyes scan across my clothes. "No, you're not dressed nice enough to be one of them."

He lets go of my hand, and blood pulses back into my fingers.

Despite the days of stubble on his face and the way his hair does a really good Medusa impression, there's something . . . nonthreatening about him. I glance at his bare arms, at the tattoos rising and falling along the contours of his biceps.

"That's not a marijuana plant," he says, pointing to the tattoo of a jagged leaf. "It's a Japanese maple leaf. You know, peace and tranquility. That's what I'm all about now, man. I'm done with that war shit. And Uncle Sam is done with me, so it's mutual. All good."

The front door opens. Cami steps out onto the porch. She's wearing her Sak & Save shirt and holding a large bag of garbage. Uncle Jimmy rushes toward her and takes it.

"I got it," he says. "Need to earn my keep somehow."

I look at Cami, and she shrugs. "I guess you two met."

"I live here," he says, launching the garbage into the trash can. "Uncle Sam put me on disability. But I can do things. I can work. See that bike?" He motions toward an old black-and-white motorcycle. "I can take that baby apart and put it back together again in less than a day. They say my brain's not right, but could a person with an effed-up brain change the oil in a truck? I don't think so."

Cami takes my arm and starts pulling me toward the house. "Speaking of changing the oil, we better let you get back to it."

"Yeah." He nods, looking at the truck like he'd forgotten it was there.

"You didn't say much in your text," Cami says once we're inside. "How was Dallas? Did they figure out anything?"

I don't know where to start or how to start.

"Kyle?" Before I know it, she's giving me an awkward hug. "It's going to be okay," she says, and I want to believe her so much I hug her back. I hold on to her until a timer starts buzzing in the kitchen.

"Frozen pizza for my brother and his friend," she says after we let go of each other. "They're in the backyard. I made them go out a little while ago because they were driving me crazy. Nine-year-olds!"

Cami opens the oven door, and warm bacon and pepperoni smells float into the kitchen like spirits taunting me. I can't remember the last time I ate pizza. Even with my arteries being one hundred percent clog free, Mom still wants me to eat healthy. It's torture.

"Want me to get them?" I ask. I need to breathe some un-pepperonied air.

"Sure."

There's a sliding glass door in the dining room. I open it and walk outside. Two kids, a boy and a girl, are sitting on the cement patio drawing with sidewalk chalk. The girl, wearing a bright sundress, has drawn several flowers with a rainbow stretching over them. The boy, Cami's brother, is drawing monsters who look like they're about to descend on the girl's garden.

"You're such a boy," the girl says.

"We should play zombies," Josh says, using a red stick of chalk to smear blood over the face of one of his creatures.

The girl stops coloring, and I'm so prepared for her to tell him how immature he is. "Do you have any guns?" she asks. "We can't play zombies without guns."

"Yeah." He stands. "I've got Nerf guns and cap guns. I've got a machine gun that sounds like the real thing." He turns around and sees me.

"Sorry, kids. The zombies will have to wait. Your pizza's done."

The girl stands up and starts to shake dirt from her dress, but then realizes her fingers are more colorful than the rainbow she's drawn. "I guess I should wash them," she says as she walks past me. "And he's *not* my boyfriend, in case you're wondering. We're just friends."

"Got it," I tell her.

"Hungry?" Cami asks me after she slides two slices onto each paper plate and sets them on the table.

"I'm good, thanks," I say. "I had a delicious walnut and spinach salad back home, followed by a handful of vitamins."

Cami gives me a sympathetic, supportive smile. "How about a can of Sprite?"

"Sure. If, that is, you don't have any pureed broccoli."

"All out." She hands me a cold can. "After you're done with your lunch," she says to the kids, "I want you to either watch television or go back outside. Kyle and I have important things to discuss."

The little girl finishes washing her hands at the sink and leans over to whisper something into Josh's ear before sitting down.

"No they're not," Josh says, his face turning red.

"We're not what?" Cami asks.

"Going to have sex," Josh says.

"When my sister says that her and her boyfriend are going to go 'talk' in her room, it means they're going to have sex. That's what Mom says, so I have to stay in my sister's room with them, or else they can't close the door." She looks at Josh. "Maybe we shouldn't play zombies. We should stay inside and keep an eye on them, or else you'll end up with a . . ." Her face squashes up as she tries to figure out what relation Josh would be to a baby his sister might have.

"We're not going to have sex," Cami nearly screams. "And I don't think your mom should talk to you about such things."

The little girl straightens in her seat. "My mom's a therapist, so we talk about everything. I know lots of stuff."

"Well." Cami flashes me a look of disbelief. "Josh doesn't know a lot of stuff, and I'd like to keep it that way, so let's not share everything you know, okay?"

The girl considers this and nods. "Girls mature faster than boys anyway, so I doubt he's ready."

Cami goes to the refrigerator and takes out a small bowl of sliced watermelon. "Eat all your food," she says, "then go play. My friend and I are going to go *talk* in my room, but we'll keep the bedroom door open so you don't have to worry."

Their talk turns back to zombies and what guns are best to kill them with.

"So," Cami says, once we're in her room with the door semi-closed. "Tell me about Dallas."

I start to talk but then see all the artwork hanging on Cami's walls. There are charcoal drawings, pencil sketches, and pastel paintings. Above her bed is a huge black-and-white portrait of her brother when he must have been maybe . . . two or three. He's asleep and has that peaceful sweet-dreams look on his round face.

There are all kinds of pictures. Trees and birds. Flowers and empty park benches. A drawing of a wheelchair sitting next to a pond pulls me in. The chair is empty, and there is no one walking or crawling or drowning in the picture. The surface of the water is perfectly still, and the chair sits forlorn and empty.

"Weird, huh?" Cami says. "I was taking a walk one day out in the country. I like to drive down dirt roads and then go walking and see if I find anything interesting to draw. That pond was probably a quarter mile from the road. There weren't any houses around. Just the pond and the chair. It was so eerie. A person could make up a hundred stories about why that chair was next to the pond. Maybe somebody got tired of taking care of his grandmother."

"Creepy," I say and shiver, but I like the feeling. There's

something normal about a teenager getting creeped out by a scary story—as long as the story isn't depicting his own life. "You're really good. I mean, *really* good."

"Thanks. I got a scholarship to study art at a couple different universities, but I'm going to spend the first two years at the community college. That way I can stay home and help with Josh, keep an eye on his new girlfriend."

"She's not his girlfriend," I correct her. "She made that very clear to me." I notice a drawing of two girls sitting on a merry-go-round eating snow cones. They look like they're in maybe fourth or fifth grade. The drawing is mostly black and white except for the red-and-blue tops of the snow cones. "Is this you and Emma?"

She comes closer and looks at the photo that's pinned just below the drawing. "Field day at school, in fourth grade. My mom took that picture. That was back when Emma lived next door to us, and we were pretty much inseparable. After my mom started chemo, she'd send me over to Emma's house so I wouldn't see her getting sick. And then when things got worse and our whole living room looked like a hospital, she'd try to send me to Emma's, but I wouldn't leave her. I was so afraid I'd come home and she'd be . . . Even after I told Emma that my mom was dying, she was willing to come to my house to play Barbies or babies. That's when I knew she'd always be my best friend."

"I'm sorry," I say, "about your mom."

"If I ever get rich, I'm going to have my breasts cut off," she says nonchalantly.

"What?"

"I'm serious. Cut them off, get fake ones, and then I'll never have to worry about getting breast cancer, or at least, I won't have to worry as much."

"Seriously?"

Cami sits on the edge of her bed. "Yeah. At least, if I have kids, I will. I'd do it for them."

I believe her. I can't imagine a woman wanting to cut off perfectly healthy breasts, but I believe her. And I have to wonder what I'd be willing to cut off if doctors said it would save me.

"So, what happened in Dallas?" she asks.

I sit down next to her. "I met both of the other Mueller babies, James and Amber. Amber died in front of me, and they're going to put a pacemaker in James to try to keep his heart from stopping."

Cami sits next to me. "I'm so sorry. What was she like?"

"She liked chocolate," I say, smiling at the memory and blinking away the burning sensation in my eyes. "James is something else. He's like a seven-foot-tall Zulu god or something. He got a scholarship to MIT. Hopefully the pacemaker will save him."

"And if it saves him, then they'll put one in you?"

I nod.

"It'll work," she says and squeezes my hand.

"Remember the guy from the diner?"

"Yeah, the guy you said was at Connor's meet?"

I take his phone out of my pocket. "This is his phone."

She lifts her eyebrows in question.

"He's dead. I saw him and started chasing him and . . . he got hit by a truck and then a car and then he died."

She's silent.

"I guess in a way, I killed him. If I hadn't started chasing him, he wouldn't have run into the alley. He's dead because of me."

Cami takes my hand. "You couldn't have known what was going to happen. You just wanted answers. You can't blame yourself."

"Then who do I blame?" I look at her, and I'm so grateful that she's not giving me some horrible stare, like I'm a killer, even though I am.

"If he didn't have anything to hide, he wouldn't have run," she says, so matter-of-factly that I feel a slight lifting of the blame I've placed on myself. "So he was watching you?"

"Somebody was watching Amber too, and I'm sure someone's watching James. They work for Dr. Mueller. Before the man died, he said that Mueller needs to know where we die so he can get access to the autopsy reports."

"But how can he get access to the autopsy reports? I mean, just because he knows what hospital they were performed at doesn't mean he can access them. And why does he want them?"

"I don't know," I say, because I don't want to say more. I don't want to tell her the rest of what Scott Stiles said.

"He must have connections—some way of accessing hospital records," Cami says. "Without having you firsthand to study, maybe he thinks the autopsy reports are the best way to get the information he needs. I feel so bad for the rest of them." Cami's head lowers, and I know she's thinking about the faces she's seen on Facebook. "At least he has more time to figure out how to save you."

I give her a weak smile.

"What about the phone?" she says. "You said you have the guy's phone. Isn't there something on it that can help us find Dr. Mueller?"

I hold the small black device in my hand. "It's locked. I can't figure out how to get into it."

"Get into what?" Uncle Jimmy presses the half-shut door open. He's wiping his hands on a towel, but it doesn't look like he's washed them yet.

I don't answer him, but I have a feeling he already knows a lot. He was probably standing in the hallway listening in and just decided it was time to make his entrance.

"You can trust me," Jimmy says. "You can't trust a marine, who the hell can you trust?"

"He was special forces," Cami says, giving me a reassuring smile.

She trusts him, and I trust her, so . . . "I need a way to access information from this phone, but it's locked."

"Whose phone is it?" Jimmy asks.

"This guy was following him, kind of stalking him."

Jimmy nods like he sees the whole picture. Like he was there and knows everything that happened. "So you killed him and took his phone?"

"I didn't mean to kill him," I say, and I wonder how many confessions start off with that exact same phrase.

"It's okay." Uncle Jimmy shrugs. "It's all good. Sometimes you have no choice. Kill or be killed. It's cool. So who's this doctor he was working for?"

I was right. Uncle Jimmy must have been listening for quite a while. Maybe some of it's paranoia, the need to know what's going on around him, or maybe he's just a bored marine. "My brother and I and some other kids were developed by the same doctor in the same fertility lab. He's had people watching us, trying to pinpoint when and where we'll die. Most of us die around our eighteenth birthdays."

"That sucks!" he says and starts pacing. "You don't know where the doctor is?"

"No."

Jimmy nods. "But you think he might be able to help you?"

"His research might."

He nods again, and I can see excitement growing in his eyes. "You need a hacker. That's probably what he has. A good hacker can get into hospital records with no problem. A really good one. And a good hacker could get into that phone."

"Do you know any good hackers?" Cami asks. "Maybe someone you knew in the marines."

A broad smile grows on Jimmy's face. "Yeah. As a matter of fact, I do."

"**H**ow do you know this guy?" Cami asks as we watch various people, mostly burly-looking men, coming in and out of the truck stop.

"I told you, we served together in Afghanistan." Jimmy glances at his watch. "He's probably just running a little late."

A waitress puts down three small glasses of water, one with something floating on top of it.

"We've got another one coming," Jimmy says, and the waitress leaves to get another glass and one more menu. "We didn't fight together. He wasn't even supposed to be in Afghanistan. He was supposed to be stationed in Germany, but the intelligence guy serving at our base had a breakdown, so they sent Matt in. He was pissed, too. Guy's a genius. Wasn't supposed to be anywhere near combat zones—that's the deal his recruiter made him. But there he was in the thick of it. He spent two weeks at our base, then the higher-ups realized their mistake. We were transporting him out when we got hit."

"Got hit?" I ask.

"IED blew the shit out of us, but I was lucky compared to Matt."

Lucky? What could be worse than chunks of metal in your brain? "What happened to him?"

"Lost his left leg and some other parts us guys are particularly fond of, if you know what I mean. He was supposed be getting married to his high school sweetheart, and she dumped him while he was in the hospital. Who does that?" He clears his throat just as a man in his midtwenties comes through the door. Jimmy waves, and he comes toward the table.

Matt's wearing jeans and a shirt buttoned up oddly high for the warm weather. He walks with a noticeable limp.

"Man, it's been too long," he says as the reunited marines give each other a quick but firm embrace. They both sit down.

"This is my niece, Cami," Jimmy says, motioning across the table. "And this is her friend Kyle, the one I told you about."

Matt extends his hand to each of us. He doesn't look like a computer nerd. His shoulders are broad, his arms muscular. His blond hair is cut short next to his somewhat tan face. He reminds me of an older version of one of Connor's friends. I can totally see them shooting hoops together or going for a run. Of course, it might be tough for Matt to do those things with one leg.

The waitress steps up to the table. "Do you need another minute?" she asks, looking at Matt. "I can come back if you do." She's probably in her early twenties, with long brown hair pulled into a ponytail. She'd be prettier if she put some effort into it, but I can see why she doesn't, working here. Still, the way she's looking at Matt, I bet she wishes she had.

"I'll just have a cup of coffee," Matt says, avoiding the eyes that are trying to meet his.

She looks at me. "And you?"

I lift the menu, and my fingers slip on the greasy film covering it. The place is busy, but it's the only place on Interstate 70 for several miles, so the number of patrons probably has nothing to do with the quality of the food.

"I'll just have a Coke," I say.

"A lemonade," Cami adds.

Jimmy looks at us like he doesn't quite understand why we chose to meet at a truck stop at lunchtime if nobody's ordering any lunch. When no one offers him an explanation, he shakes his head. "I'll take a Dr Pepper and a piece of apple pie." He picks up the glass with something floating in it, uses a spoon to fish it out, then takes a long drink.

"Do you have the phone?" Matt asks, reaching over the table.

I want to hesitate. Jimmy knows this guy. He trusts him, but I don't know him. Hell, I barely know Jimmy. And I'm handing over the best chance I have to find Dr. Mueller. I give Matt the phone.

"And the guy's name is?"

"Scott Stiles," I say, "but that might not be his real name."

"Probably isn't." Matt pops off the back of the phone, takes out the battery, looks at the serial number, then pops the battery back in and slips the phone in his pocket. "Chances are if he was doing some type of covert work for this doctor, he was using an alias. And Jimmy said something about autopsy reports?"

"Yeah," I say. "The doctor who designed us needs access to the reports."

"But people died in different places. That means different coroners, different hospitals."

I nod.

"So he's got someone hacking into different hospital servers. Do you have a list of the people who have died and where they died, what hospitals their bodies were taken to?" Matt asks.

"I can get that to you."

Matt takes a small pad of paper and a pen from his pocket and slides it across the table. "Write down everything you know. If I can get a list of the names and hospitals, I might be able to find a link between whoever is hacking their system and where that information is being sent."

"You can really do that?" Cami asks. "You can hack a hacker?"

Matt smiles. "I can do anything," he says. "Of course, it was easier when I had military clearance. But then the military decided they didn't need me anymore, thanks to their own fuckup. I went from the being the best programmer they had to being unemployed."

"Unemployed? You don't need a leg to be a programmer. You just need a brain," I say

Matt gives Jimmy a nudge. "So you didn't tell them our whole sordid bromance, huh?"

Jimmy shakes his head.

"We were both in the humvee that got blown up, but we didn't really know each other until we ended up being roommates in a hospital in Germany. Our relationship really blossomed in the psych ward after Jimmy had a bit of a PTSD psychotic breakdown and I tried to kill myself, hence Uncle Sam doesn't have much faith in my brain these days either. And when companies look at me and my not-fully-honorable discharge, they're not sure they can trust me with all the shit they have stored in their systems. So I might be teaching computers 101 at a community college this fall. Looks real promising. Hooray." He shrugs.

The waitress comes with our drinks and Jimmy's pie. She hesitates, having heard this last bit of information. She is young, but a sudden sadness on her face makes her look much older.

"You boys veterans?" she asks, looking at Jimmy and Matt.

"Marines," Jimmy says.

She thumbs through the orders on her little pad of paper, tears off the one for our table, and puts it in the big pocket of her apron. "It's on me today," she says. "Glad you made it home." She rushes from our table, and it's clear that somebody she knew, somebody she cared about, didn't make it home.

"We should have ordered more," Jimmy says.

Matt smiles and shakes his head. "I've missed you, buddy," he says. "And I'm really glad you got ahold of me on this." He looks at me. "I'm good at what I do. I'm damn good. I'm not sure how long it will take me. Different hospitals use different security programs, but I'm sure I can get around them. As far as the phone goes, I'm not sure how hard that's going to be, but I'm sure I can do that too. Let's just say I'm Santa Claus, and if I'm going to give you just what you want for Christmas, what exactly would that be?"

"Dr. Mueller's real name and address," I say. "But please tell me I'll get my present before Christmas." *And my seventeenth birthday,* I think.

"I should have something to you in a few weeks, maybe a month."

"Really," I say. "That's great." And it is great. But I hope it's sooner. Scott Stiles said I wouldn't make it to my seventeenth birthday. Connor and I were born nineteen months apart. I turn seventeen in December. It's the middle of July now, so I have, at most, five months.

"Write it all down," Matt says, pointing to the paper and pen. "Everything is stored electronically nowadays. An autopsy report goes somewhere; I just have follow its path. See where it went, and you'll have your man. If I were you"—he takes a sip of coffee—"I'd enjoy what's left of summer. Spend some time with this pretty girl here." He winks at Cami, and I feel for the guy.

He's good-looking. He could probably get just about any woman he wants, until he tells them the bit about missing a leg and . . . his manhood.

"So," Cami says, "should Kyle consider that an order?"

I look at her and roll my eyes, like I really need to be *ordered* to hang out with her. Hell, who else would I hang out with?

School starts in one month, and it's not like I want to spend it hidden away in the basement playing video games. Last year that's exactly what I did. But it's different now. I think of Amber and the way she kissed me. I think of how emotions have a taste to them and how treasuring a moment and being desperate at the same time can create the most exquisite, unbearable taste.

She only had a few days to deal with the possibility of death, of never growing up or falling in love or any of it. Stiles had had no time to contemplate his death. He was fit and healthy and running one minute and then he was dead. I guess when it comes down to it, nobody knows how much time they'll get. I do know I'm ready to hand this over to Matt, to let him look for Dr. Mueller for a while.

I'm ready to get a sunburn and a snow cone brain freeze. I'm ready to step on hot cement in bare, damp feet, and I'm ready to forget, for just a while, that this may be my last summer.

I never realized how the gravitational pull of the Earth impacts water, specifically water soaked into swimming suits. Bikini bottoms and baggy guy trunks reach toward the pavement, and their wearers seem oblivious to the various amounts of ass being exposed. Of course, judging by the bikinis most of the girls are wearing, being exposed is the goal. Crescent-shaped butt cheeks are everywhere, and the old saying that if you don't see the nipple it doesn't count should really be revised.

I've seen more tits in two hours at the water park than a dairy farmer sees in a lifetime and, occasionally, nipples included. Not that I want to see them, but . . . it's not like you can help it. I wish the lifeguard where Josh is playing would stop turning around to look at Cami. At least she's not hanging out of her suit. She has the good sense to leave some things to mystery, but they're mysteries I'm pretty sure he'd like to solve.

"Who is that guy?" I ask as he supervises little kids trying to make it across a path of lily pads in water that's probably about three feet deep. He's tall and muscular and bronzed.

"That's Ryan Jameson."

"Does he go to our school?" I ask. I feel something bubbling up in my stomach, and it's not the plate of nachos Josh and I shared an hour ago.

"No. Josh took swim lessons this spring at the rec center, and Ryan was his teacher. He was always hitting on me."

Jealousy. No, that's not what it is. But then again, my dreams have morphed away from images of Emma to glimpses of Amber to Cami. But that's just because I spend so much time with her. I mean, that's what dreams are—your brain filing away the day's events into certain categories. I've been spending a lot of time with Cami. She's helping distract me while Matt works his hacking magic. We watch movies together, take Josh to the park, and play endless hands of Uno. Of course I dream about her.

Cami picks up the towel she's been lying on, rolls it up, and shoves it into an oversized bag. She looks at me with her sunglasses lifted to see me better. Then she looks over at Ryan Jameson, who just so happens to be looking at her. She smiles. "Are you jealous?"

"Of him?"

"Yeah. He's hot."

"And he's checking you out," I say, and for the first time, okay, maybe not the first time, I check Cami out myself. Jameson's not the only guy who enjoys a little mystery, and all the *really good stuff* is hidden. Of course her legs are pretty good. They're slender but shapely. Her stomach is definitely nice too. It's not completely flat and hard like girls in workout commercials. There's a little curve to it, a nice soft curve.

She's standing now, the bag draped over her shoulder. She clears her throat and then does a turn so I can take it all in. So does Jameson.

"You *are* jealous," she says. And I think I hear her add "about time" under her breath. "I'm going to get Josh. My dad will be home tonight, so I'm free if you want to watch a movie at your house or something.

Cami's dad's not a big fan of leaving Josh alone with Uncle Jimmy, so we hang out at her house a lot, especially during the day. But I like to spend most evenings at home with Mom and Dad, so it's nice of her to volunteer to come over.

"Sure," I say.

She looks back over at Ryan. "I can see if he's busy if you want. Maybe he can come over too, and the three of us can hang out."

"You think it takes two guys to handle you?" I say, enjoying our playful flirting, but at the same time wishing I could rewind and think things through a little more. Cami's great. She's pretty and smart and unbelievably responsible. But there's the whole "you won't make it to seventeen" thing. Is it fair to flirt with Cami? Aren't I being selfish just spending time with her when I don't know what's going to happen?

Water splashes both of us, and we see Josh giggling in the three-foot section. She doesn't yell at him or even look mad; she just takes a semidry towel from her bag and holds it, using it to signal him that it's time to go. He dog-paddles through the water to where we are and lifts himself out of the water. He takes the towel, then shakes his body like a wet dog.

"I gave you the towel for a reason," she says, then pretends like she's going to throw him back in. Josh laughs and starts drying off.

Suddenly I feel like I'm inside a box—a box made of thick glass. I can see everything, but the sounds are muffled, and there's a definite feeling of being disconnected. It's like I'm trapped inside a television and the actors, the scenes, and stories are happening on the outside of it.

Earlier, there was a young girl with no hair in the kids' pool. She looked like she was twelve or thirteen. The water only came up to the top of her knees. Several times she looked toward the deeper pool where kids her age were splashing and doing somersaults in the water. But she never left the kiddie side. She just sat down so that the water lapped up against her chest. She closed her eyes like she was pretending she was part of the laughter, like she was part of the life being lived where the water is deep.

She was in the box. I know that now. Does everyone who is so sharply aware of mortality feel the box? Do we try it on while we're living so that the permanent box we'll be planted in won't be so frightening?

"**H**appy birthday eve," I say, and James's smiling face fills up my monitor screen. "I'll tell you happy birthday tomorrow," I add, because I will tell him happy birthday tomorrow, because I'll be able to because the pacemaker will work, and he will be alive. And the next day, we'll Skype again, and I'll wish him a "happy day after your birthday."

"Thanks," he says. "So, how's my brother from another mother but the same mad scientist doing?"

"Okay," I lie.

"Bullshit," he says but keeps smiling. "This sucks balls."

I nod. "How's the pacemaker?"

"Pacing away. I'm all healed up. Don't stress it when you get yours. It wasn't really a big deal, and some of those nurses taking care of me were hot."

"NILFs?"

James laughs. "Some of them were. And some of them definitely were not."

"You nervous?" I ask because I know his family is being positive, telling him that the pacemaker will work and there's nothing to worry about. But it doesn't matter how many times someone tells you something; it doesn't mean you believe it.

James shrugs and attempts a smile. "Yeah. I just want it to be over, you know. I want to be eighteen and a month old. I don't know what it's going to be like, if I'll feel my heart stop and then start again, or maybe I won't even notice. I hope I do. I want to know that this thing in my chest worked."

"How are your folks doing, and your brothers?"

"They all keep staring at me. I'm surprised Mom and Dad aren't in my room right now, sitting on my bed, watching me. Creeps me out."

"My folks do the same thing. They try not to make it obvious, but I catch them all the time. It's like they're trying to memorize us."

"I feel bad for them."

James lives in Kansas City, Missouri, just on the other side of the Kansas border. He's miles away, but he's right in front of me. I can see into his eyes. I can see the fear and the hope in them.

"Watching your family hurting makes it so much worse," he says. "I think if they were shitty parents, and they didn't care so much, didn't love me so much, it'd be a little easier."

"I sent you a birthday present," I say, wanting to lighten things. "I mailed it yesterday, so you'll probably get it late." It's a T-shirt with the MIT logo on it.

His smile widens, and I notice for the first time that the corners of his mouth have small dimples like little apostrophes that accentuate his grin.

"You want me to tell you what it is?" I ask.

"Nope. It's fine. If it's a day or two or three late, I'll still get it." He nods, and it's so strange to see vulnerability in such a strong, perfect face. "Ever since I was a little kid, I thought turning eighteen would be so awesome. You're a man at eighteen. You can vote, get married, and buy cigarettes. You can gamble in Oklahoma. Oklahoma's not that far."

I laugh.

"I figure if I'm alive next week, I've beaten the odds and it's time to pay for my college books with a trip to the blackjack table. How about we take a trip together once you're eighteen? We'll drive across the Kansas border and show those Okies how 'superior' people do it."

"Deal," I say, hoping our luck extends far beyond the blackjack tables. "I think I might find out Dr. Mueller's real name soon, and where he lives."

"You serious?"

"Yeah, I met this marine. Ex-marine. Medicated and slightly brain-damaged marine. He has a friend who's a computer whiz. He thinks he might be able to find him by hacking into hospital computer systems. I checked in with him just yesterday. He thinks he's getting close."

"That's great." James leans in excitedly. "What kind of systems is he hacking into?"

"Hospitals."

I can see the gears in James's head start to turn, and I don't want him to make this connection, not tonight, not until he's eighteen and a month old. Shit, why did I even say anything?

When I was talking to the police about Scott Stiles, James was getting prepped for his pacemaker. I never told him about us being watched or why. I figured it was too much for a Mueller baby with an approaching eighteenth birthday to handle.

"Hospitals, as in not just the hospital in Dallas?" He nods his head, and it's too late. "Autopsy reports."

I nod.

"That's a good plan. I guess it would make sense that if he's still out there somewhere, he'd want to know what's happening to us. But he's not going to get mine," James says, a faked confidence in his voice. No doubt he's gotten good at reassuring his parents, at reflecting their optimism. "You find out who he is, you let me know. We'll pay him a visit together."

"You'll be the first one I call."

"You know that bucket list thing?" James asks.

"Yeah," I say, and I have to admit, I've given a little thought to what I'd like to do before I die, that is, if the pacemaker doesn't work and I don't find Dr. Mueller. But then I tell myself that it's going to work and we're going to find the doctor, and there's no need to have a bucket list because I'm not going to die. Not for a long, long time.

"Well, it's bullshit," James says. "Don't waste any time thinking about who you'd most like to have sex with or what exotic food you'd like to eat on what exotic beach. When it comes right down to it, there's no better place in the world than sitting at the table eating your mom's cooking. And stick a supermodel across from me, and I'd still just be looking at Mama's beautiful face. Home. You think you might be dying, you think time's running out, there's no other place you'll want to be. Remember that."

"You can remind me tomorrow and the next day. And no wussing out on me when I turn eighteen because you'd rather be with your mom than hitting up those casinos in Oklahoma. That's how I'm spending my birthday, so no backing out."

He nods. "Yeah. That's the plan. Remember, though, if things don't go according to plan, you got some time to figure it out. And if I'm not there with you, you put down twenty bucks at the blackjack table for me, all right?"

"You'll be there," I say, wishing I felt as confident as my voice is sounding.

James gives me a smile, his best smile, and then he logs off.

"**J**ack! Jack!" she cries out in a harsh, raspy voice, like her tonsils have frozen in her throat.

Why the hell did I pick *Titanic* to watch? I couldn't have grabbed something a little more upbeat, a little happier? Maybe *Jaws* or *The Boy in the Striped Pajamas.*

"You know there are actually websites that show how Jack and Rose could have both fit on the door," Cami says, delicately eating one piece of popcorn at a time.

"Seriously? Like someone actually spent time researching that?"

She nods. "I know it's stupid. The writer obviously wanted Jack to die, or he or she would have made the door bigger, or maybe had a giant dinner table floating next to them. But people won't let it go. They want a happy ending."

I grab the remote from the coffee table and turn the television off. I don't need to see a young version of Leonardo DiCaprio frozen solid and sinking to the bottom of the ocean. I don't want to see the passengers bobbing in the ice-cold waves either. I have something in common with the *Titanic* victims—having been frozen. But I survived. I was just an embryo and didn't feel the hellish sensations that come with flesh turning to ice. I can't imagine *feeling* that. The body is made up of around 70 percent water. When water freezes, it expands. I can't imagine feeling the molecules in your skin expanding, the molecules in your organs and muscles and brain. I can't imagine the excruciating pain of every cell in your body being torn apart from the inside out.

"Your parents seemed kind of tense tonight," Cami says.

"Well, they went to bed right after the ship hit the iceberg. That's pretty intense."

"I don't think that's what's on their mind." She's sitting on the couch beside me. She's wearing shorts that can't be seen from under her oversized shirt, and her feet are bare, since she left her flip-flops by the front door. Her toenails aren't painted. I'd noticed that the first time she came over for a movie marathon. I don't know why I noticed—I guess it's because I'd seen Emma's feet so often draped over Connor's lap as they watched television or a movie, and her toenails were always painted. I had begun to assume that baby girls were born with pastel-colored toes.

"You want to talk about it?" she asks.

"About what?"

"What tomorrow is? August seventh?" she asks, and at first I'm surprised that she remembered, then I'm not, because Cami would remember. "If you need to talk, I'm here."

I don't know what to say. Tomorrow is James's birthday.

Even if he survives it, he won't necessarily be okay. He has to have a heart attack, and the pacemaker has to save him. The others didn't all die exactly on their birthdays, so he could live a day or maybe a few days after. He could be packing for MIT a week from now and drop dead carrying his mini fridge to his dorm room. "In the words of James Murphy Monroe, 'it sucks balls.' The whole fucking situation. And what about Matt and the phone? Why don't we hear something?"

Cami pulls her knees in close and drapes her shirt over them. "He said it would take a while, maybe even a month. He's only had the phone for three weeks."

"I'm just sick of waiting. Of not doing anything. I need to find Mueller."

"You're doing everything you can to find him," Cami says.

"But not fast enough to save James, not if the pacemaker doesn't work." *And not fast enough to save me,* I think. My birthday's approaching like the damn iceberg. Just a little over four months to go.

"The pacemaker is going to work. And Matt's going to hack into the phone and the hospital records, and he's going to find Dr. Mueller. You're not going to be eighteen for a while. That's plenty of time to—"

"Cami." I stop her. God, I don't want to tell her, but she deserves to know. She deserves to protect herself from getting hurt any more than she already will if I die. I don't want her to stay away from me. Truth is, I think I'd have gone crazy by now if it weren't for Cami. I don't want to lose her, but it has to be her decision. I shift myself on the sofa so that I'm facing her. "I haven't told anyone this, but the guy in Dallas, the one we saw here in town?"

She nods.

"He told me something before he died. He told me that I was 'made different' from the others. I don't know what that means exactly, but he said I won't make it to my seventeenth birthday. So even if the pacemaker works, even if I get mine put in next week, if I'm different, how do I know it's going to save me?"

She stares at me. "But . . . are you sure that's what he said?"

"Yeah," I say, because the moments before Scott Stiles died are recorded in my brain. All I have to do is think of him, and it's like pushing a Play button and reliving each second.

Cami keeps staring, and I want to pull my eyes away from hers, away from the fear and hurt I already see there, but I can't. "You're not going to die, Kyle McAdams. I won't let you."

Suddenly she's across the couch, her arms wrapped tightly around my neck. We hold on to each other for a long time, her head tucked in that space between my shoulder and neck. I know we're going to kiss. It's as easy and natural as falling down. Our mouths move against each other, and there is the same flavor of desperation that I'd tasted when Amber kissed me, but it's different too. It's sweeter, because Amber wanted to kiss *someone* and Cami wants to kiss *me*.

"Are you ready?" she asks once our lips part.

I look at her. "Ready for what?"

"Me." Her voice starts to falter, but she's gathering strength from somewhere, strength that will keep the tears contained and her voice strong. "You're stuck with me. No matter what. You're mine, Kyle McAdams. And my terms are simply that you keep living until I'm tired of you—and I'll never get tired of you. Do you agree to my terms?"

I want to agree. I want to sign my name in blood to a contract that says I can't die because my girlfriend won't let me. My girlfriend. Something inside me smiles at that.

But there is no such contract, and no matter how much Cami or my parents want me to live, no matter how much I want James to live, death holds all the power.

"I'll try," is all I can say back to her, but it must be enough, because she takes my face in her hands and kisses me again and again and again.

I try not to think. I open my eyes, get dressed, and hop on Facebook to send James a happy birthday message. I'd like to say this feels totally normal because I have so many Facebook friends that I've sent so many birthday greetings to, but the fact is, this is my first one. I log on, and my heart dips a little because James isn't online. It's nine A.M. He might still be asleep, but I doubt it. Most likely he's having a birthday breakfast with his family. Why not start celebrating early, especially when you don't know if you'll make it to the birthday cake and presents.

There's a light knock on my door, and it opens. It's Dad, and I know instantly from the expression on his face.

"His brother called this morning," he says.

I look at the screen, at the *Happy Birthday* I just typed. I look at the multitude of other greetings, and I look at his picture. He's not dead. James is not dead. He can't be. I talked to him last night. I saw his face on the screen last night, and he was so alive, and we're going to go to the casino on my eighteenth birthday, except I won't have an eighteenth birthday. I won't have a seventeenth birthday. James is dead.

He's dead.

A pain as real as a knife shoots through my heart, because his parents are going to get a package in the mail. A late birthday present. An MIT T-shirt. Maybe his mom will have finally stopped crying, and she's going to open that fucking box, and . . .

"Kyle?"

I've been mad before. I've been upset before. But I've never literally felt like I could explode. Dad comes toward me, attempts to put his hand on me, but I wave him away. If he touches me, if anyone touches me, I'll detonate. All I see is the door and how I have to get out of here. I have to *do* something.

I move past Dad. I don't look at him, but I know the expression on his face. I've seen it a thousand times before, that look of sympathy and compassion—pity. Only now it's magnified a million times, and it's not because Connor won another award or another race. It's because I'm going to die. But I'm not.

I stop at the bottom of the stairs and look back at him standing in my doorway. "I'm not going to die." I mean it, and he nods in agreement because he thinks we have time. He thinks we have a year and a half, but I know better.

I go outside to the driveway, and I'm ready to take on the world. I'm going to drive to Cami's house, get Matt's address, and if he hasn't figured anything out, I'll make him work faster. We'll work together until I have a fucking name.

I hit the Unlock button, and the pathetic chirp of the doors of the Smart car unlocking brings me crashing back to reality.

I'm going to go force a handicapped ex-marine to give me secret information he might not be able to get, and I'm going to get there in a car that I seriously think I can pick up and throw across the lawn. I want to throw it because I shouldn't be driving this car, because Emma should, because Connor should be alive, and I shouldn't have this fucking cemetery in my brain with its newest plot of freshly churned earth.

I make a fist and pound it against the top of the green, eco-friendly piece-of-shit car because it can't save the world, not when the preferred method of transportation in the Midwest is still giant gas-guzzling four-wheel-drives. One little clown car isn't going to make a difference. It's not going to change anything, and whoever thinks it will is delusional and stupid. I hit the top of it again and totally expect it to buckle like a crushed pop can.

"Kyle!"

I hear my name, but I ignore the voice as I hit the car again.

"Kyle!" Cami grabs my arm. "I've got it."

I stop and look at her. She's holding a piece of paper in her hand.

"Matt called Jimmy this morning. His name is Richard Sharp. Dr. Richard Sharp."

I fall against the side of the car.

"He's willing to meet with you. I have his address. He lives in Wichita, Kyle. He's not even thirty minutes away."

Wichita. The man who knows that we're dying, the man who is my only hope for living, was James's best hope, lives thirty minutes away. And of course he would. He'd want to be close to the majority of his creations.

"James is dead," I say, and I hate the words. I hate them, and I hate Dr. Richard Sharp.

"I'll drive you, okay?" Her voice is soft, and I nod because I don't trust myself to drive. How can I drive if I rip the fucking steering wheel off because I'm so . . . ready to rip his fucking heart out? Dr. Richard Sharp. I swear I could rip out his heart, but first I have to know if he has one.

Dr. Sharp's condo is in the center of the city. The five-story building, made of sandstone, used to be a high school back in the early 1900s. I remember watching the news with Dad and hearing an architect talking about how the place was being renovated into upscale condos. I remember because I thought, what rich person would want to live in an old high school? But they've done a great job. The large windows of sectioned squares have been replaced with large plates of glass. The cement stairs students used to climb are gone, having been replaced by a smooth sidewalk lined with snapdragons and marigolds. At the end of it is a tinted glass door that only slides open for those who know the code to the keypad beside it.

I have the code. I look back at Cami, sitting in her truck. I want her to come with me. I need her to, but I'm to go alone. That's the deal. Dr. Richard Sharp will talk only to me.

Inside the door, I expect to see a lobby, but there isn't one. There's no desk, no sofa or chairs. On one wall is a row of mail compartments. Each is the size of a large shoe box. On the other side is an elevator. I'm about to press the Up button when it makes that chiming sound and a woman walks out. She looks like the kind of woman who would live in a high-dollar condo. She's thin with pale yellow hair cut stylishly around her slightly wrinkled face. She looks at me, gives me an awkward smile, and then hurries toward the front door.

I step into the elevator, glance down at the torn sheet of notebook paper, and press the button for the fifth floor.

The elevator opens into a wide corridor with cream-colored carpet that sinks with every step. The walls and the ceiling are the same color as the carpet, giving the feeling of walking through a squared tunnel. There is only one door at the end of the corridor, and beside it is a security pad. I punch in another number. A light flashes from red to green. I turn the doorknob.

The thick carpet ends in the hallway. The floor of the apartment is dark wood, the walls painted a deep brown. There is a portrait hanging in the entry of a young woman wearing a gold gown that matches the color of her hair. She's holding a red rose, and her skin is white. She looks like a corpse, like someone's beloved bride died, and he propped her up and quickly painted her before decay marred her beauty.

In the living room is an antique sofa, framed in ornate, gold-painted wood. Thick burgundy curtains block out the morning sun. A floor lamp in the shape of a half-naked woman leans over the sofa. The light is turned on but barely gives off more than a whisper of a glow. The coffee table is marble, and there are no magazines or television remotes on it. On the other side are two chairs with straight oval backs upholstered in tightly pulled fabrics that look like medieval tapestries.

A woman, probably my mom's age, comes out of the kitchen. She's wearing beige scrubs.

"He's very tired, so I don't want you staying long." Her full face is a mixture of concern and annoyance.

"Is something wrong with him?" I ask. My heart literally skips a beat like it's practicing for when it will stop and never start again.

She scoffs at my ignorance, but then her eyes soften behind the thick blue frames of her glasses. "Pancreatic cancer. It's spread to his liver and his lungs."

"How long?" I ask.

"One month, maybe two."

"His mind?"

"Dr. Sharp's mind is as brilliant as ever. But he tires easily, and he's always in a great deal of pain. He wouldn't take his pain medication this morning because of your meeting. He said he wants his mind to be clear. So, please, don't keep him any longer than you need to." She points toward the hallway leading away from the kitchen. "It's the last door."

I feel totally unprepared. I should have a notebook and a pen to jot down any tips he's going to give me: tips on how to save my life. I press against the door. At first it feels heavy, like it's made of solid stone. But then I feel as though I'm not alone, like Connor and James and the rest of them are here with me—all of us anxious to see this man, this demigod who created us. The door gives easily under my touch and glides in across a thick rug.

Dr. Mueller, I mean Dr. Sharp, looks small standing in the

middle of the spacious bedroom. He is thin, a frail specimen of a human being. He's wearing pants that pucker beneath the belt that holds them in place. The dress shirt is tucked in, but hangs from his bony shoulders. He's standing with the help of a gold-knobbed cane, and I can see a bandage on the back of his hand, where fresh blood seeps from the site of a recently removed IV.

"You didn't have to get dressed up for me," I say, startled and grateful for the strength in my voice.

"Of course I did," he says. His face is smooth and hollow, and while his eyes should seem large in the recesses of his skull, they look like black pebbles laid in the places where eyes should be. "I've wanted to meet you for some time. I'd planned on it, actually, though I wasn't sure at what point would be best. Then the gentleman who works for me, the one who helps me access certain bits of information that I need, detected a . . . presence. In short, my hacker discovered that he was being hacked. I contacted the young man you were using to find me." His thin, cracked lips curve into a smile. "I believe he thought finding me would be much easier, but I employ only the best. I guess I'm trying to say that this meeting would not be occurring if I didn't want it to."

"But why now? Why wait until after James is dead?"

"It seemed best. The pacemaker was a variable thrown into my experiment. While I knew the chances of it working were . . . well . . . minuscule at best, one has to let these things play out. Find out for certain what the outcome will be before proceeding further. But there was little doubt in my mind that it wouldn't work. When DNA tells the heart to stop, a burst of electricity is not going to start it again."

"You knew it wouldn't work. You didn't want it to, did you? You wanted James to die."

"Of course. No scientist wants his experiments to fail."

His experiments. Is that all any of us are to him? An experiment?

He shakes his head a bit sadly. "What did they tell you? That it was a mistake? That you have some strange genetic sequence they've never seen before, and they don't know how it got there?"

"A mutation," I say. "The genetics specialist said it's a mutation because of all of the DNA you manipulated in us."

His thin, white face hardens. "You know that when Einstein first presented his theory on black holes, the scientific community thought he was crazy. Still did long after his death. You place genius right in front of someone, and they can't see it. In front of educated people, no less—it's infuriating. Cancer is a mutation—a mistake. I don't make mistakes."

"What are you saying?"

His black eyes meet mine. "I genetically modified you—yes. That's what my financial investors were interested in. They wanted to know if it was possible to make someone tall or smart or talented or good-looking. And yes, as a researcher, the possibilities fascinated me as well. I won't lie. And that part of my experiment went quite brilliantly. My investors are very pleased. The world should expect to see several world records in sports being shattered in the coming decades and IQ scores soaring. Of course, only the richest will be able to create luxury children to ride around in the luxury cars, but that's no concern to me. My legacy is the other part of my research, the part that has nothing to do with my investors."

"What part is that?"

"I wanted to know if I could control a person's aptitude for intelligence, beauty, and athleticism. Why not see if I could control mortality as well?"

"You killed us just to see if you could?"

His smile is wide this time, pushing the little flesh over his cheekbones into the hollows of his skull. "A scientist's calling is to push the boundaries—to see what is and isn't possible. The genetic sequence inside you isn't a *mutation*. It's an expiration date, a date of execution, an end to your existence."

"You programmed us to die," I say. "How many of us? How many exceptional beings did you create just so you could watch them die?"

"Do you really want to know? I normally don't ascribe to the notion that ignorance is bliss, but in this case, you might want to stay ignorant."

"How many?"

"Twenty-five. You are my last living creation."

The cemetery in my brain grows exponentially, and it hurts, like pieces of my soul are being torn out to make room for the bodies of people I don't know, but care about just the same.

"Why?"

He looks at me like I'm five and I've just asked *why* balloons sail into the sky when you let go of their strings or *why* camels have big humps.

"Because we're human," he says. "As the most intelligent species on the planet, it's our duty to *try* everything. It's why we climb mountains, why we had to master flight and go to the moon and split the atom, and why in several countries, including our own, I'll wager, humans are being cloned. We do it because . . . we ate the apple."

"The apple?"

"In the garden of Eden. The devil told them they could be like God. All they had to do was eat the apple. And they did, because it is in our nature to *be* God. To create life and to decide when it should end."

I look at him, at the man who made Connor so that he could fly over the bar when he pole-vaulted, at the man who made Connor a whiz at math and debate. But he didn't make Connor a good person, a kind, caring person. Our parents did that. And this man, this brilliant scientist, is nothing but a frail, cancer-riddled body in baggy clothes.

"You're not God," I say. "You can't save yourself, can you?"

He struggles to draw a large breath into his sickened lungs. "I want to. You don't know how much I want to. Mostly because of you."

"Me? You're sad because you won't be around to see me die, to read my autopsy report."

"Sad, yes, but my interest in you is purely scientific. You

have the same sequence as the others, but yours is just a little different. He couldn't tell, could he, your genetics specialist?"

I shake my head, and his face illuminates like a Halloween skull with a flickering candle inside.

"I knew he wouldn't. The difference is so small, so minute. And they didn't find the other difference, did they?"

"What difference?"

His bony hands knead at the golden knob on the top of his cane. "The most inconsequential change is in your expiration date. I hate loose ends, and your parents wanting to freeze you for two years extended my experiment past a deadline that I was comfortable with, so I programmed you to die at seventeen, instead of eighteen. I could have programmed you to die sooner, keeping more within the parameters of my study's time line, but then you'd have been the first to die, and somehow I didn't want that for you. You're special."

"Special? I'm going to die in four months because of you, but I'm special?"

He takes a step toward me, and I recoil.

"Your parents' decision to freeze you offered me more time to manipulate your cells. I added another sequence, one hidden away in what's come to be known as junk DNA. I knew it wouldn't be detected there. I would very much like to see if it works. If I were healthy, if my brain were functioning normally, I might be able to come up with a way to save you, and thus see if my other experiment worked. But I'm not healthy, and as you so eloquently point out, I can't save myself. Thus, I cannot save you. You and I are both going to die very soon, and I'll never get to find out if the sequence for immortality I placed inside of you will work. Such a shame."

"Sequence for what?"

"Immortality, virtual immortality. A life span of anywhere from two to three hundred years, I suspect. I could try to explain it to you, but even though I made you intelligent, I didn't make you a genius. Let's just say that this sequence works on the brain, regulating the growth of new neurons and the release of neurotransmitters—chemicals. The fountain of youth isn't hidden away on some island somewhere. It's in the brain's ability for neural plasticity—its ability to grow new brain cells.

"If the brain constantly generates new cells, replacing itself, so to speak, then it won't become old. Dementia, Parkinson's all happen because the brain starts to deteriorate with age. As cells break down, they don't create the same amounts of neurotransmitters, of hormones as they did in youth. But keep the brain replacing its own cells, keep it young, and it keeps the rest of the body young. That's what the sequence will do. That's the simplified version, anyway." He makes a gesture of modesty with his hand, like mastering mortality is simple for someone like him. "The genetic sequence that will kill you simply tells your heart to stop beating. This sequence, the more complex one, is programmed to begin once the body reaches full maturity—around the age of twenty-one or twenty-two. But you'll be dead by then. Neither of us will ever get to know if my immortality sequence works."

I'm in shock. That's it. I can't be hearing this right.

"How does it feel?" he asks, looking around for a moment like he might want to grab a pen and paper and write this down. "It must be quite perplexing to hold both imminent death and immortality in the same body. To know that if you could just live past the age of seventeen, you could live indefinitely."

"Fix me. I don't want to die. Please."

He smiles, almost nostalgically. "I cannot." He shrugs.

"Please," I say, moving toward him and fighting the urge to grab hold of him. "You have to help me!"

"Or what?" He grins.

I smell the bitterness of medicine on his breath; I smell it seeping through the pores of his skin.

"Will you kill me? That might be nice, actually," he says. "The pain of this is getting to be a bit much. But do you really want to spend your final months caged in a cell? I should highly doubt that."

"You're crazy." It's all I can say as my legs start to buckle beneath me, and I push him away. He teeters but somehow manages to continue standing, his hands cupped over his cane.

"On the contrary," Sharp says. "I'm quite rational. I'm not doing this for my own gain. I'm doing this to save humanity." Sharp's skeleton chest tries to inflate, but the very act of filling his lungs with air causes him to cough violently. "Seven billion people," he says, drawing out each word as he tries to catch his breath. "A mere three hundred years ago, the world was home to less than one billion people. At the current rate of population growth, we'll see catastrophic levels of pollution, starvation, disease, climate change. All life on Earth will be in danger of extinction, including human life. Something has to be done."

"So, what, you plan on giving every person on Earth an expiration date?"

"Yes," he says, matter-of-factly. "Well, my successor will. I'm far from perfecting my research, but I'm hopeful that the doctor I turn it over to will succeed."

"But how? That's impossible."

"Do you know how HIV works? It uses the DNA in our cells to not only replicate itself, but also to actually plug the virus's genetic information into the cell. It's quite a remarkable process, and it's this process that will deliver my genetic sequences into billions of people. We simply have to bind it to a common virus that replicates itself in the same manner as HIV. It will enter the body, alter the genetic structure of cells, and eventually be passed down from generation to generation."

"But HIV doesn't get passed on genetically, so why would your virus?"

"It's not the virus that will be passed on, but the genetic sequence loaded into the cells, the sequence that will level the playing field. It will be inherited just like a child inherits eye color or height. Within a generation or two, people will all get the same amount of time. Say . . . sixty years—barring any accidents, that is. Get hit by a delivery truck in an alley, and it doesn't matter what your DNA says." He looks at me, his black eyes narrowing. And I know he's thinking about Scott Stiles, his former employee.

"You seriously want to make billions of people drop dead when they turn sixty?"

"I know—sixty may be too long. Especially considering the current levels of water contamination. Might be best to cut it back to fifty years. Just think, no more overpopulation, no more sick, elderly people draining the system of resources. Health care costs will plummet, and it will be so much easier for individuals to get their affairs in order, because they'll know exactly when they are going to die. I know it's hard to truly see my vision, but I assure you, it's the only way to save humanity from itself. In the end, every species wants to survive. But sometimes it takes someone of strong mind to help lead the way."

"Then why create an immortality sequence?"

He considers me with eyes so clear, so alive in contrast to their decaying frames. "To see if I could, of course." His smile carries a hint of sadness. "We are going to die. I suppose we could make a race of it, but I think I have an unfair advantage." He tries to laugh but starts coughing instead. "It's best we both accept our fates."

"I'm sixteen, and you want me to accept that I'm going to die?"

His slight cough intensifies, becoming more and more out of control. He takes a white handkerchief from his pocket, holds it over his mouth, and I watch as white turns to red.

I feel nothing, nothing but a burning sensation in my eyes, as if the fluid that constantly bathes them has been turned to acid. My legs are gone. Even my heart seems to be frozen in silent disbelief. I am nothing but eyes looking at a half-dead man and feeling the angry spirits of dead teenagers all around me. They didn't want much. They never asked for perfection of mind or body. They just wanted to breathe, to feel, to live. That's all I want.

"Connor was a great person," I say, and I see him, his smile and charisma. "James was amazing too. Triagon had a great sense of humor. I never got to meet him, but I know from his blog. Alexis and Hannah and"—I feel a special stabbing in my chest—"Amber were beautiful, gifted women. You had no right to kill them. And you have no right to kill me. At least give me a copy of your research. Maybe I can find someone who can use it to save me."

"I will give this part of my research, my very sacred research, to the person I deem worthy of continuing it. But no matter who that person is, he or she won't be able to help you. There simply isn't time. I'm sorry. And just in case you're wondering, it's quite secure. No one will be able to access it without my consent."

"I'm begging, all right? Is that want you want? You want me to beg to you like you're God? Okay. Fine. Just help me!"

Dr. Richard Sharp walks toward me on thin, faulty legs. When he's close enough, he stops and places his palm against my chest. "Your heart *will* betray you." He turns and walks toward his bed. "I'm getting tired," he says, sitting on the edge and sliding his feet out of his slippers. With great effort, he reclines against the mattress. "Can you send in the nurse on your way out? I need my pain medication."

I walk to his bedside and am surprised that his eyes are closed. I could easily lean over him, take a pillow from the bed, and press it to his face. He wants to win the race, why not let him win now—today. He deserves to die. But he's right, I don't want to spend what time I have left locked away. I want to spend it figuring out how not to die. I'm not going to die. I refuse. I don't care what he says. He's not God. I'll figure it out, then once I do, I'll figure out what to do with the next two or three hundred years.

Cami's asleep. She tried to fight it, tried to hold her eyes open and keep me company on the way home from James's funeral, but about an hour from town, she lost the battle. Truth is, I'm kind of glad. I needed quiet. I needed, still need, time to process everything.

Seeing James displayed in the entryway of the church was . . . I still can't believe it was real. There was a receiving line like after a school play, when all of the actors line up in the hall so people can congratulate them on a job well done. But no one was congratulating James on his heart attack. No one was shaking his hand or embracing him, or even talking to him. They just filed past. Some tried to look at him, but turned quickly away as they wiped their eyes. Others stared for a long time, like they were waiting for his chest to rise, for his eyes to open, for his mouth to curve into one of his glorious grins.

Cami looks so peaceful sleeping, but I keep looking at her chest, making certain that it's rising and falling, because Death seems to be everywhere now. He stands beside me, and if he gets bored, he might just reach out with his scythe and take her or Mom or Dad. He might as well take them if I die. They won't live through losing another child.

I haven't told anyone about my conversation with Dr. Sharp. Cami wanted to know everything, and I told her that he's working hard, trying to come up with a solution, but that he's old and sick, and maybe she shouldn't get her hopes up. Maybe I should have told her the truth. Maybe I still will, but that morning after I left Sharp's condo, she was so hopeful and I couldn't tell her. Not then. And not today.

"We're home," I say, slipping my hand into hers.

Cami yawns and stretches her legs out as far as the Smart car's interior will let her. "Sorry I fell asleep."

"It's okay. It's been a long day. I'm just glad you went with me."

For a moment, we just stare at each other, then I lean over and softly put my lips to hers. We get out of the car, and lightning bugs flash on and off around the yard.

"You coming in?" she asks.

"Just for a little bit," I say. We'd left early this morning for Kansas City. I need to go home and see my parents, but I also want to talk to Uncle Jimmy.

He's in the living room sitting on the floor next to Josh. They're playing video games but not *Call of Duty* or *Black Ops.* They're playing *Mario Kart,* racing around on the deck of a cruise ship.

"Who's winning?" I ask.

"I am," Josh yells, and I have to smile, because Uncle Jimmy picked Princess Peach and Princess Daisy as his characters and they suck. He's obviously letting Josh win. "Will you play me, Kyle?"

"Maybe in a few minutes," I say. "I kind of want to talk to Uncle Jimmy for a second."

"I'll play you," Cami says. "Just let me change real quick."

Jimmy stands. "Want a beer?"

"He's sixteen," Cami says, then looks at me and smiles. "But he's mature for his age, so . . ."

"No thanks," I say.

Jimmy opens the fridge, takes out a bottle of beer, offers me a bottle of water, and I take it.

"You want to go outside?" he asks.

It's nice outside for early August, and the neighbors might be thinking so too. They might be sitting out on their decks or patios with citronella candles keeping the whine of mosquitoes away. They might be able to hear things spoken in neighboring backyards.

"How about your room?"

Jimmy looks at me, intrigued. "Yeah, sure."

Cami's coming out of her room wearing a large nightshirt. She looks at us, somewhat concerned, as we enter Jimmy's room, and he shuts the door.

The room isn't exactly how I would have expected it. The walls are painted a deep blue, and Spiderman wallpaper borders the ceiling. The bed's small, a single size. The sheets are Spiderman, but not the red comforter that somehow ended up on the floor.

"It's the kid's room. He's sleeping with his dad while I do a little work in the basement. Then I'll head down there, and he'll get his Spidey room back." Jimmy sits in a kitchen chair next to a folding table with a laptop on it. I sit on the edge of the bed. "Matt wanted me to tell you that he's sorry it took so long. He was really frustrated, and marines don't like being frustrated."

"It's okay. I know he did his best. Dr. Sharp seems to have some pretty intense security. But there might be more he can do for me, if he's interested."

Jimmy smiles. "Why don't we ask him?"

He pops open his laptop and starts tapping on the keyboard. In a few minutes, Matt's face is on the screen.

"Jimmy!" he calls, a big grin on his face, then he sees me kneeling in front of the screen. "Hey, Kyle. Man, I'm really sorry about your friend. But I'm glad to see you too. Did you get my message, Kyle?"

"What message? I've been away from my computer all day."

"At the funeral?" Matt asks. "So rotten. Only eighteen years old. Sucks. But I wanted you know that even though I ran into some major firewalls with that doctor, I think I finally figured out how to get around them. He's got a master computer guy working for him, and let me tell you, he pissed me off when he 'gave' me the information I've been working my ass off trying to get. But it just made me more determined to hack into their system. And I think I've finally done it. Or at least I'm close."

"Seriously, that's awesome. I need to find out how to get his research."

Jimmy looks at me, confused. "I thought you met with him," he says. "He's trying to help you, right?"

"I met with him, but he's not trying to help," I say, and now

Jimmy knows I lied to Cami. "He planted a genetic code in all of us so that we'd die at the age of eighteen. But he wanted to hurry me along. I'm supposed to die at seventeen. That gives me about four months. And he doesn't care. His experiment was to see if he could kill us, and it worked. But if I can get hands on his research, maybe I can find someone who can help."

"You are not going to die," Jimmy says, placing a heavy hand on my shoulder. "Not on our watch. Right, Matt?"

"Yeah," he says. "If the research is stored in a computer file, I'll find it."

"He said something about finding a successor, someone to carry on his work," I say. "If you can access his contacts, maybe you can find out who it is. Dr. Sharp's got terminal cancer. He won't live that much longer. He's looking for someone he can trust to carry on his research, and it's not good. Killing all of us was just the start. This guy wants to kill everyone, and I mean everyone. He wants every person on Earth to have this genetic sequence that will make them die when they're fifty."

Matt's staring hard, and I can feel the intensity of Jimmy's stare from beside me. "You're fucking kidding, right?" Jimmy says.

"I don't think so," Matt answers. "I've seen the kind of security this guy has. It's better than some of the military stuff I've run into. Even the phone was some type of special Android that normal programs couldn't hack into. But maybe I can find a path to who he's considering giving his research to."

"What if Dr. Sharp finds somebody as crazy as he is? Somebody who thinks it's a good idea to put a kill switch in every person on Earth? How can we let that happen?" I ask.

"My dad just turned fifty," Matt says. "We just had a big party for him. He's still got twelve years before he plans on retiring, and some asshole scientist thinks fifty years is enough. I'll figure it out, Kyle. I promise, man. I will find whoever this is, and we'll get that research."

Even on the screen, Matt's a good-looking guy. It's Friday night, and he's at home alone on his computer. He should be married now. He should be the golden boy for the military, but he's not. And he's not wearing a button-down shirt like he was at the truck stop. I never asked Jimmy what method Matt had used to try to kill himself. It didn't seem right to. But now I can see the place where a rope had tightened around his neck, had torn through his skin and scarred him. No leg. No sense of manhood, and a constant reminder that there was a time when he didn't want to live anymore.

I like the light I see in Matt's eyes, and I love the determination in his face. He's alive, and for now anyway, he wants to be. And he wants to help me.

"I'm not going to your funeral, Kyle," Jimmy says. "I've been to enough of those. Matt, if there's anything I can do, you tell me. Anything."

Matt runs both his hands over his short blond hair and grins. "Commence Operation Save Kyle and Everyone over Fifty."

I know it's too small of a word. But small words can sometimes be the most powerful. Words like *hope* or *hate* or *love*. And so I say the only word I can think of for this particular situation: "Thanks."

"**C**laudia Bartholomew," Matt says, and this time he's not on a screen in Uncle Jimmy's bedroom. He's sitting at the kitchen table in Cami's house.

"Who's she?" Cami asks. She knows everything now. Not so much because I told her, but because I filled in what she missed when she was listening in through Jimmy's bedroom door.

"When I finally got into Sharp's phone records, her name came up the most," Matt says. "There are a couple of other possibilities—an immunology expert in Boston who looks promising, and a super-smart guy who graduated from medical school when he was eighteen. Dr. Sharp has had contact with both of them, but this Claudia Bartholomew, she's a genetics specialist from Saint Louis, and she's made several trips to Wichita over the past few months."

Matt opens a large manila envelope.

"Before you get your hopes up too much, she might not be coming to Wichita to see him. I know for certain they've had several phone conversations, but she's been seeing patients at the VA hospital here and in a few other states. She's working on some way of helping veterans by using stem cells."

The door leading from the garage opens, and Cami's dad walks in. He tosses his briefcase on the kitchen counter, then turns to look at the four of us sitting around the kitchen table.

"Hello," he says.

"This is Matt," Jimmy says, standing. "You met him when I was in the hospital."

Cami's dad, a slender man with short brown hair, comes forward and shakes Matt's hand. "Yeah, I remember. How are you?"

"Okay," Matt says.

"Glad to hear it."

"And you sort of know Kyle," Cami says, getting up from her chair just as Jimmy sits back down.

Her dad shoots me a smile and a wave.

"I saved you some dinner," she says. "I can warm it up."

"That's okay. We ordered pizza for the producers' meeting. I'm beat." He gives us a weary smile. "I think I'll see if Josh wants to watch some cartoons with his old man. Let you guys get back to whatever you're up to." He heads for the living room, but not before giving Cami a one-armed hug.

Matt looks at me and gets back to the business at hand. "I found a picture of Claudia Bartholomew online." A photo slides from the envelope. In it, Claudia Bartholomew is standing behind the podium at some sort of conference. I pull the photo closer, and I'm struck by how familiar she looks. Then it comes to me. She's the woman who came out of the elevator at Dr. Sharp's condo.

"I've seen her," I say. "She was at his apartment the morning I went to talk to him."

"Are you sure?" Matt asks. "I hacked into the records at the airport, and she took a flight into Wichita on August third. What day did you go to Dr. Sharp's?"

I glance at the calendar stuck to the front of the refrigerator with a pineapple-shaped magnet. "It was August seventh. That's when I saw *her* coming out of the elevator. She had to have been seeing him."

"So when is she due back in town?" Jimmy asks.

Matt pulls another paper from the envelope. He glances over various dates and times. "She's got appointments again at the VA in two weeks."

"Then I can talk to her," I say.

"And say what exactly?" Jimmy asks.

Matt lifts his brows in agreement. "If you ask her about Sharp, about his research, if she is involved, she's liable to lie and say she doesn't know what you're talking about. His master plan isn't exactly legal, and if she's buying into it, who knows what kind of a person she is."

"Then I need proof," I say. "If I can find proof that she's involved, maybe I can blackmail her into helping me."

"What? Threaten to go to the police?" Matt asks. "You'd have to have some pretty solid proof. How are you going to get that?"

"You said she'll be back at the VA in two weeks, right?"

Matt nods.

"She'll probably be meeting with Sharp again. Maybe he'll even give her his research then. Do you know if she has an office at the VA?" I ask Matt.

"I'm sure she does."

My heart's beating faster. It's talking to me, telling me to do whatever I need to so that it can keep beating.

"I have to find a way to break into her office," I say. "Is there any way to find out exactly where it is?"

Matt thinks for a moment. "I doubt she has a permanent office. It's probably just one she uses when she's in town. But I know some people at the VA. Me and Jimmy are a little more familiar with that place than we'd like to be."

Jimmy frowns. "I don't know what you're talking about." He leans back in his chair, both hands going to his head, and I'm not sure if he's scratching his scalp or feeling for the scars left by the IED.

"I can talk to some people," Matt says. "See what they know."

"If we can find out when she'll be there and where her office is, I'll sneak in and take a look around. Maybe she'll have something on a flash drive or in her briefcase or something."

They all nod like it's a great idea. Truth is, it's an idea, and right now, I'll grasp at anything.

"We'll come up with a plan," Jimmy says. "We'll get you into that office. And even if you don't find much, any connection might be enough to scare her into helping you."

"Or maybe," Cami says, "she'll help you because it's the right thing to do."

I force a smile, but right now, my faith in doctors isn't exactly at an all-time high. What I really need is faith in myself. It might take a genius to figure out how to keep me alive, but I'm going to have to be the one to convince him or her to do it.

I look at Matt's text message, holding the phone under the desk so my teacher doesn't see it. *Dr. B at VA, 8-25.* Today's August 21. In four days, Dr. Claudia Bartholomew will be at the Veterans' Hospital, and I'll get into her office, hopefully.

"Where's your homework, Mr. McAdams?" Mr. Olson flips through pages of graph paper, no doubt looking for my name on our algebra assignment, but he doesn't find it.

I sit up straighter at my desk and slip my phone into my pocket. I so don't need this shit. Who gives out homework the third day of school, anyway? All I care about is getting through the next four days. According to Matt, Dr. Sharp's been in contact with at least a dozen doctors and researchers, including Claudia Bartholomew. But she's still our lead contender. She's the one he calls the most, and she reciprocates. To make matters even more interesting, Matt found out that Dr. Sharp recently booked a one-way ticket to Saint Louis, where Claudia Bartholomew lives. Maybe he's planning on spending his last days with her, combing through every detail of his experiment.

And Mr. Olson wants me to spend my evenings graphing math problems. Fuck that. "I didn't do it," I say, not disrespectfully, but honestly and with little emotion.

"Why not?" He tries to match the calmness in my voice, but the vein that runs cockeyed down the center of his broad forehead is starting to protrude.

"Let's just say I had a few more important things to do." Like having Jimmy teach me how to pick locks in case Dr. Bartholomew's desk or filing cabinets are locked. And spending time with the people I care about because I might not have that much time left with them. But spending time with algebra? Hell no.

"More important things to do. Like video games, I suppose. Or searching for your dad's *Playboy* magazines?" The other students laugh.

"My dad's more of a *National Geographic* kind of guy. And I don't play Xbox much these days. I prefer reality. So no, I wasn't playing by myself or with myself."

Some students around me snicker again, and I hear a distinctive "Oh, shit!" from the back of the room.

Mr. Olson puts his hand on his blossoming waist. He's a big man. His chest is thick. He was a linebacker for the school in his glory days, but take away the practices and weightlifting and keep the eggs and bacon for breakfast, and you get a mammoth-sized math teacher.

I do feel a little sorry for the guy. I mean, he and I are probably going to die from the same thing, but he doesn't have to. He could put down the bucket of chicken and self-pity and go to the gym. He could get a different job if he hates this one so much. He could live a long life. He has a choice.

"What do you plan on doing with your life, Mr. McAdams? Really? Are you going to live with Mommy and Daddy until the day you die because you don't want to be bothered with learning anything?"

I laugh, feeling the irony down to my bones. "Actually, Mr. Olson, that may be exactly what I do. How about you? You need to sit down? Your heart doing okay in there?"

His cheeks turn red, and his chest heaves in and out with great effort. "You know," he puffs, "I had a lot of respect for your brother. But don't think that the world is going to give you a pass because he died."

I smile, even feel like I might tear up a little, but that feeling passes quickly. "You were at graduation, weren't you?"

He nods.

"Well, as someone who respected and admired my brother, I'm sure you'll appreciate this quote from his speech." I give him the finger.

"Would you like to go to the principal's office?" he asks, the vein protruding even more, and I'm pretty sure I can see it pulsing with each beat of his heart.

"I've been to the principal's office a few times. It's not very stimulating."

He slams the homework on his desk. "That was a rhetorical question, Mr. McAdams. I wasn't actually asking you if you wanted to go to the principal's office."

"Oh, sorry. I misunderstood."

He gestures toward the door, but my eyes stay fixed on his tense, forty-year-old face.

"Do I need to call security?"

"Rhetorical?" I ask, complete with a perplexed look on my face. "I mean, do you really need to call security just to deal with me?"

His fingers curl in against his palms like he's ready to punch something, or someone. He steps a few feet closer to me and stands, feet planted, between two rows of desks. "Do you think your brother would be proud of you right now? Don't you care what he'd think?"

Cool air has been rattling the metal vents, but suddenly the rattling and the hum of the air-conditioning system stops. Every person is still and silent. Waiting.

"Well." I throw my voice into the quiet. "He doesn't think anything because he's dead and cold and buried in the ground. And you know what?" I stand. My hands are shaking as I grip the edge of my desk and flip it over. "You might want to make that call to security after all."

The sky is a thick, solid gray. I've always hated the brightness of the artificial turf on the football field, and now, with the dark clouds and the heavy drops of rain, it seems even brighter, even more fake. I'm in the doorway of the football locker room. Separate from the school itself, this is the place where players line up before running onto the field and tearing through the long banner the cheerleaders make for each home game.

The season won't officially start for a few more weeks, but in two hours, the football team will take to the field for practice. Last year, Connor would have been counting down the minutes of his trigonometry class or Spanish 4 or maybe forensics. He'd have been anxious to get on the field and start practicing with his team. He loved football. He loved the way the crowds in the bleachers would scream and stomp their feet to cheer him and the other players on. Now rain is pelting the long strips of metal seats. It's running down the stairs and onto the artificial grass that doesn't need rain to stay green.

I like the sound of the rain hitting the metal roof of the small building that has only two rooms, one for each team. I like the way it collects in the gutters and falls to the ground in a steady stream just in front of where I stand. And I like the way the sound fills my head, leaving little room for thought. I'm tired of thinking, but I can't stop doing it. Even when I'm sleeping, I dream about Dr. Sharp, about him and me sharing a coffin and how even in death I can't rest, because he's constantly coughing, constantly spraying my face and my white satin pillow with his blood.

When I got sent to the principal's office, she was nice enough to ask me which parent I wanted her to call. I told her to call Dad, even though he'd have to leave work and I knew my mom was at home, probably mopping spotless floors or dusting dust-free furniture. Mom's kind of been on autopilot since James died a few weeks ago. She does things; she never stops doing things, and it doesn't matter if they need to be done.

I can't get Dad's expression out of my head. He wasn't angry or bewildered. He was sad. I'd rather he'd been angry. I wish he'd shaken his head in disappointment and told me that when we got home, I was really going to get it. I'd be grounded and the Smart car taken away and no more television or video games or going to see Cami. But you don't punish the dying. You don't ground those who are about to go in the ground. And he thinks I still have almost a year and a half left. How can I tell him and Mom that I don't?

Principal Wiggins explained what happened. Dad listened, nodding his head and not once looking at me with the outrage she was expecting. Then he asked me to step into the hallway for a moment while he talked to her in private. When the office door opened and I was invited back inside, she wasn't looking at me with that "I'm disappointed in you" expression anymore. The woman who had been pissed at me a few minutes earlier, ready to refer me to both grief counseling and anger management, looked at me like she was . . . sorry. She promised not to share my "condition" with anyone else and changed my two-week suspension to three days. Dad went back to work. I told him that I would take my time getting home, since there were still a few hours of school, and it might be good to wait until he got there to tell Mom about my suspension.

I wasn't sure where to go. And then I found myself here. It's not quite the same as visiting Connor's grave, but it's close.

"There you are," Cami shouts from beneath the overhang of the concession stand. She runs across the field, and by the time she reaches the locker rooms just past the end zone, rain clings to the curls in her hair, and her soaked T-shirt is pressed against her body.

"Why aren't you all wet?" she asks, once she's safely beneath the overhang.

"I was here before it started raining," I say, watching her shiver. "Come on."

The door labeled HOME TEAM is locked, but Connor had a key to it. I try a few different keys on the key ring until one opens the door.

I'm not sure what I'm expecting when I go inside. I mean, this is the home of the Mighty Panthers, but it really looks like a giant, glorified bathroom. There are sinks along one wall.

Above them is one oblong window with frosted glass. Toward the back of the room, there's a dry-erase board and two rows of benches.

"Give me your shirt," I tell Cami. She hesitates, then sees the automatic hand dryers on the wall. She peels the T-shirt off. I mean to look away, but I don't. I see the white skin of her belly leading to the thin skin-colored bra she's wearing, and I can't look away. I take off my own shirt, and still staring, hand it to her. Then I hold her shirt up to the dryer. "How'd you find me?" I ask.

"Your dad called. He told me what happened. He's worried about you, so I told him I'd try to find you. Even though your car is kind of little, it's easy to spot in a pretty empty parking lot. And don't worry. I already called and told him I found you."

"Thanks, but aren't you supposed to be in class?"

"I'm in class: Kyle McAdams 101." She smiles, looking adorable in my blue striped T-shirt. "I was lucky to get in, actually. It's considered advanced studies."

"Really," I say, pushing the button on the dryer again and shivering just a little at my own bare torso. "I had no idea I was so complex."

Cami comes toward me, wraps her arms around my waist, and presses herself against my back so we can both benefit from the warmth of my shirt. Her hands are on my stomach. They feel amazing, driving everything from my mind except thoughts of her. She's still shivering. She steps away, slips her hands behind her back and under the shirt. Then she reaches into one sleeve and pulls out one strap of her bra, then does the same thing on the other side, only this time, her entire bra comes out the sleeve of my T-shirt. It's like the best magic trick I've ever seen.

"It's pretty wet," she says, taking it to the other dryer and pushing the button.

I watch her, and all I can think is how much I wish I hadn't given her my shirt. Shit, I almost feel weak-kneed at the thought of her standing there, bare from the waist up, then I wonder if once her clothes are dry, she'll be able to use the same trick to put her bra back on. I don't think so. I could close my eyes. I should, but . . .

Cami starts laughing.

I push the button again and talk loudly over the noise. "What?"

"The expression on your face. You look like Josh right before he unwraps his birthday presents."

My face is heating, and I'm not sure if it's from the hot air blasting toward me or something else. "Are you implying that I want to unwrap you?"

She lays her bra across the sink, comes toward me, and takes her semidry shirt out of my hands. Her hands go back around my waist. My fingers slip into the damp curls of her hair, and I kiss her harder than I mean to, but I can't help it. She's kissing me. She loves me. Even with everything she knows. Even though *we* might not last because *I* might not last, she hasn't backed away. She's never backed away. I kiss her harder. The iron taste of blood starts to mingle with the taste of her.

Our lips part, and I stare into her face. I know it so well: the depth of her brown, almost black eyes, the subtle blush of her cheeks, the lips that aren't long and thin, but small and full and perfectly arched.

Cami's fingers grip the hem of the shirt she's wearing, and she begins to peel it away but hesitates. She's breathing deeply, and I know her heart is pounding, just like mine is. She starts moving her hands upward again, but I catch them in mine.

"Wait." I pull the shirt down. "I love you. And I *want* you, but when we do it, *if* we do it, it won't be in a place like this. I'd have to be the world's biggest dick to take advantage of you in a locker room."

Cami dons a look of confusion. "Did you say that you *are* the world's biggest dick or that you *have* the world's biggest dick?"

I laugh. I can't help it, and that's what I love about her— one of the many things I love about her. She's always trying to make me feel better. No matter what. I tightly grip her arms and shake her gently to make sure she's looking at me and knows that I'm serious.

"Camille," I start, "I love you. I am in love with you."

She takes my face in her hands. "I love you, but don't call me Camille. I hate being called Camille."

Moments.

I don't think it is the number of years a person lives that matters, but the number of moments they experience and how those moments come together to form who you are, or were, and what your life meant. This is a moment. Standing in the stadium locker room, the rain pounding against the metal roof.

With Cami's hands pressed against my cheeks and her eyes smiling and weeping at the same time, because she loves me.

I kiss her. The taste of fear and love and optimism is intoxicating, and I wish I could drink this moment, this kiss, into my body somehow and taste it forever.

It's too intense, and Cami steps away. She takes her nearly dry shirt and turns around. I watch as she pulls my shirt off, and without putting her damp bra back on, pulls her shirt over her body. Then she turns around.

"It's probably good that we didn't make love in here. If we did it on the floor, instead of athlete's foot, we might have gotten athlete's ass."

I grimace in disgust, but laugh. "Whatever happens, I just don't want you to have any regrets."

"You never answered my question."

"What question?"

"Are you the world's biggest dick, or do you have the world's biggest dick?" She's smiling, blushing.

"Well." I kiss the underside of her wrist. "Both would be true, actually. I mean, I am genetically enhanced."

"**Y**ou remember the plan?" Jimmy asks.

"Yeah, but I still don't like it."

We're parked at the veterans' hospital. It's a mammoth brick building. The east and west wings are three stories high, while the center is four with a white steeple rising from its center.

"Well, tough shit, kid. Matt and I went over and over it, and with her office being in a secured area, this is the best way to get you in."

"But what about you?" I'm okay with the part of the plan where Matt has an actual appointment with the doctor, thus assuring that she stays out of her office for a while. But I'm not comfortable with Jimmy's part in this. Not comfortable at all.

"Did you know I wanted to be a teacher?"

"Yeah, Cami told me."

"Uncle Sam was supposed to put me through college. I was going to be a good teacher. I was going to make kids feel capable, you know?"

He looks at me, and in his deep brown eyes, I see the spirit of a dead dream floating around. Lost.

"Instead of an education, I got a fucked-up brain. I worked so hard just to learn how to turn letters around in my head so I could read them, and now by the time I get to the end of a paragraph, I can't remember what the first part was about." His face, covered with thick stubble, smiles. "But I can do this. I can help you. And, hey, a few days of Klonopin and cartoons won't be so bad. Won't be the first time."

"What if they—"

"Give me a lobotomy and a dose of electroconvulsive shock therapy? Nah. I'll just act crazy for a little while. Once I turn all normal again, they'll hold me for observation, give me a few dozen pills, then save Uncle Sam a buck by sending me on my merry manic way."

I'm not comforted. Jimmy's *normal* isn't exactly normal. "Why are you doing this?" I ask, genuinely. "Something could happen to you. You might not get out as easily as you think."

Jimmy looks at me with clear eyes. "How much time do you have left?"

"At most, maybe three and a half months."

He nods. "You join the military, they send you to a place like Iraq or Afghanistan, and you don't know how long you're gonna live. You hope you'll go home, hope you'll see your family again, but the truth is, you could get shot waiting in the damn chow line. Nobody knows how much time they have, but your best chance to survive is to depend on your buddies.

We watch out for each other. We have each other's backs. And you're my buddy."

Jimmy slaps me on the arm, then squeezes it, and my chest swells with emotion.

"Okay," Jimmy says, opening the car door. "Time to get my crazy on."

We go through the massive doors leading to massive hallways. The place is old. I don't know how old, but I wouldn't be surprised if some World War I veterans once hobbled down these halls on crutches or were pushed down them in wheelchairs after losing their sight to mustard gas. The place is cold and creepy.

I can almost see clean-cut World War II ghosts eyeing the bearded, tattooed Vietnam ghosts. I can see ghostly nurses mopping up ghostly blood and vomit and other bodily fluids from the tile floors. It's eighty degrees outside, and while the air conditioner seems to be working quite well, I have to wonder if the numerous ghosts passing through the halls add to the frigid feel of the air.

And this is where Jimmy is willing to spend the next few days—if all goes well.

We walk down one hallway, turn left, and walk down another. Jimmy knows right where to go, and we end up in front of a brick wall where there is a door labeled RESTRICTED: PSYCHIATRIC WARD. The door is made of thick glass. Next to it, halfway up the wall, is a large window that slides open.

"You ready?" Jimmy whispers, and I'm not sure what I'm

supposed to be ready for. I've never seen someone having a psychotic breakdown, but Jimmy's about to demonstrate.

"Can't you hear them?" he asks me, his voice loud, his eyes staring up at the ceiling. "They're coming to get me. They're laughing, can't you hear them?" His fingers are moving nervously against one another. His torso is rocking back and forth.

A bald man in blue scrubs slides the window open. "What's the problem?"

"My uncle," I say. "He's been here before. PTSD and some other shit, I don't know. I came home from school, and he was like this. He's not making any sense. He's really freaking me out."

"What's his name?" the man asks.

"Jimmy. Jimmy Williams."

The man closes the window and comes around to the glass door. He punches a code into a keypad. A buzzer sounds, and the door opens. "Hey, Frank," he hollers to a thin African American man behind him, "I'm gonna need your help with this one." He approaches us with his palms up in a nonthreatening stance, but he's a big man with a thick neck, and any stance he takes looks threatening.

"It's okay, Jimmy," he says.

"No it's not!" Jimmy grabs hold of me, like he's terrified, and I have to wonder just how familiar he is with insanity, because he's doing a hell of a job. "Don't leave me. Don't leave me!"

"It's okay, buddy," Frank says. "You want your nephew to come with you?"

Jimmy nods.

"You okay?" Frank asks me.

"Yeah, sure," I tell him. "It's okay, Jimmy. These men are going to help you. But we have to go in here, all right?"

The two men back up as I lead Jimmy through the steel door.

"That's great, Jimmy," the bald one says. "You're doing great."

Once we're inside, Jimmy looks around like he's Frodo getting his first look at Mordor. "I don't like it here," he says. "You're bad guys! You're bad guys!"

I half expect him to start lashing out, to grab a chair and throw it at them, but Jimmy knows what's he's doing. He wants to be evaluated, not harpooned with a sedative and strapped to a bed.

"Do we look like bad guys?" the bald one asks. "We're the good guys. I did two tours over in Afghanistan. How many did you do? I bet more than me."

Jimmy eyes him. "Four," he says. "Hate that fucking place."

The man laughs. "Me too, buddy. They can keep their fucking desert. But we ain't there no more. We're home. Ain't that right. It look like the desert around here to you?"

Jimmy shakes his head.

"You want to come with me. I know a nice quiet place we can go. You and me can talk about things. Things only you and I know. Like having to wash our own goddamned laundry because those assholes the government hired don't know shit about doing laundry."

Jimmy smiles, and for a minute, I think he's falling out of character. He lets the guy lead him down the hall.

"You hang out here," the other one says to me. "We'll get him settled, then I've got some paperwork and questions for you."

I nod. "You bet."

I sit down and watch as they turn a corner; then I stand and head for the elevator. According to Matt, the entire east wing of the hospital is restricted. It's the wing where the majority of staff offices are and where the mentally ill patients are kept. Once you get past a security door, you're in. You can travel between floors and still be in.

I start to push the Up button on the elevator, but stop myself. There's a good chance someone may be getting off on this floor, and they'll wonder what I'm doing here. To the right is a door leading to the stairs. I climb to the second floor, then the third.

I stand there for a moment, listening. There's a conversation going on between at least two people, both females, waiting for the elevator. One's talking about her kid, how he just started pulling himself up and walking around the furniture. The other woman oohs and ahs at how cute that stage is. I hear the elevator door ding and the voices grow distant, then silent. I close my eyes, envisioning the map Matt showed me.

From the stairs, take a sharp left turn, then go straight to a hall labeled 3B. Turn right, go past the men's restroom and a water fountain. Then there's another hall but go straight. Dr. Bartholomew's office is on the left side of the hallway. There's a chance her name won't be on the door, due to the fact that it's only used when she's in town, so don't forget that it's the second door from the far end of the hall.

I glance at my phone. Matt's appointment is in five minutes. She has three other appointments scheduled before his, and another two after.

Cracking open the door from the stairwell, I listen for voices or footsteps. I don't hear anyone, so I push the door open. There's a man in a doctor's coat at the end of the hall, but his back is turned, so I follow Matt's directions until I get to the office that is not labeled. Every other door has a nameplate on it, but on this one there is only a faded rectangle where a name should be.

Her office isn't locked. It's evident that this is just a place for her to dictate information in private and make phone calls while she's visiting patients at the VA. I can imagine that her office in Saint Louis is much larger and actually decorated and carpeted. This room is bare. The walls are beige, and the wood floor is covered by a fine layer of dust.

There is a bookshelf that stretches from the floor to the ceiling, but it's mostly empty. And there is no filing cabinet. The desk is my only bet. Other than a cup of coffee and an outdated dial phone, there is nothing on the desk. I open the center drawer and see paperclips, a pen that's sprung a leak, and what look like Oreo crumbs.

The top side drawer has a few envelopes with a silhouette of the hospital stamped in the corner, next to a notepad with the same silhouette. There are rubber bands, a fingernail file, and an abandoned pack of nicotine gum; someone must have started smoking again. The only other drawer is large and has a keyhole.

I hold my breath as I grip the top of the drawer and pull. It doesn't budge. I take the small tool set Jimmy gave me out of my pocket and choose a flathead screw driver. I slip it in between the top of the drawer and the desk. I might be able to flip the latch and open it. It won't budge. I put the screwdriver back, and this time, I select a slender instrument like what my dentist uses for those hard-to-reach places. I tilt and turn the instrument inside the lock the way Jimmy taught me when we practiced last night.

Footsteps sound in the hall, and I duck down behind the desk. A man is talking, and I wait to hear who he's talking to. When there's only silence instead of a reply, I realize that he's on a phone. My heart slows back to a frantic pace, and I start working on the lock again. After what seems like minutes, but according to the clock was only thirty seconds, I hear a click and the drawer opens. There is no neatly labeled flash drive with blinking neon arrows pointing to it, just an oversized leather handbag.

I always assumed all purses were filled with dirty Kleenexes, loose change, a lint-filled hairbrush, and a stick of gum so brittle it shatters if you try to bite into it. But not Dr. Bartholomew's. I empty the contents onto the top of the desk: a thin leather wallet, a silver compact with a matching silver cylinder of lipstick, and an appointment book.

I start flipping through the appointment book. It's filled

with names and times. I flip from page to page and then back again, but nowhere do I see the name Richard Sharp. I flip back to the last pages, the pages where names and phone numbers and addresses are kept. Still no Richard Sharp. I go through the book again and again. I look through the drawer again, even feel around the bottom, because I've seen things hidden there in movies. Nothing.

I lean back in the chair and want to scream. If I scream loud enough, maybe the two guys taking care of Jimmy can run up here and take care of me. I wouldn't mind a cup full of pills, or maybe even a shot in the ass, if I could forget about everything for a while.

But not for too long.

The door opens.

We stare at each other. Dr. Bartholomew's expression is one of anger and outrage that I'm sitting behind her desk going through the contents of her purse. Then it's as if she recognizes me, and her expression shifts more to curiosity. She closes the door.

"I've seen you before," she says, coming forward and sitting in the chair in front of the desk.

"I was going into a building you were coming out of," I say. "I was visiting Dr. Sharp."

Her thin lips tilt in a slight smile. The hair that settles against her shoulders in one giant curl seems a bit more yellow now than it was. She's wearing her white doctor's coat over a petite frame, and there's something so familiar about her, something more than just the fact that I saw her coming out of Sharp's building.

"That's not where I know you from," she says, "although I do remember being a bit startled when the elevator opened and there you stood. I don't know why I was so surprised, really. I knew he wanted to meet you. He was very curious about you."

"Was?" I ask, and even though I know he said he'd never help me, I want him to be alive. I want there to be a chance that he might change his mind.

"I'm afraid he passed shortly after your visit. It's a blessing, really. My brother was in a great deal of pain."

"Your brother?" I almost choke on the question.

"You didn't know? I thought he might have told you his true identity. If I were dying, I would want people to call me by my given name. His was Edward." She says the name deliberately.

"Do you know what he did to us? To me and my brother and the others?"

She closes her eyes, and when she opens them again, I see the resemblance. He was so emaciated when I saw him that the only family members he could resemble would have to have been long dead, but eyes don't lose weight in a dying body. They don't fade, and she has the same black, birdlike eyes as her brother.

"Confessions are part of the dying process," she says, "although I don't think Edward was confessing as much as bragging about the success of his experiment."

"Do you have his research?" I ask.

She leans forward, placing her hands on the edge of the desk. "Yes, Kyle. I do. Had he not taken a sudden and drastic turn for the worse, he might have had time to give it to someone else. He had a list of researchers he was considering, but he couldn't decide. How do you know who to trust when your ultimate goal is mass murder?"

"So you don't agree with your brother's vision of the world?"

"No." She presses her palms against the desk. "I suppose I understand his logic, but there must be more humane ways of dealing with humanity's problems. I suppose someone as brilliant and intelligent as Edward was would look for the most intriguing and challenging ways to address a problem. And, perhaps, the most practical."

Her eyes soften as her narrow face lights with memories.

"As children, Edward and I were fascinated by science. Our father was a scientist. He would tell us about his work sometimes, and it all sounded so intriguing. When Edward was only eight, he was diagnosed with a rare form of childhood cancer. He went through years of treatment, sadly leaving him sterile. I think that's why he was so fond of all of you. He had pictures, so many pictures of you all—files filled with them—like you were his own children."

"He killed us."

"Yes," she says, looking at me and offering no excuse or explanation. "After his illness, he became obsessed with medicine, with physiology and genetics. I, too, became fascinated with crossing the bridge between science and medicine. We both became doctors—scientists—but our interests took us down different paths. At first I respected his work. He was fascinated by the human genome, with the ability to create humans who wouldn't have to suffer as he'd suffered. But then he started manipulating genes to create a different type of humanity. Not just healthy, but superior." She shakes her head and gives a short, unbelieving scoff. "My work centers on helping people live full lives, but creating a 'super' race is just . . ." She sighs and folds her hands tightly together. "What I didn't know until recently was that his research into gene manipulation was to help fund his other interests, his true research."

"Killing people," I finish for her.

"Yes." She looks at me. "I still can't believe what he did to you and the others. He only confided in me once his illness had progressed to the point that he found it difficult to function. I was, at best, appalled. But by then, what could I do except beg him to give me access to his research? At first he refused. I tried to trick him, tried to appeal to the vanity that scientists sometimes have, saying how awed I was by his work. How it would be an honor just to look at it. He saw right through me, even in the fog the pain medications created. But as his illness progressed, it was easier to manipulate *bits* of information out of him, until I finally knew where his research was and how to access it. I wish he had given it to me freely, but he knew I wouldn't use it as he intended. He thought he still had time to find the right person, but he had a stroke." She dabs at her eyes with her white sleeves.

Since walking into this old hospital, I've felt ghostly fingers running up and down my spine, my arms, the sides of my throat. Now I feel them gripping me, pulling at me. It's like they can see the days counting down on my forehead, and they want me to join them, to be friends with them and haunt these wide halls together.

"Can you save me?"

Dr. Bartholomew considers my request, but it's not a request.

"Save me," I demand.

"I haven't had the research for very long, and to be honest, much of it is difficult to decipher. I have a group of researchers, people I trust completely, going over it as we speak. Ever since I first learned of your existence, it has been my goal to save you. It seems the least I can do under the circumstances. But as of this very moment, I don't know how to. And if there is a way to keep your heart from stopping, there is the immortality sequence to consider."

I think I see the envy in her eyes. She's older than my mom. I'd guess midfifties. At best, her life is half over. She's a doctor who saves lives, and in another twenty or thirty, forty years, she'll be dead or in a nursing home. I'm sixteen. I have no aspirations of saving anyone's life but my own, and I could outlive her by centuries. Or I could be dead in less than four months.

"Can you figure it out—how to keep my heart from stopping? You can take out the other sequence too. I don't care about living forever. I just want to make it past seventeen."

"We don't have much time." Dr. Bartholomew stands, staring at me, coming closer, like I'm part of her brother's research, like I'm cells in a petri dish and she wants to shove me under a microscope. Her beady black eyes narrow over her slight nose. "I can't remove the sequence that will slow your aging," she says. "It speaks directly to the brain, and the brain controls all bodily functions. To tamper with that, I'm quite certain, would lead to your death. I don't know how to keep the other genetic sequence from stopping your heart, but I promise I will find a way. No one in this world, Kyle, is more important to me at this moment, than you are."

I stand, feeling like I have to. Like I need to move, like I need fresh air because the cold air coming from the vents is filled with some type of anxiety-inducing drug. My insides feel like they're boiling, while my skin feels cold. My heart is racing—no, it's begging.

She offers me her hand. It's small and smooth, and I take it. "I know how incredibly dangerous his research is," she says. "You have my word that I will destroy it as soon as I fulfill my promise to save you. Until then, why don't you relax a bit? And avoid breaking the law." She gestures toward the contents of her purse still on the desk. "Curing you might prove difficult if you're locked in a juvenile facility."

I nod in agreement.

"I promise, as soon as I know something, you'll know."

I want to believe her. I want so desperately to believe that she's the answer to my prayers, the miracle I've been looking for.

"**W**hat'd you find out?" I ask Matt's image on my computer screen. He's thumbing through pages of material about Dr. Claudia Bartholomew.

"She seems all right. No ethical violations or felonies. Two speeding tickets and a fine for driving with a taillight out, but that's it. I didn't find anything suspicious. She's part of a research group doing work on using stem cells to grow human organs and, eventually, limbs. So far they've been able to create kidneys and bladders. They hope to use the same processes for livers and maybe even hearts."

"What about her personal life?" I ask.

"She got married when she was twenty-six. They divorced a year later, and she took back her maiden name."

"Any kids?"

Matt shakes his head.

"You met her," I say. "What'd you think of her?"

He backs away from his screen a little, settling in his chair. "She seemed nice, professional. She can't help me with my issues, at least not right now. They can't grow what I need, not yet, anyway. But hey, at least it's nice to know there's someone out there trying."

"Yeah," I agree. "It is nice to know there's someone out there trying. I just hope it's the right someone."

Matt leans toward the camera. "If you're worried that she's a singularly goal-driven psychopath like her brother . . . I just don't see it. There's been some controversy about stem cell use, but I seriously can't find anything questionable about her. I think you can trust her."

I want to believe him, and maybe I do. I don't know. My life is really in her hands, and if I were Matt, I'd want to trust someone who might be able to make me a complete man again. I guess when it comes right down to it, I don't have any choice.

"How's Jimmy?" Matt asks. "Did you see him today?"

"I went this morning. Cami and her dad are going to see him after her dad gets off work."

"How is he?"

"Medicated," I say. "He's so doped up, he couldn't even eat his breakfast without help."

Matt nods. "I bet you didn't know that Uncle Sam was such a drug pusher. Guy loves giving out the meds."

"It's not going to hurt him, is it?" I hate seeing Jimmy like that. He seriously couldn't hold his head up for more than a few seconds.

"He'll be fine," Matt says. "Once they release him, we'll get him off all that shit."

I look at him doubtfully, because it can't be that easy.

"I'm going to go see him tomorrow," Matt says. "Hopefully

he'll be out in a few days. It's not like he hasn't been down this road before."

"But he went down it because of me."

"Hoorah," he says. "Being a hero isn't supposed to be easy."

"Yeah," I agree, because Jimmy is my hero.

My phone starts to ring.

"I'll catch you later," Matt says. He gives me a little wave and goes offline.

"Hey," I answer.

"Have you checked Facebook lately?" Cami asks.

I'm surprised, because she knows that I don't get on Facebook anymore. Not since James . . .

"You might want to. I think you have an invite. Emma said she sent you one."

"Emma? Invite to what? Isn't she still gone?"

"Her parents' wedding anniversary is next week, and she's coming home for it. She invited me to the party and said she sent you an invite too."

"Why me? I'm the reason she moved."

Cami doesn't say anything. She doesn't have to. Maybe the months Emma has been away have strengthened her. Maybe she's gone on lots of nature hikes around Minnesota's numerous lakes and found peace with losing Connor, so seeing me won't be a big deal. Fat chance.

She's not over him. No one could ever get over him. So maybe that's why she invited me.

"You don't have to go," Cami says.

"I do." I have to go because Connor can't. He can't make

sure that she's all right. And if seeing me somehow brings her comfort, then . . .

"I love you," Cami says, making me smile, even though I don't feel like it.

I want to go find Connor and tease him because he has to go to some boring anniversary party. I want to see him in a pressed shirt, a tie, and uncomfortable dress shoes. I want him to come home and tell me how everybody kept asking him when he was going to pop the question to Emma. I want them to have the future they should have had, the future I was jealous of.

I want Connor alive.

I want Emma happy.

I think about how people carve their names or initials into tree trunks or get them tattooed into their skin. Connor + Emma = Forever. It's as true as $2 + 2 = 4$. It can't be changed. Two can't be added to another number and equal four. Emma plus any other person can never equal what she had with Connor. Never.

"Are you there?" Cami asks.

"Yeah," I say. "I'm here."

I'm here for now, I think. And I can't help but wonder what Kyle + Cami will end up equaling.

I feel like I'm suffocating in Emma's living room. There are people everywhere, all of them dressed to the hilt and holding a beverage of some sort. Some sip from thin-stemmed wineglasses, others from short, fat glasses filled with orange juice and vodka or deep circular glasses with the rims dipped in salt to offset the flavor of the festive green margarita mix.

I've never been drunk before. Okay. I've been buzzed. In eighth grade, I met Scott Henderson behind the Ferris wheel at the county fair. He had a bottle of his mom's peach schnapps, and we got a little wasted. Enough to lose our corn dogs and the schnapps on the bumper cars.

I'm not drunk now. At least I don't think I am. I asked Emma's dad for a Coke. He gave me a large glass, and in the heat of all the bodies in the room, I downed it. When I asked for another one, he laughed. I watched him as he put a few more ice cubes into my glass, then he doused them with rum before adding Coke from a two-liter bottle.

"Shit," I said out loud, making Emma's dad, a chiropractor with a thin face and graying hair, laugh again.

He gave me the drink, slapped me on the shoulder, and said, "I won't tell if you don't."

Emma's family has a nice house. From the living room, a person can see into the dining room and the kitchen. The granite counter dividing the kitchen from the dining room is covered with various bottles of liquor, and a blender is constantly whirling and crushing. There's music playing, and while no one is outright dancing, not yet anyway, people sway as they mingle, holding clear plastic plates with appetizers on them.

Emma is standing in front of a potted tree, its branches strewn with tiny white lights. She's wearing an off-white dress with a ribbon that encircles her torso just below her breasts, which are pushed up so the top crescents of them are visible. Her shoulders are bare, and her legs practically are too, the dress stopping midthigh. She's wearing thin-strapped, high-heeled shoes, and her hair drapes over her shoulders.

"Having fun?" Emma shouts over the music being piped in through her dad's surround-sound speakers.

"Yeah," I lie.

"I'm sorry your parents couldn't make it," she shouts. "I told Mom and Dad not to invite them. I'm sure they're not up for a party. I told them not to invite me either, but . . ." Her bare shoulders shrug. "Cami's not coming," she says, not knowing that Cami had called to tell me that nearly two hours ago. "Her dad's working, and she found a babysitter, but then Josh started throwing up. But it's okay. I'll have plenty of time to see her later."

"You will?" I ask, wondering how long she's going to be in

town and how many classes she can afford to miss back at the community college in Minnesota.

"You came." She lifts her hand and brushes it against my cheek. "It's so hot in here, and loud."

"Yes," I say emphatically. And the floor shifts under my feet just a little.

"Are you drunk?"

"No," I insist, then look at my half-empty glass of rum and Coke. "Maybe."

"You lightweight." Emma laughs and takes my hand. "But it's okay. I'm a little drunk too. Maybe more than a little."

She leads me to the stairs, the temperature decreasing with each step. The basement is huge. There's a giant flat screen on one wall, and sports posters and memorabilia hang on the others. A couple of people are shooting pool, and I don't like the sound of the balls cracking into each other.

"Still too crowded?" Emma asks.

I nod and follow her down a long, dark hallway.

"Welcome to my abode," she says, opening the door to a large room bathed in soft violet light.

"This is your room?"

There's a square, black-lacquered table in the center. The inner blob of a lava lamp dances next to a tray of sand and pebbles and a bonsai tree. In the corner of the room, a giant bean-bag chair sits next to a stack of paperbacks. Mother-of-pearl wind chimes dangle from the ceiling, a breeze from a small fan making them move in a constant, clinking motion.

Against the wall is a large bed covered by a dark, faux-fur

blanket. Above the bed, a poster of Bob Marley looks down on a pile of satin pillows.

"Do you like it?" Emma asks. "My parents remodeled it for me. Well, they repainted it. Mom and I went shopping and I added a few personal touches. I think they're hoping I'll move back home."

"Where are the cheerleading trophies and the calendar with the cute puppies on it? This looks like a hookah bar."

Emma smiles, like "hookah bar" is exactly the look she was hoping for. She sits on the bed, unfastens the thin straps on her shoes, then slides them off.

"Was Connor ever in here?" I ask. "Before it looked like this?"

It's too dark to see if the mention of his name makes her flinch, but I don't think it does.

"My parents don't allow boys in my room. But I'm in college now. I'm not a little girl anymore. Besides, they're busy with their guests. And"—she slips from the bed to the door—"there's a lock."

She turns the deadbolt and leans her back against the door. "Did you know that Connor and I never made love?"

Between the weird lighting and the rum, my head is starting to spin a little.

"We never did. I was willing, but he wanted to wait. I thought it was romantic." She's smiling as she takes a step toward where I'm standing, just a few feet from the bed. "He had this vision of us going on a ski trip with other college students. We'd all share some big cabin in the mountains. There'd be a

243

huge fireplace and a hot tub. And one day, when the others all decided to go skiing, we'd stay behind."

The smile fades.

"You always think you have time," she says. "Time to make things just right. Time to make them romantic and lovely, but you don't." Emma looks at me. "You don't know, when you say good-bye to someone, if you'll ever see him again." Her hands reach behind her back, and with a slight shimmying motion, her dress slips from her body. Her strapless bra looks violet in the lighting. Even her tiger print thong is purple, and the image of a great purple tiger roaming the plains of Africa pops into my head, then pops right back out again.

The air was cool a moment ago, but now my skin feels like it's heating from the inside out. And those damn wind chimes are giving me a headache.

She comes forward and takes my face in her hands.

Her smell is incredible, and her mouth tastes like strawberries. She pulls me onto the bed, and we sink into the thick black fur. I run my hands over her legs as they curl around mine.

"I don't want to wait anymore," she says, her breath hot against my neck.

"Me neither." My hands cup beneath her bare hips. Our mouths find each other, the flavors of rum and daiquiri fusing on our tongues.

"I want you so much," she says, tugging at my clothes.

"I want you. God, Cami, I want you."

Her body stiffens beneath mine. Emma's body. Not Cami's.

"Oh, shit!" I scramble from the bed.

"Cami?" Emma's voice is more air than sound. "You and Cami . . ." Tears burst through the clouds in her eyes.

"You were the one who kept bringing us together," I say, wanting to remind her that I'm Kyle. I'm the one with Cami. Not Connor. Connor could never be with anyone but her.

I sit on the bed, wrap the blanket around her, and hold her. I hold her tightly, as tightly as I can, but I know I can't make her feel better, just like I couldn't make her feel better after Connor's funeral. She needs *him*.

"I'm sorry." My voice is soft against the top of her head. Emma looks up at me, then squeezes her eyes closed, and I wish I were brave enough to throw acid in my face, so she wouldn't have to see Connor anymore.

Suddenly I see Dr. Sharp standing in the violet light of the room. His skin looks even nastier now as it clings to his slightly exposed skull. He's a skeleton in baggy clothes with black beaded eyes and a mouth made of exposed teeth and bone. Volcanic anger and sadness rise in me, and hatred.

I won't let him get me. He took Connor and James and the others. He dragged their families, everyone who loved them, down into hell with him. But I won't let him take me. Dr. Bartholomew told me she'd find a way to save me, and whatever way she finds, no matter what I have to do or what pain I might have to endure, I'll do it. I'll survive. I won't let Cami end up like this, and in whatever way I can, I'll be there for Emma. Even if it's just to hold her and to tell her how sorry I am and that I miss him too. I'll do it for her, and I'll do it for Connor.

Emma was asleep when I left her. Between the alcohol and the crying, she was exhausted. I'm exhausted, but I don't want to go home. Not yet.

The front porch light is on, and a strip of light shines from a gap in the living room curtains. I knock on the door, and Cami's there almost instantly. I know I must smell like Emma's perfume, but if Cami can smell it, she doesn't seem to care. She pulls me inside, and we wrap our arms around each other.

Cami leads me into the living room and directs my eyes toward the sofa, where Josh is sound asleep in his Spider-Man pajamas, a plastic bowl by his side. "He finally stopped throwing up about an hour ago. Poor little guy. He's exhausted." She's covered him with a blanket. A penguin-shaped pillow supports his head.

Cami's wearing an oversized nightshirt. Her feet are bare. Her hair is freshly washed and allowed to do what it wants, which is curl haphazardly around her face. She isn't wearing any makeup, no lipstick or eyeliner, and she isn't genetically altered.

She's the most beautiful woman I've ever seen.

"Come on," she says, then kisses me softly, sweetly. Her hand clasps mine. She starts to lead me down the hall to her bedroom, but I stop her.

"I need to tell you something," I say, but she puts her fingers across my lips.

"I know you, Kyle McAdams. There's nothing you need to tell me."

She does know me. She knows me, and she trusts me, and she loves me.

I wrap my arms around her and pull her in to me until she backs away and takes my hand again. We reach her room. I don't know how many hours I've spent here. Lately, Cami's bedroom feels more like home than just about any place, but tonight, as I watch her lock the door, I feel like I've never been here before.

"What if he wakes up?" I ask, surprised by the trembling in my voice.

"He won't."

"What about your dad?"

"He'll be stuck at the station until at least nine thirty tomorrow morning." Cami sits on the bed. Her nightshirt slides toward her hips, and I can see her pink panties.

"We don't have any protection," I point out, not certain why I keep coming up with reasons not to have sex when I really, really want to. It's not just the raging, almost-seventeen-year-old hormones either. And it's not the whole "I don't want to die a virgin" thing. It's her and how I feel about her.

She's the one.

If everything were normal, if *I* were normal, Cami is the one I'd marry someday. We'd have children together and cart them around to soccer practices and piano recitals. We'd get our first gray hairs together and complain about getting older, but we wouldn't really mean it, because there would be something graceful, something . . . profound about aging alongside the person you love. And when my face began to wrinkle and my hands turned thin and cold, it would be her eyes I would look into—her hand I would hold.

I want that, and I swallow down a sob because no matter what, I can't have it. I can't grow old with her. But we have right now. We have this moment.

Cami opens the top drawer of her nightstand and removes a box of condoms. "Dad gave them to me for my sixteenth birthday. It's never been opened," she says, lifting the lid and revealing two dozen individual packets. "I hope they haven't expired." She closes the lid again and starts looking for an expiration date on the box.

"You know, we don't have to. You don't have to. It's okay if . . ." I want to say that I'd rather die a virgin than leave Cami with any regrets, but I don't get the chance because she's grabbing me, kissing me. She's squeezing me so tightly, I can hardly breathe, but I don't care. I want her to hold me tighter. I want her to be so close to me that her heart starts beating for my body too, and we can tell death to go fuck himself.

"I love you so much," she whispers, her voice trembling.

I kiss her, running my fingers through her still-damp hair, then over the delicate lines of her face and throat.

"Tonight there's no such thing as time," she says. "No seconds, no minutes, no years. The world has stopped for us. Time has stopped." She closes her eyes, and I do the same.

Cami loosens my tie and slips it over my head. Then she unbuttons my shirt, peeling it from my shoulders. When she sees my bare chest, she stops and presses her palm over my heart. She can feel it beating against her hand, then against her cheek. Then she presses her lips against my skin and holds them there as the seconds stay frozen, suspended.

She steps away from me and grips the bottom of her nightshirt, pulling it over her head. Her skin is pale. Her breasts are small but perfect.

She comes toward me and takes my hand. I feel dizzy, not just with passion, but with the sharpness of it all. My body feels like it's being pressed with thin needles. I'm in a kind of glorious pain that I know will be relieved with only the greatest pleasure. But more than the physical sensation is the intensity of knowing time hasn't really stopped. It doesn't. Not for me, not for anyone. I'm moving toward a cliff, and seeing the edge coming closer and closer makes everything I feel somehow . . . more. Cami and I . . . we love each other more because of the cliff. And tonight, we will cling to each other, press against each other with more intensity because we take nothing for granted.

Tonight is everything.

"**A** little help," my mom shouts from the door leading from the garage to the house. Her arms are filled with grocery bags, and I rush to take them. Vegetables, I bet. The bags are filled with vegetables and a highly nutritious array of organic fruits.

"Put the milk in the fridge," Mom says. "I'll start dinner in a minute. The store was packed. I guess a lot of people are planning on camping over Labor Day weekend. I didn't see Cami there."

"She's off today. She went with Emma's parents to the airport," I say, feeling a twinge of guilt because I'm glad Emma's going back to Minnesota.

Mom opens a bag of dark red apples, places them in a glass bowl, and offers me one. I don't want it, but it's healthy and supposed to be good for my heart, so I take it.

"Dr. Fabos called earlier today," she says, but it doesn't mean anything. Considering how much my parents call him, I'm surprised he hasn't changed his number.

"What did he say?" I ask, and try to sound interested, even

though he never says anything when he returns their calls. Just the usual "we're working on it."

"They have a new kind of pacemaker," she says, and now Dad is standing in the doorway of the kitchen.

"It's better than the one they used in . . ." Dad pauses, but he can't rewind his words. "It's better than the one they used in James. It's got a higher voltage. They think it might work."

What do I say? Do I have a pacemaker put in just to make them happy? Just to give them hope, when I know it won't work? Or do I tell them the truth? Tell them who Dr. Mueller really was and what he did to their sons and other people's sons and daughters? Do I let them know that they'd better hurry up and get used to the idea of me dying? Do I make myself get used to the idea?

It's September. The only word I've had from Dr. Bartholomew is that her team is working around the clock. But the clock keeps ticking, and I've got three and half months left—pacemaker or no pacemaker.

My parents have aged at least ten years in the last few months. They've been clinging to a tiny boat out in the ocean. Before Connor and I were in the boat, they were sharing it with Chase. But a giant wave came, and even though they tried to hold on to him, they couldn't. Then Connor and I came on board, and the ocean calmed. It stayed calm for so long, they forgot that sometimes you have to hang on to those you love, because giant waves are still out there. One came, and it took Connor. Now it's just me and them. They're both hanging on to me, and I wish it were enough. But the fact is, when and if the wave comes, it will take all of us under.

The doorbell rings.

"I got it," Dad says, relieved, I think, to have a moment to gather his thoughts once he sends whoever it is away.

I pick up a box of breakfast cereal that has a picture of every grain known to mankind on the front. It's going to taste like shit. I might as well drive a mile outside of town and go graze in a field. On the bright side, if I have to eat shit like this for the next three months, dying might not seem so bad.

The front door opens. I slide the box into the cupboard next to the other boxes of high-fiber and no-fat cereal, then I hear a voice. A familiar voice. My hand starts shaking, and I drop the box onto the counter. Mom gives me a puzzled look, and we both walk toward the entryway.

"Hello, Kyle," Dr. Bartholomew says. She's wearing a pale green skirt with a thin white blouse. Without her doctor's coat, she seems even smaller, even more like her brother. Her shoulder-length hair is pulled back into a small ponytail, exposing a neck that seems too long.

"You two know each other?" Dad asks. "What was your name?"

"Dr. Bartholomew, but call me Claudia, please." She offers my dad, and then my mom, her hand.

"You're a doctor?" Mom asks as she hangs on to Claudia's hand for an awkward moment before letting go.

"Yes. Might we sit down? We have a lot to discuss."

A lot. I feel my own hope building like a massive dam strong enough to hold back any wave, even a tsunami. But she can't have figured out something already. Not when I met her barely two weeks ago.

We go into the living room. Dr. Bartholomew settles herself in the center of the sofa. Dad sits in his recliner, and Mom takes her place standing beside him, her hand clenching his. I can't sit, so I pace and wait.

"I gather from your reaction that Kyle hasn't mentioned our visit." She glances over her shoulder at me. I shake my head. "I'm not surprised. I suppose he didn't want to get your hopes up. Kyle, through great efforts, found me. You knew my brother. He's gone by several names during his life, but I believe you knew him as Dr. Mueller."

All expression drains from my parents' faces.

Dr. Bartholomew stares at them, waiting, it would seem, for them to come out of their temporary shock, for their brains to come back online. "I won't drag things out," she says. "I know you are only interested in one thing, and that's saving your son."

"You can save him?" Mom asks, and the hope in the room is both exhilarating and suffocating. "Does your brother know how to save him?"

"I'm afraid he died recently," she says. "Pancreatic cancer. It spread quite rapidly, and he knew he wouldn't be able to complete his research, so he passed it on to me." Again she looks at me, the expression in her eyes asking for my discretion. How can they trust anyone related to the man who killed one of their sons and was more than willing to kill the other one in the name of science?

"I've been methodically going through his research since I acquired it, and I do believe I can help. Though I caution, this may not be the exact solution you were hoping for."

We wait for her to continue.

"It's impossible to reprogram all of the DNA in a human body. Science is simply not far enough advanced. In two or three years, at most perhaps ten, we will be at a point where technology could save Kyle. It may be as simple as adding a new piece of genetic information into his heart to nullify the sequence that tells it to stop. I have an army of researchers and endless resources at my disposal working on this, not to mention other geneticists. Given time, we will be able to cure you."

"I don't have time," I protest. "I'll be dead in a few months!"

Shit!

Mom and Dad look at me with utter disbelief. They thought they had time. They thought a solution could be found because *they had time.* But now the date of execution's been moved up, and I never told them. I knew, and I kept it from them.

Dr. Bartholomew clears her throat, pulling us back to the main matter at hand. "I'm afraid Kyle's right. There's something different about Kyle's DNA, something different from the others." She looks at me, telling me to trust her with those small sharp eyes. "It might be a mutation due to the fact that he was frozen for two years," she lies. "Anyway, it would seem likely that he won't make it past his seventeenth birthday. But," she says quickly, "as I said, I think I have found a way to possibly save him."

"After I'm dead," I point out. "You said you might be able to save me in two to ten years."

"I do have an idea of how to save you."

"You can save him?" Mom says, bracing for the wave that's approaching much faster than she'd realized.

Bartholomew stares at me, forcing me to stand still with the intensity of her eyes. "Shortly after conception, after the egg split into two, forming you and your brother, a decision was made to keep you frozen for almost two years. What I'm proposing now is not much different from that decision. I'm suggesting that you be cryogenically frozen until the time comes that science is able to cure you."

We are silent. Questions, and a few bad movies I've seen, flood my brain, just like I know they're flooding the brains of my parents. The questions in my dad's head start to form on his lips, and then he looks at me as if he's afraid to ask them.

"Isn't that something that's done after the person dies?" Dad asks.

"Legally," she says, lifting her delicate brows, "yes. It is against the law to freeze someone who is still alive. However, if the hope is to eventually thaw and heal the body, it only makes sense that the freezing should be done before the body is completely ravaged by disease. But disease isn't my concern in Kyle's case. It's—"

"But Dr. Fabos says there's a new pacemaker that could work," Mom interrupts. "Shouldn't we try that first?"

Dr. Bartholomew gives her a sympathetic smile. "If it doesn't work, and there is no reason to believe that it will, Kyle will be dead. His body will be collected for examination and either cremation or burial, and this opportunity will no longer be possible."

I start shivering. "But the body is mostly made of water. The brain is eighty percent water. When water freezes, it expands. That would destroy all of my cells."

She nods approvingly, like I'm some budding scientist. "You're absolutely right. That's why vitrification is so important. The process is very complicated, but to simplify it, let me just say that the blood in the body is replaced with a cryoprotectant solution, sort of like putting antifreeze in your radiator. This enables the body's tissue to freeze without water molecules crystallizing and causing damage. Of course there is still some concern with what's called fracturing of tissues, but I've seen very promising research in this area. I have no doubt the damage to tissue will be minimal at best."

I'm shivering so hard now that my teeth are chattering. "No," I say. "No way. I'm not doing that. I'll just live out the time I have left. But I won't let you freeze me. Fuck that."

I swear I can hear my father's heart sinking in his chest. I can feel my mother's muscles tensing against the approaching wave.

If I'm dead anyway, what does it matter if I'm buried in the ground or if I'm frozen in some lab—again? If being frozen instead of buried makes my parents feel better, why not? It's just that . . . I can't stand the thought of being that cold. Cremate me and let science try to resurrect me like a phoenix from the ashes, but I don't want to be cold.

"What are the chances you'll really be able to fix me and bring me back?" I ask.

"It's not a hundred percent. I'm sure that's not what you want to hear, but I can tell you what is certain." Her eyes take hold of mine, and she looks at me with the tenderness of a grandmother and the certainty of a doctor holding lab results. "If you don't do this, you will die. This is a chance, a very good chance, and it is your only chance." Her eyes break from mine, and she steadies herself with a few deep breaths. "There is, however, something you need to know before you decide."

Great. Freezing me was the *good* news.

"I'm going to be very blunt," she says. "Your birthday is quickly approaching. We know that some of the others died on their birthdays, some died after, and some died before. You're a bit different, so there's no way to know exactly when your heart will stop. But it's safe to say that you won't live past your birthday, and there's a good chance you won't even make it until then." She closes her eyes for a moment. "If a young man dies, an autopsy will be ordered. All of the others were subjected to autopsies, and you will be too. You know what happens in an autopsy."

A shiver runs down my spine like the blunt end of a scalpel is pressing against the center of my back. In an autopsy, they take out all of your organs. They weigh them, examine them, and then they stick them back in, but they don't reattach anything. They just put them in and sew you up, like sticking in candy in a piñata.

"We have to make certain that does not happen, and since

there is no way to predict exactly when you are going to die, we need to act quickly. The sooner, the better."

"B-but," Dad stutters, "how long do you think he'll be frozen? How sure are you that you can bring him back?"

"We've had great success recently with freezing organs. We've tested slices of brain and found that after the vitrification process, the slices were able to send neurological signals. And there was a dog—"

"Have they ever unfrozen a person?" I interrupt.

Her head tilts sympathetically. "No, but the science is almost there. With nanotechnologies, we'll soon have tiny robots that can go into a body and repair damaged cells. And hopefully, they'll be able to plug a new sequence into your DNA—all of your DNA—to keep your heart from stopping. The advancements in nanomolecular science are staggering. My team is on the cusp of being able to prevent strokes and heart attacks, even killing cancer cells as soon as they start forming, by using this technology. This will work, Kyle. I'm certain of it. Scientific advancements are happening at such a staggering pace. Not even two centuries ago doctors didn't know enough to wash their hands between patients. Now we've mapped the entire human genetic code."

"When will I die? I mean, I will die, right? You can't be alive and frozen." I don't want to ask. I don't want to know because I don't want to do this, but my parents . . . I can see the fear in their eyes, but I can also see the hope. "Will it hurt?"

Dr. Bartholomew gives me a reassuring smile. "You'll go to sleep. That's all. You'll be given anesthesia, and you'll go to sleep.

They won't so much as prick your finger until you're completely under; I promise. Your body will be cooled gradually while certain processes are being performed."

"Like draining my blood and replacing it with 'antifreeze'?"

"Yes."

I look down at the veins in my arms. At the blood moving through them. "How cold will my body be once it's done?" I hear my voice, but it can't be me. I can't be talking or breathing or doing anything but fighting the urge to run as far and as fast as I can.

She hesitates, like she'd like to lie to me but has too much integrity to do so. "The entire cooling process takes a few weeks, but when it's complete, you'll be cooled to negative one hundred ninety-six degrees Celsius."

I was never good at converting Fahrenheit into Celsius, but if 32 degrees Fahrenheit is freezing, negative 196 degrees Celsius is . . .

"Why so cold?"

"It's the temperature of liquid nitrogen. They're experimenting with alternatives to liquid nitrogen as the primary cooling agent, but for now . . ."

I remember a movie I saw once about a caveman found frozen in the ice somewhere near the North Pole. He was really confused once he thawed out. He'd never seen an airplane, or for that matter, a person with straight teeth. He couldn't take it, and he ended up killing himself. What if it's not just a couple of years? What if they fix me, and my parents are dead and people are flying hovercrafts instead of driving cars, or what if there's a nuclear war and the scientists aren't around to thaw me out? What if there's nobody around to put the blood back into my veins?

"How soon do I need to decide?" I ask.

"Anytime before you die," she says, "but I highly recommend we proceed as soon as possible." She opens her purse and sets a thick envelope on the coffee table. "This should answer most of your questions. A story will have to be devised to explain Kyle's absence from school. My apologies for being deceptive, but I pretended to be a social worker and called the school to speak with your counselor. It was brought to my attention that your principal knows some things about your condition. I suggest that we simply say that you've gone somewhere for treatment. But we must be careful."

She gives me a supportive look.

"It's imperative that no one comes looking for you. Just as the procedures to create you were illegal, so is this course of action. It's only because I have certain connections that this is an option at all, but confidentiality must be kept. Once you are cured and revived, you need to be able to step back into your life with as little turmoil as possible. You'll tell people you were simply away for a time due to ambiguous health issues. They resolved and now you're back. I'll be able to secure transcripts showing you were able to continue your education, perhaps through an online school. If needed, I can even include a few semesters of college. But no one, absolutely no one outside of this room, can know where you really are. I have a letter, drafted by a friend of mine at Johns Hopkins, stating that Kyle is being transferred to his care and that his team will be trying to find a solution to his condition. If you agree to this plan, the letter will be sent to the cardiac hospital in Dallas. All the loose ends will be tied up." She looks at each of us in turn. "But this can only work if I have your complete trust and silence."

"Cami," I say. "I won't do it if she can't know."

"A girlfriend?" Bartholomew asks.

I nod.

Bartholomew takes a deep breath and dampens her thin lips with her tongue. "No doubt, it's a serious relationship. Can you make her understand the consequences if she tells anyone the truth about where you are?"

I nod, and she frowns.

"Very well," she says. "But she must know what's at stake. All of you must. Your life, for one, Kyle. And not just my reputation, but my freedom and my work. If anyone discovers what we're doing, I could go to prison, and countless people who could have been saved by my work will perish, including you."

"She won't tell anyone," I say, it's the only thing in the world I know for sure.

Dr. Bartholomew doesn't like it. She may not be a parent, but she has the disapproving look pegged perfectly. "Fine," she says. "But I want to meet her. You can bring her with you to the institute. She must understand the gravity of the situation. If she tells anyone, if you're discovered, you could be left frozen indefinitely, or worse."

What could be worse than being frozen . . . indefinitely? Being thawed like a turkey on the kitchen counter. Having someone pull the plug, because someone broke the law and froze me before I died, before the doctors could cut me open and weigh my organs.

"It's a lot to take in, I know, but I want you to read through all of the information. I've included a card with my phone number. Please, call me as soon as you decide." Dr. Bartholomew stands and straightens her skirt. "Don't hesitate to contact me if you have questions or concerns." She comes toward me and takes hold of my hand. "I made you a promise. But I can only keep it if you let me. I hope you will." She squeezes my hand.

I don't remember watching her leave. I don't remember eating dinner or sitting on the sofa with my parents and none of us saying anything and none of us touching the envelope that contains information about freezing a human being. I don't remember anything except wishing things were different and wishing the chill in my gut would go away.

We didn't discuss it. We didn't need to. The decision was made, because the only other choice is not an option, not to my parents anyway. Now I have to figure out how to tell Cami.

I turn on the heater in Cami's truck. She's already complained about being hot. It's mid-September, and while the evening air may be considered refreshing to many, to me it's cold. I can't stop feeling cold.

Cami takes the piece of paper she's just finished reading and starts to refold it, but stops. She looks over at me. "I'll wait for you," she says. "No matter how long it takes." She grabs my hand and tries to smile. "This is good."

She sounds like she's trying to convince herself as much as me.

"This is good," she says again. "We can have a future."

"What if it's ten years from now?"

"I'll be twenty-eight," Cami gasps.

"And I'll still be almost seventeen." I start to say more, because I want her to know everything, but I stop myself. If she's worried about being ten years older, how will she feel when she's forty or fifty, and people mistake me for her son because the longevity sequence has kicked in and I'm not aging? I shiver.

Cami's arms slip around my waist. "It's going to work," she says. "And I don't mind if people think I'm a cougar, going after a younger man. They'll just be jealous because you're mine."

"I'll always be yours," I say, trying to blink away the stinging in my eyes. "Promise me you'll stay mine. Promise me you won't freak out when you get your first gray hair and I'm . . ."

She lifts her face and kisses me.

The warmth of her does ten times more good than the truck's heater. "I just want you to be happy," I say. "And if something goes wrong . . ."

Cami presses a finger over my mouth.

I take her hand and hold it tightly. "If something goes wrong, I don't want you to waste time being sad. I mean, really— nanorobots smaller than the eyes can see are going to go around fixing my DNA? I know Dr. Bartholomew swears she can do this, but what if she can't?"

"She can," Cami says. "You'll be cured, and we can be together. But you can't complain if I get a few gray hairs or a few wrinkles before you do."

I study her face. I want to memorize it, and if my brain is frozen thinking about one thing, holding on to one memory, I want it to be this. I want to see Cami's eyes, her hair, and her smile. Freeze me with that stuck like a screen saver in my brain, and I won't care how long it takes. And when I wake up, let her be there. Please let her be there.

How do you go to sleep when you know that tomorrow your heart is going to stop beating? That you are, for all intents and purposes, going to die? How do you close your eyes and let the thing you desire most in this world—time—tiptoe past you?

Have you ever been so scared, so overwhelmed with emotions that you could feel your heart, your soul, doubling over inside of you? You feel like . . . like you just want to escape, but you know you can't.

They said it wouldn't be like dying. My heart wasn't going to suddenly stop. It would slow down gradually while I slept, while my body was cooled. Eventually everything would start to solidify until my heart, my lungs, my brain, were rendered motionless. In the letter I wrote to Cami, the one she read in the truck because I was too chickenshit to say everything myself, I left out the part about the holes in my skull the doctors will drill so they can monitor my brain responses. A healthy brain supposedly contracts under the process, while a damaged brain expands. Negative 196 degrees Celsius is negative 320.8

degrees Fahrenheit: 353 degrees below freezing. I Googled it, but I wish I hadn't. I can't imagine anything being that cold.

It's as incomprehensible as the universe, and it's going to happen to me.

My stomach growls. I'm not really hungry. Mom made my favorite dinner. Actually it was more like my favorite *dinners* and to hell with eating healthy. We ordered in pizza—pepperoni with stuffed crust, plus Mom made fried chicken and mashed potatoes and gravy. We topped it off with cake and ice cream. No one said happy birthday, but with mine being three and a half months away, it kind of felt like we should have, especially since we know I won't be home for my birthday.

Hours ago, I felt sick from eating too much. Now my stomach calls out to me. It's not because it's empty; it's because it knows it will never be fed again—at least not for two to ten years. It's the old "no food after midnight" rule. They're using anesthesia to put me out, so there's a risk of choking if anything is in my stomach. If I choke while I'm unconscious, my airways will close up and my brain will be deprived of oxygen. If that happens, I'll be thawed out and given a pass to ride that special short bus. So, no food.

In a way, I guess that's good. I can't imagine a slice of stuffed crust pizza being frozen in my stomach for two or more years. Talk about freezer burn.

I roll onto my back, and the mattress shifts around my body. It doesn't feel right. It feels off somehow, foreign, like this isn't the bed I've slept in since I made my way out of the crib all those years ago. I roll back onto my side, but that doesn't feel right either. I kick off the covers and start pacing. I pace around my bed, pace back and forth along the wall where my dresser is. Finally, I pace right up the stairs and find myself standing outside my parents' bedroom. The door is shut, but I can see a light shining dimly from beneath the door. Of course they're not asleep. How could they be?

I want to knock. I want to fling open the door and fall into their arms. Tears burn my eyes while I imagine sobbing in their embrace. I want them to tell me that I don't have to do it because there's another way. They've just discovered it, just seconds ago they had some brilliant realization of how I can be saved another way.

I can see them; Mom and Dad are sitting on the bed. They're embracing each other, comforting each other. They're fighting the urge to slip down the stairs and stare at me in my sleep, except I'm not sleeping. They know that. And to enter my domain would be to open the floodgates to a sea of emotions none of us are strong enough to deal with. So they hold each other. They hold on to their hope.

I don't go in.

I won't leave them with the memory of me scared and sobbing. I'm going to be strong.

All I have to do is go to sleep, and the gas they give me will take care of that, so really, I don't have to do anything. Negative 320.8 degrees Fahrenheit. Don't think about that. Don't. Just go to sleep and wake up. And be strong.

Be strong. Be strong.

Quietly, I knock my forehead over and over again against the frame around my parents' door. Be strong, I repeat. Be strong.

My dad's hand is on my shoulder. "It's morning, buddy," he says. "About time to go."

"Go where?" I mumble and try to get the kink out of my back. I'm in the hallway. I must have fallen asleep . . . I'm awake.

One hundred and a thousand percent awake. Time to go, he'd said.

Dad smiles down at me and offers me his hand. I take it, gripping it tightly. He pulls me to my feet, but he doesn't let go of my hand. Instead his other hand goes around my shoulder, and he pulls me to him. Mom's there too, her arms going around me, but we can't stay like this for long. We know it. We're on a tightrope of sorts. We can't make any wrong moves. There's a schedule, both physical and emotional. Right now, it's time to be strong. Time to move like robots or zombies, to move without thought, without emotion.

The emotional part will come later.

I go downstairs and get dressed, being careful not to look around my room. Either I'll see it again or I won't. If I get better and come home and get to sleep in my bed, great. If I don't, it's not like I'm going to miss it.

Cami and my mom are standing in the kitchen when I get upstairs.

"Here." Cami comes to me and sticks something in my

hand. It's an iPod. "I made a playlist of all your favorite songs. I thought that you could listen to it . . ."

"Thanks," I say, wondering when exactly I'm supposed to listen to it. Before they put me to sleep, I'll be with my family. Once the sleeping gas hits my lungs, I'll be too out of it to hear anything. But still, I like the idea, even if I only get to hear a few notes of a favorite song.

There's a strange feeling when we step out of the house, like we're going on vacation and we're sure we're forgetting something. We aren't forgetting anything. And I know my parents are just trying to memorize the feel of me at home. They never got to do that with Connor: never got to stand there and look at their son with the backdrop of the front porch. But they can do it with me. They can try to remember what it was like to be standing here looking at their son.

"Let's go to Hawaii," I blurt out. "We can be like homeless bums on the beach. It's nice all the time there, warm. We can lie in the sand and watch the waves, and when it happens, you can cremate me and sprinkle my ashes over the water."

Actually, I don't blurt that out. At least, not anywhere but in my head. I want to. I want to go to Hawaii. I want to die where it's warm, with my toes buried in the sand. But I can't say it. I can't.

I follow them out into the gray morning, and there's Jimmy leaning up against Cami's truck. He looks thin. I know he lost weight during his week in the hospital, but even though he's been out for two weeks, it looks like he's still losing, like the medications that zapped his appetite are still on duty in his stomach, refusing to let invaders in.

"Didn't think I'd let you leave without seeing you off, did you?" Jimmy says. His eyes look glassy but better than they have been, like the ice that's been coating them is starting to thaw. It looks like he's attempted to comb his wild hair, and there's a razor nick on his chin from shaving with an unsteady hand. "This is gonna work," he says. "And don't worry; I know this is top-secret shit. I really appreciate you trusting me enough to tell me. Your secret's safe. I promise."

"I know," I say, and I still can't believe what he did for me. What he's still doing for me, because his stay in the hospital isn't exactly over. It won't be until the meds have left his system and he's put back on the weight he lost. And even then, I can't ever repay him. "You're my best friend."

He smiles, his eyes tearing. "Some crazy shit, though," Jimmy says. "I mean—fuck! You're getting frozen. That's . . . that's some crazy shit. So crazy it has to work. That's how missions are. The ones you think will go smooth go to shit, but the ones you think are just too fucked up to work go off without a hitch. This will work, buddy."

He extends his hand, and I take it, expecting one of his finger-crushing handshakes, but instead Jimmy pulls me toward him and hugs me.

"Come home," he says, slapping my shoulder. "See you in two years."

"You bet. Take care of Cami for me?"

He frowns like it's a stupid request, and I give him one last quick hug.

The institute is in Nebraska. It's a four-hour drive from home. It's a miserable drive, the last hour of it on a two-lane highway. Cami and I sit in the backseat, our hands clasped so tightly together our palms start to sweat, but we don't loosen our grip. Mom and Dad keep glancing back at me in the rearview mirror. They try some idle chitchat, but give up. It seems like there should be a lot to say, under the circumstances, but I doubt anyone is ever chatty on the way to the gallows or the gas chamber, and I think that's how we all feel—like we're all about to die in one sense or another. Dad turns on the radio. "If I Die Young" starts playing. He quickly turns it off again, but not before Mom starts crying.

We ride in silence until we see the place, rising from the earth like a giant tombstone standing in a field of prairie grass and wild cedars. It is a large, gray, windowless structure. And instead of the name of a departed loved one etched on the cement surface, there is a cold, sterile name: THE INSTITUTE FOR CRYONIC SCIENCES.

I've already put on the hospital gown. Now it's time to pull on the thin cotton scrub bottoms. I'm not naïve. I know the bottoms are to make me feel more comfortable. Once I'm out, they'll come off. So will the gown, for that matter. I'll be totally naked, with a tube shoved in every orifice of my body. The doctors will create a few new ones, too. It's the holes they're going to drill into my skull that concern me the most. But I can't think about that.

I fasten the tie on the pants and put my clothes into a plastic bag so Mom and Dad can take them home. Then I wait for my parents and Cami to come in and say good-bye. But I can't think about that, either.

I look around the room. It's not a hospital room. This place doesn't deal with *live* patients. This room, with its desk, a futon, and a round table complete with three chairs, must be a sort of lounge. I can imagine Dr. Bartholomew and the others trying to figure out where to put me. They could have had me change in the bathroom, but that's not exactly an appropriate place to tell my family good-bye. There were small exam rooms, places to prepare already-dead bodies for the freezing process, but stick me in one of those without a sedative and see how long I stay.

I hate this. I hate being here, and I hate the buzz that is sending charges of electricity through the air. The staff is so fucking excited. It must be like the first time the Russians sent a man into space after sending dogs. The doctors have never had the chance to freeze a *live* human being, and I'm giving them that chance. No more freezing dogs or rats or slices of brain.

The last thing I wanted to be was a lab rat, and now that's exactly what I feel like.

But do I have to be? I could put my clothes back on and walk out of here. I could enjoy whatever time I have left. I could skip to the acceptance stage of death, and we could really go to Hawaii. We could.

There's a knock on the door, and it opens. Dr. Bartholomew steps in, wearing her doctor's coat and beige pants. She sees my hand reaching inside the sack where my clothes are, and her face morphs into one of sympathy. God, I hate that expression: the furrowed brows, the pain-filled eyes, the pursed lips. I've seen it too many times since Connor died, and she's ramping it up a notch. And why shouldn't she, considering what she's about to do to me?

"You're scared," she says. "I know I would be, if I were you." She gives a tender smile. "You don't have to do this. No one's forcing you. This is your life. Only you can decide. But let me tell you a story before you do." Dr. Bartholomew pulls a chair out from the table and sits down. "Have you ever heard of Gordon Harrison?"

I shake my head.

"He is a very wealthy landowner in Texas—land with abundant sources of oil on it. Mr. Harrison had everything, but five years ago, his wife gave birth to their third child—their first daughter. The little girl was healthy except for her kidneys. They were both deformed, barely functioning at all. Their only hope was an organ transplant, but did you know that eighteen people die every day in this country waiting for transplants, and it doesn't matter how much money or power you have? You can't jump to the front of the line. Their precious little girl would have died, but knowing before her birth that the child's kidneys were deformed, Mr. Harrison contacted me. Another doctor had read about my work growing organs from stem cells. We were able to harvest the needed cells from the umbilical cord, and I grew the child a new kidney. Since the cells came from her cord blood, there was no concern of rejection. And that little girl started kindergarten a month ago."

Dr. Bartholomew gives herself a satisfied smile and a mental pat on the back.

"You're wondering how this pertains to you." She comes to me and wraps her thin, cool fingers around my hands. "I've *helped* two congressmen, a governor, and the family member of a president. My goal is to help all people, regardless of their socioeconomic status, but helping rich, powerful, influential people is what makes my work possible. What I'm trying to tell you is that I have money behind me. I have access to the finest scientists and physicians. If anyone can cure you, if anyone can give you your life back, it's me." She squeezes my hands. "You just have to trust me. Can you do that? Can you be astronomically brave?"

I hate that she resembles her brother. The resemblance isn't great, especially since in my mental image of him, he was near death. But their eyes are so similar, so dark and small. Still, there is something different in hers—a spark of hope. I have to trust her. I nod.

She lets go of my hand and starts for the door. "I'll bring your family in to . . ." She starts to say that my family will come in to tell me good-bye, but she thinks better of it. "I'll bring your family in to wish you well."

She leaves. Minutes later Mom, Dad, and Cami step into the room, or try to. It's hard. The air itself acts like a wall they're pressing against, because they don't want to come in. They don't want to say good-bye.

Dad's arm is wrapped around Mom's waist. He's holding her up, keeping her from collapsing on the cold, tile floor. Her eyes aren't bloodshot with tears. That will come later, but not much later. She's trying to hold it together for my sake, just like I'm trying to hold it together for theirs. Cami is standing behind them, and while I know she's trying to be strong too, she hasn't been quite as successful. Her eyes are puffy and red, and she dabs at them with the sleeve of her sweater.

I can't take it.

"Let's pretend I'm getting my tonsils out," I say. "And I have really, really big tonsils, so it's going to take a while. Just make sure there's plenty of ice cream when I get home." My voice threatens to crack, but I won't let it. I won't. I can't. Not when I look at my parents and see how thin they are. Not physically, but emotionally. I can see right through them, and it's not fair. No parent should have to lose so many children. But they're not going to lose me. At least, I won't let them believe that, not today. I wish this could have been figured out sooner. If Dr. Mueller/Sharp/Bartholomew/psychobastard had died sooner, maybe his sister could have frozen all of us. There could be a whole wing of frozen Mueller babies, and somewhere in the part of our minds that can't be stilled by science, we'd exist together. I could introduce Connor to James and Amber. We could listen to Triagon play Mozart, and Connor and I could . . . We could be together without being dead.

I rush toward my mom and put my arms around her, trying to speed things up, like I'm at camp and her going all gushy is going to spoil my reputation with the other kids. Dad throws his arms around both of us, and we stand there for too long. We are giants holding up a massive weight. We are that ancient turtle balancing the Earth on the back of its shattering shell. The weight is too much. It will crush us if we don't let go, and so we do.

"Tonsils, Mom. It's just my tonsils." But this time my voice does crack. I look past my mom at Cami. She comes toward me, and I can hear her jagged breaths. She forces herself to smile despite her tears. We hold each other for a long time, until the weight comes down, and at first, we don't care. I don't care. Let it crush me. Let me die right now with Cami in my arms and no holes cut into my body. She would agree. At this moment, she would let the ceiling above us collapse and bury us in rubble just to end these unbearable feelings. But I love her, so I push her gently away.

Dr. Bartholomew comes in and straps an identification bracelet around my wrist. I'm out of time.

I open my mouth, wanting to say "tonsils" one more time. Wanting Mom and Dad and Cami to force themselves to believe that I'm only going away for a little while. That they can see me in recovery in an hour or so, and then they can spoon-feed me Jell-O and ice cream while I flip through channels on the hospital television. But I can't say anything.

A white mask covers Dr. Bartholomew's face, but I can tell she's smiling down at me from the way the lines around her eyes lift. She's wearing white surgical gear. So are her assistants. The machines and equipment they will be using are covered with white sheets. Normally they don't have to worry about their patients freaking out at the various tubes and gauges and needles, but I'm alive. Right now, I'm alive, so the technology that will hopefully save me is covered like old furniture in a haunted house.

The walls and the ceiling are white. I should be listening to Whitesnake on the iPod, stay with the theme. But I'm not. I'm listening to a song by Dr. Dre, Skylar Grey, and Eminem. I close my eyes because I don't want to see the plastic mask coming down over my face. Instead I see the music video for the song. I see the woman draped in white floating in the air as Skylar Grey sings, *I need a doctor. Call me a doctor. I need a doctor, doctor, to bring me back to life.*

44

"**J**ason."

Someone taps my cheek. At least, I think someone is tapping my cheek. I feel numb, like I've just been to the dentist.

"Jason." The tap turns into a slap. "You have to wake up. Come on. Wake up."

"Stop it." The words only sound in my head. I try again, but it's like my throat's numb. Another light slap, and I force my eyes open. "Stop hitting me," I manage in a small, rough voice.

"You're awake!"

There's a nurse standing over me. She's on the heavy side. Her hair is short and gray, and slight wrinkles are visible behind her plastic-rimmed glasses. She's smiling, beaming like I've just come back from the dead.

Oh, shit!

"Am I cured?" I ask, my voice a little stronger. I look around the room. It's bigger than a standard hospital room, and nicer. There are actually curtains on the windows, not sterile blinds but heavy fabric. "Where are my parents? How long has it been?"

"Slow down, Jason," she says. "Just take it easy."

I see something in her hand—a syringe filled with medication.

"Am I cured?" I say slowly. I lift my hand to my head and feel for the holes that were drilled into my skull, but I don't feel anything except hair that's grown longer. And I feel pain, not in my head, but my torso. "Where are my parents? And why do you keep calling me Jason?" I grimace. "And why do I hurt so much?"

The nurse's face darkens, like she'd suspected something, and now she knows it's true. "Your name isn't Jason?"

"No."

"Your parents died in a car accident. Don't you remember?"

"What? Mom and Dad?" It's my worst nightmare come true. I wake up and the people I love are gone, but how could I remember if it happened while I was frozen? "Who's Jason? My name's Kyle. And when I was frozen, my parents were alive."

"Frozen? What are you talking about? You've been in a coma."

My stomach screams in pain. I lower the blanket and lift the thin gown. Across my torso are a series of incisions, some healed, some still red but without staples. Some are still held together with small metal teeth. Just down and over from my belly button, a tube with a small cap over it sticks out of my abdomen.

"I was frozen. I was supposed to be frozen. Where's Dr. Bartholomew? What is all this?" I stare down at the horror movie on my torso.

"You're supposed to be Jason," she says. "You have a rare disease, and Dr. Bartholomew's been experimenting on your tissue, trying to figure out how to save you. She's been doing all kinds of biopsies, but I don't know what she's looking for. I just take care of you. But . . ."

"But what?"

"I've had this feeling something isn't right." She takes the syringe and lays it on the nightstand. "I was supposed to give you that. It's what keeps you in a coma. I've seen what they're doing to you. I'm not a doctor, but I don't know how cutting on you like this can help. And then I . . ." She glances at the door, then back at me.

"Then what?"

"I heard Dr. Bartholomew say something."

"What? What did she say?"

"I was in the back of the pharmaceutical room. I knocked over a box of bandages, getting clumsy in my old age, I guess, and I was bent over picking up them up when she came in. She was on the phone with someone. She said something about how long to *drag it out*. That she thought it was time to *tell the parents he's dead*. She sounded frustrated, said she was tired of dealing with them. Then she said it was time to start taking brain biopsies. She was holding your file."

My fingers curve into fists, and I want to scream, but I don't dare. Just staying still is torture. How much pain will I feel if I take a deep breath and let really let my anger out? I close my eyes, only for a second, because I know some of the drugs are still lingering in my body, and I don't want to take the chance of closing my eyes and slipping away again. "She told you that my parents were dead?"

She nods. "I wondered why nobody came to visit you, and that's what she told me—they died in a car accident a year before you got sick."

"How long have I been here? They were supposed to freeze me on September twelfth, at the cryonics institute in Nebraska. What's the date now?"

"You were brought here on September thirteenth. You're in Saint Louis. You've been here for two months."

My breath catches in my throat. Two months! Two fucking months I've been in a fucking coma while fucking Dr. Bartholomew's been dissecting me like a frog in a biology class. I have one month left. One month before I die.

"So I was never frozen?"

She shakes her head.

"And she told you that my parents are dead?"

She nods again, her hand touching my forearm.

"What's your name?" I ask.

"Virginia," she says. "Nice to meet you, Kyle." She squeezes my arm. "I'm going to help you, but first, do you know why she's doing this? I've worked with Dr. Bartholomew for years, and I just can't imagine . . ." She gestures toward my various wounds.

"Her brother experimented on me and a bunch of others. He did things to our DNA, and I'm guessing she wants to know how it all works. She lied to me, told me and my parents that he gave her his research before he died, but he couldn't have.

If she had it, she wouldn't be doing this." My head sinks into the thin pillow. Dr. Bartholomew had said that I'm the most important person to her in the world. She also said that there would never be a way to stop the longevity sequence once it got activated because of how it specifically impacts my brain. Virtual immortality. The fountain of youth, her brother had called it. Maybe that's what she wants. She tried to convince me to trust her by telling me how many rich, powerful people support her. What if she could give them immortality instead of just new kidneys?

I look up at the woman standing beside my bed. She's the stereotypical grandmother, with her gray hair, full face, and glasses. She must be pushing retirement age and probably has grandchildren she's planning on spending time with once she does. I wonder what she'd be willing to do to turn back time. To be able to race her grandchild through the park and actually win because even though she's lived decades longer, she's not aging. But Virginia's blue eyes are soft and filled with concern and compassion. Claudia's eyes have never been anything but small and black, just like her brother's.

"Dr. Claudia Bartholomew is a bitch," I say. "A coldhearted bitch."

I wait for her to start defending the great doctor, but she just nods slightly.

"We need to do some things before I move you." Virginia goes to a small metal cabinet with several drawers. She takes out a Band-Aid and a cotton ball. She quickly removes the IV needle from my forearm, then presses the cotton ball to it, followed by the Band-Aid. "Would you like to choose which one to take out next?"

"Which one?" There's the tube in my stomach, but other than that . . . oh, shit.

"Let's get the worst over with first. I won't lie. It's going to hurt; it's been there for a while. Just keep breathing and find a happy place."

"I can do it," I say, as she puts on a pair of gloves.

She peels the thin blanket off of me, and quickly takes hold of the tube and of me. "Like pulling off a Band-Aid. One, two . . ." She pulls at the catheter, and it feels like a hot knitting needle being yanked out of me.

"Fuck!" I gasp, wanting to curl up, but the incisions in my stomach stop me.

"Now for the last one," she says, rather matter-of-factly, and I'm glad she's experienced.

"Is that a feeding tube?" I ask.

"It is." She goes back to the metal drawers and takes out a handful of small packets and a large bandage. She swaps the area with one of the packets, wiggles the tube just a little, then slowly starts to pull it out. To my relief, it doesn't hurt that much, or maybe it's just that with everything else hurting, the pain blends in. When she's done, there's a hole in my abdomen about the diameter of a drinking straw. Blood and the remnants of what looks like a melted milkshake seep out of it. Virginia sanitizes the area again, then applies the bandage.

"Will it keep leaking?"

"The hole in your stomach and in your skin will heal up pretty fast."

"So that's how they've been feeding me?"

She nods. "That's how I've been feeding you. I'm so sorry. I should have suspected something sooner, but I've never had a reason not to trust Dr. Bartholomew. She said that if you weren't kept in a coma, the pain from your disease would be unbearable. Your records are stored on a computer. All your medications are listed there, and each time I give you anything, I log it in the computer file. But there's information that should be there that isn't. I could never understand that. There's not even a diagnosis or any records or surgeries or procedures. But now I know you have a separate file, one only Dr. Bartholomew has access to, the one she was holding. I even tried to get into her office to find it, but everything was locked up tight. I wanted to know for sure . . ."

I think she's going to start crying, but instead, she makes two fists and tightens her arms like she's ready for a fight.

"Time to get you out of here," she says, taking a phone from her pocket. She dials a number and waits. "Gene, I was right. Are you sure you want to help?" She waits, then nods with the phone pressed to her ear. "Let's do it," she says, then ends the call. "I'll be right back."

Virginia goes to the door and peers out into the hallway. She gives me a thumbs-up, then disappears into the hall. Within a few minutes, she's back, pushing a wheelchair into the room.

"There aren't very many patients on this floor. And visiting hours are long over, so we shouldn't run into anyone. We just have to get you down to the first floor."

She comes toward me, taking a syringe out of her pocket.

"What's that for?"

"Pain. You'll thank me, I promise. Now roll over a little."

I try to roll over, to expose at least a little of my ass to her, but the pain is too much. Then her hand is against my hip, pushing me. I feel a quick sting and hope to hell the shot works fast.

"Come on." Her arms go around my waist and she pulls me to a sitting position. It's all I can do to stay sitting. My muscles aren't used to working, and there are still sedatives lingering in my body. I start to roll backward but she grabs hold of me. The wheelchair is next to the bed now.

"I can do it myself," I say, thinking for a minute she means to lift me out of bed like I'm a baby.

She puts a hand on her round hip. "No, you can't. Come on." Her arms go under my arms, and she's lifting me. My feet search for the floor, but when they feel the coolness of the tiles, my knees start to buckle—and the pain, God! The fucking pain!

Suddenly I'm in the chair. Virginia starts tucking a blanket around me. I want to ask her how soon the pain medication is going to kick in. I want to ask her to give me another shot, but the pain has immobilized my vocal cords, so I grab her arm and look up her.

She bends down in front of me, patting my hand. "It's going to be all right," she says.

Virginia peeks into the hallway before pushing me out. And the pain medication is starting to work. My eyelids start to slip down, and I try to force them up again. I don't want to sleep. I force my head to life, force my eyes to stay open and that's when I see the camera mounted in the hall outside my room. There's a little blinking light telling me that it's working, that in some little room there are security guards watching the various hospital halls. I just hope they're watching all of them and not just mine. But even if they are, there will be a video to rewind once they notice I'm gone. A video of Virginia wheeling me out of my room. I try to say something, to warn her, but then my eyes are just too . . .

"**A**m I supposed to give him five milligrams every eight hours or eight milligrams every five?"

I press my eyes open to see a man sitting in a folding chair next to me. He's holding a phone up to his ear, and he looks frustrated.

"I know you wrote it down, but your handwriting is worse than chicken scratch. Eight milligrams. No, he's still out. Hopefully he'll wake up soon and I can call his parents get him the hell out of here!"

"I'm awake now," I manage to say.

The man with a tanned, narrow face and deep winkles looks at me awkwardly. "He's awake," he says into the phone and waits. "Hold on, I'll ask him." He turns to me. "Are you in much pain?"

I think for a second, and the answer is, mercifully, no. I shake my head.

"Good," he says. "The boy says he's not in much pain."

There's a sheet under me and blanket covering me. My arm

is hanging over the side of a . . . sofa, and something is licking my hand. I look down and see a wiry-haired mutt lying beside the sofa.

"Duke, stop that," the man yells at the dog, then gets back to his phone conversation. "You sure he should be taking two of those? He says he's not in that much pain, and one will knock me on my ass faster than a bottle of whiskey." Pause. "Fine. You're the nurse. You just make sure you call me once you get to Phoenix. And, Virginia, be careful."

He ends the call, but stares at the phone for moment, like maybe he forgot to say something important to the person on the other end.

"Was that Virginia?" I ask.

"Yeah," he says. "On a goddamned plane to Phoenix, thanks to you. I don't think she's ever coming back, either. Her daughter lives out there. I just hope whatever you got her mixed up in doesn't follow her."

I want to assure him that it won't, but I can't. "You might call her back. If Dr. Bartholomew knows that she has a daughter in Phoenix, that she might go there . . . she might want to go someplace else."

He exhales like an angry old bull, his eyes staring down at the floor. "Her daughter's married, not too long either, so she's got a different name. Virginia doesn't socialize much with the hospital people, so maybe they don't know."

I try to give him a reassuring smile and pull my arm back onto the sofa so the dog will stop licking it.

"I'd wash that hand good, if I was you," he says. "Duke's got a thing about chewing on dirty underwear. His mouth's like a sewer."

I look at my hand and don't know whether to laugh or cry. I don't even know where the hell I am.

"I'm Gene, by the way. Friend of Virginia's. And I know who you are. Kyle, the fella who got my hernia acting up because I had to drag your ass in here all by myself at two o'clock in the goddamned morning. Virginia wanted to come back here, but I took her straight to the Amtrak station. Can't be too careful these days. And when she said you'd been in a coma for two months, I thought you'd weigh less. Must have been cramming French fries up that feeding tube."

What little hair is on Gene's head is light brown, and it matches the faded freckles that disappear into his wrinkles. He looks mean, reminding me of the story my mom used to tell us about the troll who lived under a bridge and ate goats.

"You two close friends?"

Gene scoffs. "Have been for six years now. Ever since her husband and my wife died. She comes over every morning after work for coffee, and we share the newspaper. Then she tells me about you, how she's all worried and whatnot, and the next thing I know, I'm parked by some hospital door and she's smuggling you out of there. And now I don't know if I'll ever see her again."

"I'm sorry. I don't want you dragged into this. I should probably go." I force myself to sit up, and the pain, comes creeping back like I've been hiding from it and now it's found me.

"Not so fast. I seen what that doctor did to your gut. Virginia said something about them messing with your DNA. You have any superpowers?" he asks.

"No."

Gene frowns, obviously disappointed. "What did this doctor do to you, then?"

"He put a genetic sequence in me, so that I'll die before I turn seventeen."

"And when's that?"

"A little less than a month."

He sighs and rubs a hand over his sparse hair. "Well that's some fine fucking shit, ain't it? What kind of a sorry-ass excuse for a human being would do something like that to a kid? A kid!" He steps away from me, then toward me again. "You're not just walking off here. We have to *do* something about this. You know, I got shot in Vietnam. I was pinned down, and bullets flying everywhere. You know how many times I got shot?"

He waits for me to answer, his reddish-gray brows lifted.

"Three times?" I guess.

"Nineteen. Yeah. That's a one in front of a nine. But did I give up? Did I lay down in that jungle and ask God's forgiveness for the shit that I done in my life? No. I got up. That's what I did. And that's what we're going to do right now. You're going to get up and go sit down at the kitchen table. I'm going to fix you some . . . soup or something. I'll give you a Lortab, just one—she said two, but that's too many—and no more shots. We need you awake so we can figure this all out. And we are going to figure this out. You got it?"

I fight the urge to shout, "Sir, yes, sir!" But I just nod and struggle to my feet. A sudden breeze hits my backside, and I realize I'm still wearing the hospital gown. "I don't suppose you have any pants I can borrow."

I think of Virginia on a train to Arizona. I think about the danger I'm putting Gene in just by being here, and I'm not hungry. But Gene wants me to eat, so I force the tomato soup and a Lortab down, half expecting the soup to seep through the hole in my stomach.

"So what about calling the police?" Gene asks.

I remember the conversation Dr. Bartholomew and I had right before I was supposed to be frozen. She was trying to convince me to trust her because of all the influential people she'd helped, all the money she had access to.

"I don't think that's a good idea," I say. "Dr. Bartholomew has a lot of connections."

Gene slumps a little in his chair. "You know, I can see Virginia's house from that window there." He nods at the window over the kitchen sink. "Our backyards bump up against each other. While I was washing that bowl out for your soup, I saw a car pull up to the house. Three people got out and jimmied their way in the back door. I imagine they're looking for you."

"I should leave," I say. "If they find me here, they'll want to know how much you know. If they think you're a threat—"

"You're not leaving. Not unless we have a plan. Surely there's someone out there you can trust. Someone who might be able to help you."

Someone Dr. Bartholomew doesn't know about. Or maybe, someone she does know—a patient from the VA who saw her once, so that I could sneak into her office.

"Do you have a computer and internet?"

Gene smiles. "Do I have a computer and internet? You're talking to one of the most popular fellas on the Silver Fox dating website. Just a second. It's in the bedroom."

I push the bowl of soup away and wish I could push the thought of Gene Skyping in his bedroom with old women out of my mind as easily.

"Here we go," he says, opening the laptop on the table in front of him. He punches in his password and connects to the web. "What do you need?"

"I need to send an email."

Gene logs into his account, then slides the computer over to me.

I type in Matt's email address. His messages go directly to his phone, so I don't expect it to take too long to hear from him.

"What's your Skype password?"

He clears his throat. "Big Fox seventy-two," he says. "The *B* and the *F* are capitalized." He clears his throat again.

Within minutes, Matt's face comes up on the screen. "Kyle? Holy shit! Where the hell are you? Aren't you supposed to be frozen?"

My excitement at seeing a friendly face dims for a second. "How do you know I was supposed to be frozen?"

He looks confused, then a little hurt. "Jimmy told me. I

know he said he wouldn't, but since I already know just about everything anyway, he wanted to keep me in the loop. But don't worry. I haven't told a soul. I swear. And don't be mad at Jimmy. You know Jimmy."

I nod, but I'm surprised. I do know Jimmy. He said he wouldn't tell, and I believed him. "How is he? Do you know how Cami is?"

"Fine, I guess. But what about you? Where the hell are you?"

"I'm fine," I say out of habit. "No, I'm fucked is what I am. I need your help."

"You bet. Name it, I'm there. You need me to come get you?"

"Before we found Dr. Bartholomew, there were a few doctors you thought might have the other Dr. Bartholomew's research. Can you give me their information?"

"Yeah, sure. Wait—I thought she had it."

"So did I. Do you have the names? Their contact information?"

"Yeah." Matt leaves the screen for a minute. I hear drawers opening and papers rustling, then he's back. "You got a pen and paper?"

I start to rise, but the Lortab isn't working yet, and I gasp in pain. But it doesn't matter because Gene's there with a small notebook and a pen.

"Okay, I'm ready."

"You want the immunologist in Boston or the boy wonder in Chicago?"

"Both," I say.

"To be honest," Matt says, "if Claudia Bartholomew doesn't

have the research, my bet's on the kid in Chicago. I guess I shouldn't call him a kid; he's like twenty-two now. Before we thought Claudia had the research for sure, I did some digging. Your psycho doctor had quite a few phone calls with this kid, Dr. Brian Rubenstein. And Rubenstein is an expert in genetics, plus he's a genius—probably got an ego almost as big as Edward Bartholomew's—so they might have hit it off. Are you anywhere close to Chicago? I can wire you some money. Or I can come and get you. Take you there myself. What about your folks? Do they know where you are?"

"No. They still think I'm frozen." The words make me sick. The thought of my parents still trusting that bitch is like a blade slicing through my skin, making yet another incision. "They need to keep thinking that for now," I say. "It's safer that way."

"Safer? Kyle, what's going on? Let me help. It's not like I have anything better to do." He gives a slight laugh. "And we're kind of like our own little platoon—me, you, and Jimmy. We got to look out for each other."

"You are helping me," I say. "For now, I just need his phone number and address if you have them. I'll let you know if I need anything else."

Matt leans in toward the screen. "Sure thing," he says and reads off the contact information for a Dr. Brian Rubenstein.

"Thanks a lot, Matt," I say once the information's written down.

"Promise you'll let me know if I can do anything for you. Really. Anything."

I'm tempted to tell him where I am. To ask him to get in his car, pick me up, and take me to Chicago. But it's at least a seven-hour drive from where Matt lives to Saint Louis. That's too much time to be putting Gene at risk and too much time to waste. I nod and then log off.

I slump down in the seat, pulling the baseball cap Gene gave me farther down over my face. The bus to Chicago is pretty crowded. A girl around my age is sitting one seat over. I know she's looked my way a few times, but I'm avoiding eye contact. I don't want to talk to anyone.

I know it sounds stupid, but I miss Gene, and Virginia. They both stuck their necks out for me. Hopefully, Virginia will be safe in Phoenix, but Gene's going to have to read the newspaper alone every morning. And there's the bus fare and the money he stuck into my jeans pocket. His jeans, and his T-shirt, his jacket, his socks, and the tennis shoes he stopped to buy me because none of his shoes came anywhere close to fitting.

I'm going to repay him. Even if Dr. Rubenstein can't help me, I'll tell Mom and Dad about Gene before I die, so they can thank him for trying to save their son.

The bus lurches, and I grab my stomach and groan.

"Are you all right?" the girl asks.

"Yeah," I say, giving her a quick glance. "Had my appendix out a few weeks ago. Still kind of sore. I just need some sleep."

"Sure," she says. "Where are you getting off?"

"Chicago."

She smiles. "Me too. There'll be a few stops between here and there. I'll make sure and wake you up. If you're asleep, that is."

I look at her, and I know it's the painkiller Gene gave me and the drugs still lingering in my system from my two months in a coma, but I feel like crying. She's probably fifteen or sixteen. An average-looking teenage girl with straight brown hair and bangs cut slightly crooked. She smiles at me with her mouth closed, most likely because her parents can't afford braces. She's nice, and with luck, she'll live a long time.

"Thanks." I lay my forehead against the cool glass and close my eyes.

I don't sleep. I can't. Not with the pain and the people walking up and down the aisle to the restroom and the screaming baby and the stops where people get off and new people get on and, just maybe, there might be someone looking for me.

It's six hours of hell, but every time we stop suddenly or hit a pothole and the pain makes me want to scream, I remind myself how lucky I am to feel pain. How lucky I am to be awake and alive.

"We're here." The girl nudges my shoulder.

"Thanks," I look at her, and her face fills with concern.

"Are you sure you're okay? You really don't look well."
She places a hand on my forehead like she's my mom. "You're
warm. I think you have a fever."

"I'm okay," I say, and try to prove it by standing up. The air
suddenly turns black for a second as I grab hold of the seat in
front of me. Suddenly, her arms are around me, helping me
stand.

"Let's get you off this bus," she says, leading me down the
aisle, and then the steps. "My grandmother is picking me up.
Mom and I haven't been getting along since my dad left, so
Grams said I could live with her for a while. Who's picking
you up?"

My foot catches on something, and I almost go down, but
she keeps hold of me. "No one."

We walk to the side of the bus, and she leans me against it.
"Let's get your luggage and then we'll find Grams."

"I don't have any luggage," I say, trying to feel my legs beneath me.

"I just have a backpack," the girl says. She takes her ticket,
shows it to the driver, and collects her pack.

I try to stand on my own, try to balance with one hand on
the bus. When I feel somewhat steady, I let go, but I feel sweat
against my back. I want to take Gene's jacket off, but I can see
my breath. I know it's cold outside, but I feel hot.

"Let's find Grams," she says, taking my arm again. "We'll get
you to a hospital."

"No." I pull away from her and almost stumble backward.

"No hospitals. If you can . . ." Think. Think. Think. "A pharmacy," I say. "If you can drop me off at a pharmacy, that would be great. I just need my medicine. And I can call someone from there to get me."

She considers me, and I think she knows I won't get into a car with her and "Grams" unless she agrees to do what I ask.

"Fine," she says. "Let's go find her."

"**I**s he a drug addict?" the old lady asks for the second time.

"No. He has a fever. He had his appendix out a few weeks ago. I think he has an infection."

"Then we should take him to a doctor."

"He wants to go to a pharmacy."

"Because he's a drug addict," the old lady says loudly, like she wants me to know she has me figured out. "We're not taking him home with us. He'll rummage through my medicine cabinet and take all my pills."

"We just need to take him to a pharmacy," the girl says, her voice strained like she's trying not to get into a fight with her grandmother before they even make it home.

"Sorry for the trouble," I manage to say from the backseat. "I really appreciate the ride."

"Where are your parents?" the old lady asks, her voice even louder.

"It's a long story," I say. *And I'm in no shape to tell it right now,* I want to add. "I'll call them soon, I promise."

We stop at a traffic light, and she turns to look at me. Her face is round, her hair is dyed pitch-black. She's wearing bright red lipstick, and with her white complexion, she looks like a senior citizen who's gone Goth. Her mouth twitches a little.

"There's a pharmacy on the next corner. I'll drop you off if you promise to call your folks and quit using drugs."

I'd laugh if I didn't hurt so much. "I promise."

We pull into a pharmacy parking lot. The girl gets out of the front seat, comes around to the back, and helps me out.

"I'll walk you in," she says, and I realize that I don't know her name. I also realize that, at this moment, I don't care.

"It's okay," I say, lifting my arms in a ta-da motion to show her I can make it inside on my own. "Thank you. Really," I say, and my eyes start to tear because of the pain and because of Virginia and Gene and now this girl who's so nice and is so plain and ordinary, and to me, that seems so extraordinary and wonderful, because being superior sucks.

She gives me a smile, but doesn't get back in the car. Not immediately. Not until she knows I can make it inside on my own.

Thank God the doors are automatic.

The clerk at the front register is chewing away at a piece of gum as she rings up a giant package of toilet paper. She looks at me.

"Pharmacy counter?" I ask.

She stops chewing, her mouth hanging open as she points toward the back of the store.

I turn down an aisle of Thanksgiving decorations. A woman

looks at me, her eyes widening at the sight of me while the little boy next to her points at me. Do I look that bad? They're gawking like I'm the infected guy who's about to start the zombie apocalypse. I look to where the boy is pointing. My jacket is hanging open, and there is a dark spot in the middle of Gene's light blue T-shirt. Blood. I lift the shirt and see where one of the freshest incisions has managed to tear open.

"Oh my God," the woman gasps.

I pull my shirt back down. "It's okay," I say, not wanting to scare the little kid any worse. "Just need some Tylenol, maybe a Band-Aid."

I continue past the ceramic turkeys and fake autumn flowers. I make it through the cold medicine aisle and then to the pharmacy counter.

There's no one there, so I ring the bell, and a man with short red hair and a crisp white jacket appears. "Can I help you?" he says, his polite smile dropping from his face when he looks at me. "Are you all right?"

"Just need a prescription. Can you call my doctor?"

"Sure," he says. "What's his name?"

I take the piece of paper out of my pocket, set it on the counter, and write my birthday next to it. "This is his name, phone number, and my birth date. My name is Kyle McAdams."

"What's the medication?"

"Just say it's for my heart," I say, trying to look at him, but my sight is starting to blur.

"You should sit down," he says. "There are chairs over there."

"Thanks." I'm not sure where *over there* is, but I move toward the wall and when I feel something solid sticking out, gently lower myself down into it.

I can just hear him talking as my head falls against the back of the chair. I hear him say "emergency," and at first I want to get up and run because maybe he's calling Dr. Bartholomew. But she's in Saint Louis. At least, I think she is. And I'm in Chicago.

"I need to talk to the doctor," I hear him say, his voice elevated by frustration. "I don't want to talk to his nurse. I need to talk to him. This is an emergency. His patient is here, and he looks like he might not be Dr. Rubenstein's patient for much longer. Kyle McAdams. . . . He just said heart medicine. That's it."

It hurts. I remember my mom having gallbladder surgery a few years ago and them giving her a morphine drip to control the pain. She had one incision. Just one. I have . . . I don't know how many I have, and one of them is seeping blood not just into the shirt I'm wearing, but now I can feel warm liquid on my skin.

The door next to me opens. I force my eyelids to part.

"He's on his way," the man, who is still slightly out of focus, says. "Dr. Rubenstein. He said he'll be in here in about fifteen minutes. Do you need anything? I should get you some water or maybe orange juice. Are you hypoglycemic? Diabetic? You look really bad."

I smile. "I bet I look good for a guy who was in a coma this time yesterday."

"A coma? Like, a medically induced coma?"

"Bitch induced," I say, and I think I can almost make out a smile on his face.

"I've been in a few of those," he says, trying to make light but still sounding concerned. "Maybe I should call an ambulance."

"No!" I almost come out of the chair and for a split second, my vision improves. "No ambulance. Not unless Dr. Rubenstein calls one. You said he's coming?"

"Yeah. He's on his way."

I think I'm nodding, but I'm not sure. Then I close my eyes and let my arms fold protectively over my torso. No more cutting on me. No more.

"**K**yle!"

I feel a hand against my forehead, then against my neck, like someone's trying to see if I'm still alive. I wonder if I am.

"Get me a stethoscope," I hear someone say, a man. "I'll pay for one, just get it, and a blood pressure cuff."

I force my head upright. There's a man hovering over me. "Rubenstein?"

"Yep," he says. "I've been looking for you, Kyle McAdams. I thought you fell off the face of the earth. I don't suppose that bitch Bartholomew had anything to do with that."

The pharmacist hands him a box, and he slides something out of it. He slips it under my shirt, and he must see the incisions because it takes a moment for him to press the cold metal against my chest. He listens, moving the cold metal around, but it feels good, almost soothing.

"She do this?" he asks.

"Yeah," I say.

"Call my office. Tell them to send an ambulance here. A discreet ambulance."

"Discreet?" the pharmacist asks.

"They'll know what I mean. Just make the call."

"Do you have it?" I ask. Knowing he must. He has to have it, or he wouldn't know who I am. He wouldn't have been looking for me.

"I do. I've been trying to find you, so you better not die."

He is young. How old did Matt say he was? Twenty-one? Twenty-two? His straight brown hair is cut at odd angles, like maybe he'd gone to one of those schools where they train hair cutters and he'd gotten one who was off their meds.

"You're not going to die, are you, Kyle," he says, not like he's asking me, but telling me. I want to believe him. I want to trust him. Virginia and Gene helped me. Even the girl on the bus, a complete stranger, helped me. They were all complete strangers, really, and I trusted them, but can I trust him?

I don't have a choice.

His clean-shaven, boyish face grins. "I tell you what," he says, leaning in close to me. "How about I save your life, then we fly to the Bahamas. We'll stand on the beach holding up a poster that says 'Fuck you, Bartholomew.' We'll take a selfie and send it to her. What do you think of that?"

I can see it in my mind. Me and this man I don't know, standing barefoot in the sand, wearing gaudy floral shirts and Bermuda shorts. We both have one hand on the sign, and we're both tanned and healthy. "Fuck you, Bartholomew." And then everything goes black.

"Time to wake up, Kyle."

I hear the voice, but I don't want to answer it. I want to sleep. I just want to keep my eyes closed and drift.

"Kyle," he says again. "You've been out long enough, buddy. You need food. I suppose I can stick in a feeding tube."

I open my eyes.

"I thought that'd get your attention." It's Dr. Rubenstein. *The* Dr. Rubenstein, the one who has the research that can save me. He'd said that, hadn't he? He said he can save me.

I try to move, try to clear my head more. There's a heart monitor on my finger and an IV in my arm. I can hear the continuous beeping of a machine keeping track of my vitals, and I feel the blood pressure cuff tighten around my arm.

"You really scared me. Your temperature was a hundred and three when we got you here. You had a bad infection where Dr. Bartholomew had been playing tic-tac-toe with her scalpel."

"You know her?"

Dr. Rubenstein wheels the chair he's sitting in closer to my bed. It's one of those adjustable chairs, and he's got it positioned so that the seat is higher than my bed. He's tall and lanky, and his long legs dangle. "Before I met her brother, I interned under her at Johns Hopkins. She rode my ass like crazy, and not because she wanted to push me. I mean, she did want to push me, right out the door. She thought I was a snot-nosed brat with acne. No way did she think I deserved to be there. She didn't care if my IQ was a bazillion, which it is, by the way. God, it would be so sweet if I could call her up and tell her who her sociopath of a brother gave his research to. He sure didn't give it to her. Nope. He gave it to the little twit she can't stand. But it's mutual, because I can't stand her. She beats me out of every research grant I apply for. She may be petite, but she's got big pockets and a lot of influential people shoved into them."

"She doesn't know where I am, right?"

He shakes his head. I can't get over how young he is. He does not look like a doctor. He's not even dressed like a doctor. He's wearing jeans and a faded Superman T-shirt.

"It's casual Friday," he says, noticing me taking in his attire. "And the shirt kind of makes a statement, don't you think?" He jumps from the chair and puts both hands on his waist, his chin lifted. "No?" He looks at me out the corners of his eyes while he holds the pose. "Fair enough. I guess if I were really Superman, I could get a girlfriend. But even though I'm tall and devastatingly average in the looks department—no girlfriend. I bet there's nothing you would love more than to hear all about my lack of social interactions with the opposite sex. Or not."

He sits on the edge of my bed.

"Kyle McAdams, in the flesh." He shakes his head, and I

309

think I can detect a few of the scars left over from one of those bouts of acne he was talking about. "God, I am so stoked that you're here!"

"You said you can save me."

He pinches his lips between his teeth. "I did say that, didn't I? Of course, you were bleeding and feverish. Maybe you misunderstood? Not that I can't save you; it's just that it's not, like, a hundred percent guarantee that I can save you. It's more like sixty-forty. The sixty in your favor, so that's good."

"What do you mean?"

He runs his hands through the jagged layers of his hair and stands, then starts pacing. "Did I mention that I have ADD? A lot of brilliant people do, or at least, they get diagnosed with it because their brains are always going, always racing from one thing to another, and so they drive their teachers crazy and end up medicated, which really sucks because it dumbs them down. We'd probably have a cure for cancer by now if we'd just let the neurons fire away in our brains instead of saying, 'Here, kid, take this because we'd rather deal with passive zombies in the classroom than miniature hyper Einsteins.'"

I stare at him, and he stares back, almost like we're having a contest to see who will blink first.

"Can I save you?" he finally says. "Here's the deal." He hops back on the chair and rolls it forward until his legs hit against the bed. "You need a new heart. Your entire DNA has a sequence plugged into it that basically tells your heart to turn off, just like flipping a light switch. Your heart has that same DNA in it, but if you had a different heart, one that had DNA without that sequence, it wouldn't be able to communicate when the rest of your body tried to turn it off. It's like telling a Spanish person to do something, but you tell them in French. *No comprende*. He can't do it because he doesn't know what the hell you're saying.

"Problem is getting you a heart. It's not like we can go through the usual channels. For one, all the tests would show that your heart is perfectly healthy, so no way they'd put you on a list for a donor heart. Plus, people wait months for hearts and never get them. We could kill someone. God knows there are plenty of cold homeless veterans on the streets. I could offer one a cheeseburger laced with a really big dose of sedative. Whisk him back here. Take out his heart, and bam!" He grins, then immediately frowns. "But murder isn't exactly my style. Doesn't go with the shirt." He points to the Superman logo. "However, what does go with it is my bazillion IQ." He grins again. "I have already started growing you a heart."

"Growing?"

"Yep. Claudia's been growing kidneys and bladders for some time. And since I hate her, and since it's the right thing to do for the sake of humanity"—he rolls his eyes—"I've been working on growing hearts. Specifically, one for you."

The long, narrow young face, with dark eyes framed by equally dark, dramatic brows, stares at me with such intensity, I want to look away, but I can't.

"Ever since I found out about you, I've wanted to *do* something to save you." he says. "You are . . ." He struggles to find the right words. "You're the real Superman. Or you could be.

And I'm not just talking about the whole living-for-centuries thing, and yes, I know about all that. It was right there in his research, but I deleted that part. I mean, talk about tempting. Immortality would be so awesome, but really, while the guy was a nutcase, he did have a point about the whole overpopulation thing. I could open that Pandora's box." He gestures like he's pushing a button on a computer and makes a popping noise with his mouth. "I made the part of his research that could make people be AARP members for like . . . ever, go bye-bye. But the rest of it, the part where he designed you and the others, I kept all that. I mean, holy shit, that's exciting. The potential in you is so freaking amazing. Do you want to know how he did it?"

The blood pressure cuff starts squeezing my arm again, and that's good. I need the physical sensation. I don't hurt anymore. I'm not dizzy or even that tired, but my head is starting to spin just the same, trying to keep up with the guy who's giving me a sixty-forty chance to survive.

"You have multiple parents," he says, still amazed. "It's true. Nine of them. He used genetic information from eight different donors to create you. One, may I inform you, who won a silver medal in the Olympics."

"But how's that possible?"

"The Human Genome project mapped out all the genetic codes for various attributes and diseases. He used genetic material from different women, from their eggs. He took out the parts he wanted and basically plugged them into you—well, into your mother's egg. Instead of one mother and one father, you have Mom, Dad, and Mom, Mom, Mom, Mom, Mom, Mom. There's kind of some bad news about the dad part."

He looks at me like he's not sure if he should finish.

"Go ahead," I say, because it's time—time to lay it all out there. Time to know everything.

He sighs. "You have to remember, the guy was a total narcissist. Most brilliant, overly intelligent people are. Edward Bartholomew—yeah. Totally. Now, supposedly he was rendered sterile from all the chemo and crap he went through as a kid, but he used his own stem cells to create sperm. He had to use *his* own bone marrow to do that. Can you imagine . . ." He lifts his hands like he's about to stab a large needle into his own hip to harvest his bone marrow. He must feel my impatience because he stops midstab. "I digress. But science is so damn amazing, and he basically . . ." Rubenstein grimaces and grasps at his hair with both hands. "He used his own sperm to create you, not your father's, or who you think of as your father," he says very quickly.

I want to kill Edward Bartholomew. I want to build a fucking time machine, so that I can go back to that day in his condo and choke the fucking life out of him!

"Interestingly enough," Rubenstein says, "that makes Dr. Claudia Bartholomew your aunt."

"No! No fucking way!"

"Calm down," he says. "You don't want me to have to sedate you, do you?" He checks my vital signs on the display screen next to my bed.

"I know who my parents are," I say calmly, because I don't

want to get knocked out again, and because I do know who they are.

"Look on the bright side. He was really intelligent, which means so are you. The whole having the pharmacist call me and ask for heart medication, that was brilliant. You have no idea what your potential is, especially if you end up living for a few hundred years. Think of the knowledge you could obtain. Things I can't even imagine. That's why I really don't want you to die. You're the only one left, and the potential inside you is so amazing!"

"Can you take the sequence out? Change it so that I'll live a normal number of years, if the new heart works, that is?"

He looks horrified, shocked. He even turns around to look behind him like maybe I'm talking to someone else, about something else, because who wouldn't want to live for hundreds of years?

"You're kidding, right?" He laughs. "Seriously. I mean . . ." He pulls at his hair, as if he actually wants to rip it out. "Do you have any idea how brilliant, fucking . . . Einsteinish this sequence is? Yes, I destroyed his research about it, but I did glance at it just little bit before I hit the big Delete button. This sequence is like . . ." He searches for the right words. "You won't age. You'll be a hundred and fifty, swimming laps and shooting hoops and having sex with twenty-year-olds!" Suddenly he looks troubled. "Okay, that means you'd being having sex with someone who could potentially be the same age as your great-great-great-grandchildren. That's a little creepy, but not as creepy as Mick Jagger doing it with a twenty-year-old, because you won't look like the Crypt Keeper. You'll look like you—now. Young and healthy and vibrant. Who wouldn't want that?"

"Me." I think about Connor. He got eighteen years. Not a day more. Amber didn't even get that. Why should I live for hundreds of years? Why would I want to live without Cami? How could I watch her grow old in front of me and not be able to grow old with her? All I want to do is get better. All I want to do is live so I can take her on dates, real dates, not watching movies in the living room. I want to marry her, and it doesn't matter that I'm saying that when I'm only sixteen, because I'm not sixteen. After everything I've been through, I'm already ancient, and I don't want to live forever.

Dr. Rubenstein sighs. "Sorry, kid. No can do. I can give you a new heart. That will take care of the whole killing-you sequence, but the genetic sequence for longevity controls the neurons in your brain. I can't give you a new one of those. If you want to die, we can forgo the heart transplant. You can call your folks, your friends, girlfriends, and you can all spend what time you have left together. Let's see, that's what . . . three weeks at most." He sighs. "Three weeks or three hundred years. Your call. Of course, remember, the whole heart thing isn't a given. Maybe we try it and let fate make the call."

"You said there was a sixty-forty chance that the new heart will work."

"This is all experimental. We know how to clone stem cells into heart tissue but not into outright hearts. I've been experimenting with ghost hearts—where you remove a heart from someone who obviously doesn't need it anymore. It's *washed* to strip away the cells, leaving a sort of heart skeleton, or what we call a ghost heart. Now, ideally, you then use stem cells from the person needing the heart, and eventually those stem cells turn into heart tissue. Then you have a heart that is a genetic match for the person needing it. This is great because then the recipient doesn't have to take medications to prevent rejection. But this won't work with you because you need a heart with different DNA. We can use a ghost heart made with stem cells from another person. It won't be a genetic match, so you may have to stay on antirejection drugs until we can figure out another option. This will buy us time, and quite a bit of it if all goes well. But it's tricky. I've got a great transplant team, but ghost hearts are new, and new means risk."

My head sinks into my pillow.

"These are all uncertainties, but . . . if anybody can save you, I can. I do not want you to die."

"I don't want to die."

"Then we're agreed. You need to get stronger. I want you healthy when the heart's ready, and hopefully, it will be before the switch gets flipped. I'll work on the heart, and you rest. Then we'll see what happens."

"How long have I been here?" I ask.

"Two days."

More time lost. More fucking time just gone.

"I'm going to save you," he says, and I can't help but think of the promises Dr. Claudia Bartholomew made me right before she put me in a coma and started hacking away.

"Why did he give his research to you?" I ask.

He smiles. "You're super intelligent. You tell me."

I look at the baby-faced genius. "I can think of two reasons—no—three."

"They are?"

"Number one, Edward Bartholomew wasn't going to find anyone more intelligent than you are."

Dr. Rubenstein taps his nose like we're playing charades, and I've gotten his first clue right.

"Number two is the fact that you're so young."

His brows lift. "And why would that make me a good candidate to rid the world of 401(k)s, breakfast discounts, and the increasingly popular undergarment that old folks can do their business in?"

"Because fifty seems like a long way off to you. Other doctors he was considering probably are fifty or over. They're dreaming about how much they'll enjoy their retirements, so it would be harder for them to imagine killing off people their own ages. They can't see the big picture because they're *in* it. But you're not."

"The Mensa membership goes to. . . Kyle McAdams." He applauds, then stops. "What's your third reason?"

"He knows his sister doesn't like you, so it was his last chance to stick it to her, because he thought she was a bitch too."

He laughs and heads for the door. "And the prize goes to Mr. McAdams! Yeah! The crowd goes wild."

"What's my prize?"

He thinks for a moment. "Food. Anything you want."

Other than the soup I had two days ago at Gene's house, I haven't eaten for two months.

Everything sounds good.

"I could send out for Chinese food if you want. A pizza, double cheeseburger?"

I think about what my mom would say if she heard him. "Shouldn't I be eating a little healthier than cheeseburgers?"

He shakes his head. "If we get you a new heart, you're going to live a long time. But remember, you're not bulletproof or car-wreck-proof. The sequence for longevity, I assume, will only protect you from aging and diseases associated with getting older. And considering how long it's been since you've eaten and the fact that there is that chance you'll die no matter what I do, you might as well eat what you want."

It's exactly what Cami would say if she were here. "Ice cream. A banana split."

"God, I haven't had one of those for like . . . a week. Maybe I'll have one with you. I'll just find one of my minions to go and fetch a couple. You want nuts or no nuts?"

"No nuts," I say.

"Whipped cream?"

"Hell yes."

"Double whipped cream." His eyes do a little dance. "And double cherries. I shall return shortly," he says, performing a weird sort of bow as he approaches the door.

"Did he pick the right doctor?" I ask, before he can disappear into the hall.

"You want to know if I plan on carrying out his evil plan?"

"Yeah, I do."

He leans against the door frame, his arms crossed over his chest. "We just established that you are very wise," he says. "So being that you are wise, you have to know that I'm going to tell you what you want to hear, whether it's the truth or not. Right?"

I nod.

"So the answer is . . . of course I'm not going to use his research for evil. I have only the greatest of respect for humanity and would never dream of doing anything to cut any human's life short. Now it's up to you to decide if my answer is A: sincere, or B: total bullshit. I'm guessing you'll go with A, because let's face it, you need someone to trust right now. Am I wrong?"

"No," I say, because I do need someone to trust.

He turns toward the hall. "You can trust me, Kyle." He points to his shirt again and grins. "I'm Superman."

"It's amazing, isn't it?" Dr. Rubenstein says, coming up behind me in the lab. "See these?" He points to the four plastic tubes running into each section of the heart that's suspended in fluid. "These are delivering endothelial precursor cells, cells that usually make up the lining of blood vessels and are, in this case, going to make heart muscle cells."

The theme song from *Star Trek* starts playing. Rubenstein takes his phone out of his pocket, looks to see who's calling, and presses Ignore. He's about to put the phone back in his pocket when he notices me staring at it.

"You want to call your folks," he says. Then he tucks the phone in his pocket because I can't call them. "Last month, I had your parents followed," he says. "My guy—I have a guy, a few guys, actually—followed your parents to the cryogenics facility in Nebraska. They were going to visit you. Well, visit the long cylinder they thought your body was being stored in. I knew immediately you weren't there. There was no way Claudia was going to freeze you. Not with what you have locked inside you. But your poor parents had no clue. That was when I knew they were a dead end to finding you. But I kept trying. I had people watching Dr. Bartholomew's movements, where she traveled, who she talked to. But she was so careful. Then you called me. *You* found *me*." He puts a hand on my shoulder. "With you on the loose, you know she's watching them. I guarantee your mom can't drive to the grocery store without someone following her. And no doubt there are people listening in on every phone call on the chance you'll try to contact them. Then, of course, there's the matter of their safety."

"As long as they think I'm frozen, they're not a threat to her." Every time I consider calling Cami or my parents, I think about Virginia. She fled her home because of what she feared Dr. Bartholomew would do to her, either as a way to find me or because she knew too much. If my parents find out the truth about Bartholomew, what's to keep them from having a car accident because the brakes failed? Or maybe Cami will be walking to her car after the Sak & Save closes and some masked man will . . .

Dr. Rubenstein pulls up a chair for me to sit down in, then rolls another one over for himself.

"Why?" I ask. "I mean, I get that she wants the longevity gene. She wants to know how to make people live longer. She can make billions of dollars if she can sell it to people." I lift my shirt, looking at the incisions that are starting to morph into scars that will always be with me. "So this was all for money."

"Money is a pretty powerful motivator. But for her, I think it's more about redemption."

"Redemption."

Rubenstein leans forward, his elbows on his knees. He seems calmer than usual. Maybe it's because it's late evening and he's tired. Maybe it's because being in a lab filled with floating hearts requires calmness. Or maybe he took his ADD meds today.

"I spent a lot of time with Edward Bartholomew before he died. He wanted to get to know me before bequeathing his research to me. So I got to know him pretty well. His father, their father, came over to this country after World War II. I thought it was interesting that your parents knew him as Dr. Mueller, because that was his father's original name. It was changed when he was brought over to the States as one of the many scientists who were divided up amongst the Allied nations. People were horrified by the medical experiments conducted in the concentration camps, but there was also this sense of intrigue about what their torturous work might have yielded. Dr. Mueller was settled in a small town in New Mexico, where the government supplied him with a new set of patients, who were being exposed to radiation. He was young, handsome, intelligent, and after some years in the States, he managed to win the heart of pretty young secretary.

"They married and had two children. Then eight-year-old Eddie got cancer, and his mother started thinking that maybe her parents, who'd been against the marriage, had been right. She decided that Eddie's illness was God's way of punishing her for her disobedience and her husband for his sins. She took the kid. Drove him to some shit hotel in Arizona and told him they were going to stay there until he died."

Eight years old. I don't want to sympathize with Edward Bartholomew. I won't sympathize with him, but I can't help but feel badly for a sick little kid with a crazy mom and an evil father.

"Daddy came to the rescue. He found them. Brought Edward back. As part of Mueller's working for the United States Government, little Eddie got the best of care and survived. Mom, however, decided to swallow some cyanide. Nothing like a little irony."

"So what happened to Claudia?"

"She wasn't very happy. The way she saw it, if Eddie had been allowed to die, then her mom would have lived, and what little girl wouldn't choose Mom over her brother? What was most weird was how the two kids came to see their daddy." Rubenstein's eyes widen. "They both saw him as a hero of sorts. He was a scientist, trying to help mankind. It wasn't his fault that he was given Jews to experiment on. If it hadn't been him cutting away at them, burning them, injecting them with chemicals and viruses, it would have been someone else."

He laughs. "It wasn't until my little conversation with Eddie that I realized why Claudia hated me so much. I mean, the thought that she was anti-Semitic never crossed my mind. Not in this day and age. But Eddie made it sound like his sister might have a white robe to go along with her white doctor's coat. He said that she blamed the Jews for their father not getting the respect he deserved. That such a big deal shouldn't have been made over a few Jews being experimented on. A few Jews . . ." He shakes his head and clears his throat. "Well, that's when I understood why she had it in for me, besides the fact that she hates that I'm smarter than she is. Anyway"—he drums against the table for a few beats—"as I was saying, Eddie and Claudia went different directions—scientifically speaking.

"They both wanted Daddy to gain some respect. Even with his work at Los Alamos, they saw how people treated him. I think they both wanted to redeem him somehow. Eddie planned on being the savoir of humanity by killing billions instead of the meager millions the Nazis killed. But at least in his head, he had a just cause, and he was willing to kill everyone without discrimination. But Claudia." He shakes his head. "I can't explain it." His face twists with disgust. "She's hungry, and there's no delusional higher cause. She doesn't want to help anybody. She wants money, power, prestige. Years." He stares at me.

I shiver because I know he's right. No matter how she smiled or how she tried to reassure me that I could trust her, there was always something, or a lack of something, in her eyes: compassion, caring.

Cold. They were just cold.

"You know you're safe here, right?" Rubenstein says, wheeling his chair so close, our knees are touching. "I'm a resident at the hospital two miles from here. I have an office and a receptionist and nurses. But this place is off the grid. It's my own special little work space. Only a few select people know it's here, and Dr. Bitch-tholomew is not one of them. And she's not going to find out." He looks up at the heart suspended by artificial vessels and floating in clear solution. "I'll save you, then we'll call your parents. And then we shove it in Claudia's pinched little face. But after that"—he looks back at me—"you and your family have to disappear."

The smell of Chinese food lingers in my room, along with a bag of microwave popcorn. I've been here almost a week, and every night Rubenstein brings in dinner and watches television with me. Tonight, it's basketball.

"They're going to win," Rubenstein says. "My Bulls are not losing to the Thunder. No way." He's standing in front of the recliner I'm sitting in, blocking the television, but it doesn't matter, because he won't be in that exact spot for very long. He never stays anywhere very long. "Get it to Rose! Get it to Rose! Get it to Rose!"

Rubenstein jumps a good six inches off the floor, like it's him making the jump shot. The buzzer sounds, and Rubenstein comes crashing down, landing first on his feet, and then his knees. He lies down on his back, hands over his face, shaking his head.

"Did you see that?" he asks. He's wearing sweats, a Bulls T-shirt, and Converse shoes.

"No, actually," I say, because I couldn't see through Rubenstein's imaginary jump shot.

"They lost!" Rubenstein gets to his feet almost as quickly as he'd gotten off of them. "He had a clear three, and he missed." He stares at the television for a moment, like maybe there was a last-minute foul. Then he looks back at me. "Not a big fan?" he asks, when I don't seem to share his level of disappointment.

"Not really."

"Shit! Why didn't you tell me? We could have watched something else. Some raunchy reality show, wrestling, a sci-fi movie."

"It's okay. I just appreciate you hanging out with me. I'm sure you've got better things to do on a Saturday night. To be honest, I don't think I could focus much on anything anyway."

He does this weird thing where he purses his lips together and moves them back and forth. "Seventeen days until your birthday," he says. "And no more than fourteen until you get your early present."

I nod, like it's a given because the heart's growing and Rubenstein keeps assuring me it'll be ready. But no matter how many times I visit it in the lab, I can't get used to the idea that the floating skeletal heart, which is supposedly growing day by day, is going to save my life. It still doesn't look like a heart. It looks like what they call it—a ghost heart. It looks like what I'm probably going to become in seventeen days or less—when I die.

"I sense doubt in the young lad's eyes," Rubenstein says, attempting a British accent.

"Doubt you?" I try to smile. "Never."

He tries to smile back. "Have you thought any more about

what we talked about? Stupid question. Of course you have. Have you decided anything?"

He's talking about disappearing. About spending the rest of my life with a fake name, living, most likely, in another country so that Dr. Bartholomew won't be able to find me and resume her dissection.

"Just my parents," I say, surprising myself because my voice cracks a little.

Rubenstein sits on the edge of the bed. "You don't want to let her decide for herself?"

I shake my head, my throat filling with emotion. "It wouldn't be fair. She's got her family, her dad, and her little brother. They need her, especially her brother. I can't make her choose between them and me. I can't do that to her."

"That's very noble of you," he says again with the accent, but while his accent may be fake, his expression is one of genuine caring. "You're a good guy, Kyle McAdams. And on the bright side . . ." He stands. "Maybe someone will drop a house on Claudia." He looks off toward the ceiling, and I know he's envisioning her sensible, low-heeled shoes sticking out from beneath the house instead of ruby slippers. So am I. "With that thought, I bid you sweet dreams."

Rubenstein comes toward me, and for a moment, I think he's going to lean in for a hug, but instead he puts out his fist and we fist bump.

I can't sleep. Rubenstein took the empty cartons of Chinese food and the half-eaten, half-burnt bag of popcorn with him, but the smell is still present, and for some reason it serves almost like a sound, keeping me awake. Cami and I used to make popcorn when we watched movies at her house or mine. We shared boxes of it when we went to movies with Connor and Emma. And then there was that little Chinese place where Mom and Dad liked to get takeout.

If I live, I know Mom and Dad will do anything, move anywhere, to keep me safe and to be together. But I'll never see Cami again, no matter what. I'll never hear her voice. Never kiss her.

Who knows how long we'll have to hide away so Bartholomew can't find me? Years, would be my guess. She won't stop looking. Not when Rubenstein destroyed the research on the longevity sequence.

It only exists inside me. And she'll never stop trying to get it.

I get out of bed and do what I do almost every night—go down to the lab and stare at my heart. This place, Rubenstein's "work space," as he calls it, isn't very big. There are a few offices and three labs. I'm pretty sure my room was once an office or a storage room that was hastily made into a hospital room of sorts. A bed was moved in, a television, nightstand, and the wonderful machine the nurse, Rosemary, uses to check my vitals.

At night, there aren't many people around, except Rosemary, who assures me that Dr. Rubenstein is never more than a phone call away if I need him. She's young, only twenty-five, and she calls her husband every night at eleven. She has a pretty face and long brown braided hair, and when she's not checking up on me or talking to her husband, she's reading some novel.

Lab techs are everywhere during the day, but only Jerry works the nightshift. He reminds me of a babysitter, watching over the sleeping organs, making certain they're constantly bathed in stem cells so that one day they can grow up and save lives.

"Coming to relieve me?" Jerry says, looking at his watch. It's almost eleven, the time he ducks out for a late-night lunch. He's a little guy, barely over five feet tall, and thin. He's got short brown hair and dark plastic-rimmed glasses—the look just screams "nerd," and he loves to talk about video games.

"Where to tonight?" I ask, like I have for the last two nights when I couldn't sleep.

"Maybe IHOP. I did Denny's last night. I can bring you back something," he offers, just like last night and the night before.

"No thanks," I say. Jerry looks at me like he wishes I would tell him to bring me back a stack of pancakes or a piece of pie because then he could *do* something for the kid who could be dead in a few weeks. And he makes me think of Connor. Connor always wanted to bring me back something if he wasn't dragging me along. And I always said no. I wish I had said yes at least once. I wish he could have handed me a paper sack with fries and a hamburger in it, and I could have thanked him.

Jerry slips off his white lab coat and replaces it with a thick winter coat. "You sure you don't want anything?"

I nod and watch him disappear into the hallway. For the last few nights, I've stood in front of the large round heart aquarium. But tonight I go to Jerry's laptop.

He always leaves it open on his desk, and he never logs off. I go to Facebook and type in Cami's name. I just need to see her profile picture. I know I won't be able to see anything else, since it's blocked, but if I can just see that picture, just one picture.

She's changed it. Her profile picture used to be one of her and Emma pretending to be sleeping, their heads resting on each other's shoulders. Now it's a picture of her and Josh that I took with my phone and sent to her.

They're in a small wading pool in the backyard, splashing each other. Hundreds of droplets of water are frozen around their laughing faces, and I almost laugh, remembering the moment like it was yesterday, because for me, it practically was. But that's what happens when two months of your life are stolen from you.

I stare at the picture, and stare at it and stare at it, until my head gets heavy, and I rest it on the desk next to the image of the girl I love.

"**K**yle."

I feel a hand against my shoulder.

"Wake up."

I know the voice. I must be dreaming.

"Kyle." The hand is more forceful this time, pulling at my shoulder.

"Matt?" I open my eyes, and it's him. Matt's standing in the lab. He's wearing a baseball cap and a jean jacket, and he has a gun pointed me. The grogginess in my head vanishes.

"It's time to go," he says, his voice flat as he glances for a second at the screen, at Cami and Josh.

"What are you doing?"

"I'm sorry," he says, gesturing toward the screen. "I knew sooner or later you wouldn't be able to resist. Welcome to the modern age of no privacy. Uncle Sam taught me. You just watch the bait." He nods at the screen again. "Then wait. Once you enter the site, you're traced back to the source. I already knew you were in Chicago. I figured Rubenstein's private lab would be within a three-mile radius of his office and the hospital where he works. I just had to wait for you to enter the trap."

I look at the time on the screen. It's just after midnight. "Jerry?"

"He's fine," Matt says. "Just taking a little nap in the hallway. I could have left him outside, but I didn't."

I look at the gun, in disbelief. "Why?"

"She's going to help me."

I lift my shirt. "Like she helped me?"

"I'm sorry," he says, looking away for a moment from the scars. "Dr. Bartholomew, Claudia, made sure she knew everything about you. So when I went for my *appointment* at the VA, she knew about the connection between me, you, and Jimmy. I know I told you she couldn't help me, but I lied. She made me an offer."

"You've been working for her ever since then?"

"I can't live like this," he says, his voice raised. Matt takes off the baseball cap; sweat beads on his forehead. "You don't know what it's like. She said I'll even be able to have kids someday."

"Well, good for you," I say. And I know she can make him a kid or two in a lab. The guy doesn't have balls, but he can have kids, just like fucking Edward Bartholomew was sterile and he . . . I stare at Matt, my eyes cold enough to freeze him, I think. "I'm sure your kids will be really proud of their dad. Why don't you take a picture of me? Then you can show them who you sacrificed so that they could exist." I laugh, my incisions starting to ache like they know Claudia's waiting to reopen them. "Even if she can help you, she won't. The only person she cares about is herself."

"She *is* going to help me." The hand holding the gun is shaking, which seems odd for a marine. But then, his hand wasn't meant for guns; it was meant for computers. "She's going to help a lot of other people, other guys like me missing arms and legs and other parts. I'm sorry, Kyle, but you're a necessary casualty—unless, that is, you can tell me what Rubenstein did with her brother's research."

I'm forming a lie in my head. The research is somewhere in the hospital where Rubenstein works, or in his office locked in a safe behind a poster of Kirk Hinrich doing a jump shot. It's—

The door to the lab starts to open. "Are you in here, Ky—"

The bullet hits the center of her chest. She looks down at it for a second, confused, shocked. Then her knees give way, and she's on the floor. I run over to her.

"Rosemary! Rosemary!" She's dead. She and her husband were trying to have a baby. She likes cooking shows and her favorite author is Nicholas Sparks and blood is spreading across her pale pink scrubs. I wish I were a doctor. I wish these hearts were all ripe for the picking and I could grab one, take out the heart that's been torn by Matt's bullet, and plug in the new one.

I look up at Matt. His mouth is hanging open.

"Another casualty?" I ask, and I want to rip off his prosthetic leg and beat him to death with it, because taking his gun and shooting him would be too goddamned unfulfilling.

"Let's go," he says, holding the gun steadier now, even though his face is tinged with green. "Let's go!" he yells.

"Okay." I stand, and all thoughts of lying to him are gone. I won't let anyone else get hurt because of me.

I don't have a coat on. The cold air hits me as soon as we step out of the building. I think of Jerry and his warm coat, and I wish I'd taken it off him. He was lying in the hall beside the door, just like Matt said. He didn't look hurt, just asleep.

My breath clouds in the air and disappears quickly in the cold wind. I start shivering like crazy, and I'm afraid the incisions are going to start tearing open again.

"Here," Matt says, halting me. With the gun still in hand, he slips one arm, then the other, out of his jacket and hands it to me. I put it on and follow him past the Volkswagen Beetle that's parked at the front of the lot, close to the building; I bet it's Rosemary's. I start shivering again, despite the jacket.

I hear him push a remote, and lights flash on a dark sedan. "Get in," Matt says, his arms held close against his body now.

As directed, I get in. "Have you ever killed anyone before?" I ask as Matt turns the key and air blasts forth from the heater vents.

"Shut up," he says, and pushes a few buttons on the GPS screen.

"So you're taking me back to Saint Louis?"

"Claudia is." He gestures toward the screen. "There's an ambulance waiting on the outskirts of town. She doesn't trust anyone but herself and her assistants to take you back, so we're meeting them."

"Are you going to drive and hold a gun on me the whole way there?"

"Open the glove compartment."

I open it. The only item inside is a syringe.

"Take it out."

I take the syringe in my hand, and even though it's slender, I know that the sparse amount of liquid is enough to turn my brain off.

"Inject it into your leg."

I keep holding it.

"Now." He points the gun at my head.

"You won't shoot me," I say. "Claudia wants me alive." I hear voices approaching the rear of the car. One's complaining about the cold. It's the cleaning crew. They come for a few hours every night to empty trash cans and mop floors. I've never met them, but I know one of them, the man, likes to hum to himself.

"You're right," he says. The dome light in the car still glows. This summer, I remember, I felt sorry for Matt. So young and good-looking and alone. I never noticed the desperation in his eyes, the clouds amongst the clear shade of blue. And there's something else in his face, a hardness that wasn't there when he first woke me in the lab.

Because now he's killed someone. Killed for his cause. There's no backing out now.

"Inject yourself, or I'll shoot one of them," he says, his eyes moving between me and the couple walking past.

I slip the cap off the needle.

"The man or the woman. Your pick."

"I'm doing it," I say, seeing a bead of clear liquid forming at the tip of the needle as I bring it toward my thigh.

"Now!" He steadies his hand against the dashboard, the gun pointing at the man's back.

I think of Cami and my parents, and how if I do this, I'll never see them again. I'll never see anything ever again.

"Now," he says, looking at me, wanting to make certain I do it right.

I lower it toward my leg just as the man playfully grabs the woman, making her scream. Matt looks up, and I act. I jab the needle into his stomach and start pressing the plunger. He grabs my hand, pulling out the syringe.

I know I got at least some of it in him, but how much, and how much does it take?

He lifts his shirt like looking at the injection site will somehow tell him if he's about to pass out or not. But he doesn't have to wonder for long. He shakes his head in a vain attempt to clear it, then slumps against the steering wheel.

I put the gun on the dashboard, and once the two-person cleaning crew is in the building, I get out of the car. I lean in across the passenger seat and pull on Matt. He's heavy, but I manage, slowly and painfully, to slide him across the seat. Then I get behind the wheel. I turn onto the street and follow the directions on the GPS, the directions that will take me to Claudia Bartholomew.

My destination is six miles away. My gut feels like it's on fire from the strain of moving Matt, but I'm thankful for the pain. It's both the proverbial fire in my gut and the literal one. I'm so angry. And I want to stay angry.

I take the gun from the dashboard and set it in my lap. Claudia's not getting me. She'll never lay a hand on me, never again. I glance over at Matt, slumped against the door like he's sleeping, his mouth slightly gaped and a surprisingly peaceful look on his face. His baseball cap is on the floorboard, and I wait until I'm at a stoplight to reach down and pick it up. I put it on my head.

Five miles.

There are streetlights and stoplights and lights shining from office windows and businesses. The streets are filled with cars, and I know back home in Rose Hill, the streets are mostly empty. But this isn't some small town. This is Chicago, and I fight to focus among the glaring lights or oncoming traffic and the occasional car horn.

Four miles.

Another red light. A guy in the car next to me is jamming to very loud rap music. I turn the heater up another notch and roll the window down to hear it better. I could turn on this car's radio, but I don't want to. I don't want music clouding my mind. I just want a small dose of it, a reminder of what life is supposed to be like. Of what life could be like if Claudia Bartholomew were out of the picture. If she were dead.

The light turns green, and the car makes a right turn, but I go straight. I follow the directions on the screen and listen to the voice telling me which way to go.

A short melody comes from the seat next to me. I glance over at Matt, then reach into his jeans pocket and take out his phone. He has a text: *Do you have him?*

When I first got my license, I promised Mom and Dad never to text and drive. But traffic is moving slowly, and this is a rather special circumstance. I push Reply.

On our way.

I put the phone down and settle my hand over the gun.

Three miles.

The traffic is getting lighter as I drive through a business district. First the buildings are tall and covered in glass. Then they become shorter, with no windows except for maybe one or two. Factories and warehouses line the streets, becoming more and more sparse until they are gone altogether.

Two miles, and there's nothing but a two-lane highway with the lights of houses here and there gleaming in the dark.

One mile. The voice instructs me to turn left on a gravel road.

Of course she would want somewhere discreet. Someplace a bystander wouldn't see a body being carried from a car to an ambulance and think it was odd and perhaps call the police. My hand clenches the gun as the tires move across the gravel, and then I see it. The ambulance is pulled over, hugging the ditch. The hazard lights are blinking, and as I approach, I see people getting out. There are three of them, squinting against my headlights. One of them, a man, waves for me to turn them off, but I don't.

I pull the baseball cap down more over my face, knowing that the second I open the door, the dome light will come on. With my head tilted downward, I open the door.

"Finally," I hear Claudia say. "Henry, get the gurney." She comes toward the car while two people, a man and a woman, open the back door of the ambulance.

I get out of the car and push the Unlock button on the door with my left hand, keeping my right hand and the gun close to my side.

"I hope you didn't have any problems," Claudia says as she approaches the passenger side. "You've certainly caused me enough problems, Kyle, but still, no hard feelings."

I lift the gun, but she's behind the car and the angle is off. I hear the man's voice, Henry's, telling me to drop the gun.

I look over at him, at the back of the ambulance, and I see that both he and the other woman are armed and pointing guns at me. It seems ridiculous in a way—the three of us, standing on a dirt road in the middle of a freezing cold night with our guns like we're in some late night movie. They squint a little in the glare of the car's headlights, and I inch forward, trying to get a better view of Claudia. Then I do what people do in late-night movies, I point the gun at the one in charge. "You drop your guns, or I shoot her."

Claudia laughs and starts clapping her hands, the sound muffled by her thick gloves. "You *want* to shoot me," she says. "They know that. They know what I've done to you, what we"—she motions to the man and woman, as if they've all taken a turn with the scalpel—"have done to you. If you plan on shooting me no matter what, they might as well shoot you right now."

She looks at the man. He's large with broad shoulders. The woman is tall and lanky. They're both wearing black pants and black jackets and holding black handguns.

"How about you all fire on the count of three?" Claudia says. "I might possibly die, depending on how good a shot you are, Kyle, but considering the dark and your lack of experience with a real gun, and the fact that both of my associates are not only doctors, but skilled marksmen, I think my odds are much better than yours. Or you could put the gun down. We could have a nice conversation. It doesn't have to be this way, you know. I can still save you, Kyle."

I laugh. "Don't you remember that your brother made me intelligent? Okay, sure. I wasn't smart enough to see through you at first, but then sociopaths have reputations for being charming and cunning. Matt's smart, and he bought it, so I guess I shouldn't feel too bad. Just out of curiosity"—I keep the gun trained on her—"did you really have any intention of helping him? Can you seriously grow him a new penis? Give him testicles? Or were you just saying what he wanted to hear so you could use him?"

She opens the passenger door, and Matt falls onto the dirt road. With the door open, I can see her face even better. She's smiling as she looks down at his unconscious body.

"I just love desperation," she says. "I love how it turns people into putty that you can mold into anything you like. You and your parents were willing to have your body frozen. Frozen! *This* sorry excuse for a person turned on his friend like Judas delivering Christ." She kicks Matt, not hard, but she kicks him. "And for what? For the pleasure of having sex again, the ability to spawn children? Do you think I would really waste my time on such pursuits?"

I can't see where Matt's lying on the other side of the car, but I know she's wrong about him, at least partly. It's about being normal, about feeling whole. It's about wanting to love some-one with every part of your being and about getting back what was so unfairly taken away.

He's desperate, and she took advantage of him. It's because of Claudia Bartholomew that Rosemary is dead.

"One."

I start the countdown, because as much as I want to live, I know I can't, not as long as she's alive.

"Two."

Suddenly Henry's head and gun turn toward Claudia. I see a flash from the woman's gun, and I duck without thinking. There's a searing pain in my shoulder. I prop myself up against the car and try to look through the still-open driver's door to where Claudia was standing. I can't see anything. I climb into the front seat. I want to grip the gun with both hands, but my left arm won't move, so I hold it as tightly as I can with my right. I lie flat on my stomach, trying to keep my head down as more shots fly. I scoot forward on the seat, and then I see Matt. He's still on the road, but he's not lying unconscious anymore.

His body is straddling Claudia's, his fingers wrapped around her neck. Her gloved hands are pulling at his arms, but it's no use. He's choking the life out of her, strangling her so thoroughly, his arms are shaking with the effort. Her hands keep pulling at his arms, then they start reaching for his face, trying to gouge at his eyes. She keeps reaching, her back arching with the effort, and then something snaps. Her arms fall to her sides.

Matt moves back, away from her body. He stares at her for a moment, then he looks up at me. Tears are streaming down his face. Then a bullet pierces his forehead, and I start firing.

55

Someday, I want to wake up in my own bed. It's not a lot to ask. I don't need to be rich or famous. I just want my head to rest against my own pillow. I want to open my eyes and see *Call of Duty* posters on the walls. I want my own blanket. I want to hear the washing machine churning in the laundry room and the buzz of the dryer when the clothes are done. And I won't be annoyed like I used to be when those sounds woke me up. Instead, I'll call out to my mom, and she'll push the door open and smile at me because I'm home.

I'm not home. I can hear hospital-intercom voices from the hallway. I can feel the thin mattress beneath my body and tubes sticking into me. I'm scared to open my eyes. Scared of where I'll find myself. I feel dampness at the corners of my eyes, then feel tears moving down my temples. There is a hand, and it wipes at the tears. It moves to my hair, combing through it like when I was little and had a stomachache or awoke from a bad dream. The tears come faster, and I force my eyes to open.

Mom. She's here. She's staring down at me, and Dad's

standing behind her. They're both smiling, both leaning over me, trying gently to embrace me.

As they move away, I see someone else on the other side of me, and I don't believe it. I can't believe it. She can't really be here.

Cami leans over and lightly kisses my forehead.

I try to speak, but my throat hurts and nothing comes out.

"It's okay," Mom says, holding my hand tightly in hers.

"Don't try to talk," Dad says. "You've been on a ventilator, so your throat's pretty tender. But you're all right." He smiles. "You're all right."

I can hear the sounds that have become too familiar to me. The beeping and hissing and humming of machines.

I look at my dad. At his brown eyes and his balding round head. He's my dad. That's all there is to it. And Mom. Her eyes are red from crying, and her face has grown thinner since the last time I saw her. But she's my mom. My only mom. I look at my parents, and even though I can't talk, they know what I'm asking.

"You have a new heart," Dad says. "And you're seventeen and two days old. You're going to be okay."

A nurse appears behind my mom, and she's putting something into the IV bag. I want to stop her because I don't know who she is, and I don't trust her, but a warmth comes over me, spreading through my body, and as I fight to keep my eyes open for just one second longer, I see Cami again standing at the foot of the bed.

• • •

It's dark in the room. The lights are turned off except for the lone fluorescent bulb glowing on the headboard. I hear all the sounds again, but they don't bother me. Just like the technology in the lab helped to form me, these humming, beeping machines are helping me stay alive.

"Belated happy birthday, buddy. You've been out for a while. I put you in a bit of mini coma. Just needed your body to have a chance to heal."

Dr. Rubenstein is sitting in a chair next to my bed.

"You did it," I say, giving him a drowsy smile.

He looks good. The awkward layers of his hair are combed, and he's dressed like a real doctor. He's not wearing a white coat, but his black suit jacket over his gray shirt looks good. "We did it. Actually, more like you did it. You saved yourself."

"You saved me," I say, because he did. I'd be dead if it weren't for him.

He bites at his lower lip, while he looks for the right words. "The ghost heart wasn't ready. You getting shot sped things up a bit, and we couldn't wait."

Shot. That's right. I got shot. I remember that now. And I remember . . . "Claudia's dead," I say. "And Matt."

"And Claudia's two henchmen. You got one of them, and one of my guys got the other."

"I hit one of them?" I ask, and I don't remember. I remember seeing Matt's head snapping backward. I remember the sound of gunfire, and I remember pulling the trigger over and over again, until I don't remember anything else.

"Where did you get the heart?" I ask, and I'm not sure I

want to know, because she was related to me. She was my biological aunt. What if Rubenstein—

"It's not hers," he says quickly. "No way I'd use her heart. I might cut it out and burn it in my chiminea, but I sure as hell wouldn't put it in you."

My heart, my new heart that never belonged to Claudia Bartholomew, settles in my chest a little.

"Whose, then?"

"Turns out your buddy Matt happened to have type-O blood, which means he's a universal donor—he could donate to anyone with any blood type. You're just lucky I put that tracking device in you when I was stitching up your incisions. If it weren't for that, you would have bled out or gotten shot again. As soon you left the premises, an alarm sounded, and we tracked you. Matt was barely alive, but we were able to stabilize him long enough to get to the hospital and take his heart."

Rubenstein puts down the railing on the bed and leans forward against the mattress. "Do you know who those people were, besides Claudia?"

I shake my head.

"One was Dr. Jessica Dunlap, Claudia's most trusted associate. The man was Dr. Henry Boggs. Besides a doctor, he's pretty much her business manager. He handled her investors, grants. The three of them were like the three heads of the Hydra that was never going to stop hunting you down."

I look up at the ceiling, at the shadows cast against it.

"I don't think she would have trusted anyone else with the

secret of what's inside you. That means nobody but you and I know."

I feel his hand against my arm. I feel him squeeze it, because even though we haven't known each other long, there is a bond between us.

"You can go home, Kyle. You can live your life."

"What about the police?"

"The police believe that Dr. Bartholomew and her colleagues were in Chicago to pick up a patient; however, they were unable to discover the identity of that patient. They believe that on the way to the hospital, they were carjacked, probably for drugs. The ambulance had been ransacked, medications were missing—the weapons used in the killings were never found."

"What about Rosemary? Is Jerry okay?"

"Jerry's fine." Rubenstein looks down and for the first time since I've known him, he seems at a loss for words. He clears his throat. "There was a break-in. Jerry was assaulted in the parking lot. He takes a breath. "The murderer took Jerry's security badge and gained entrance to the facility. He was startled by one of the staff, shot her, then in a panic, fled. Motive was, again, most likely drugs."

"I'm sorry."

Rubenstein attempts a smile and squeezes my arm.

"Thank you." I say the words, but they're not enough. I'm not just thanking him for my life, but for all that life will mean. All the holidays with my parents, the family dinners and conversations and being able to watch them get older because now they'll want to live to watch me grow up. To see what I make out of my life. And I know that at some point, I'll have to tell them that there's a reason I look twenty when I'm forty. But we'll save that for later. Much later. "You saved my life. I owe you big time."

His lips suck in against his teeth, his eyes narrowing in a sort of guilty child's expression. "You, my friend, don't owe me anything," he says. "But you should know that I, um. . . . will be going away for a while. But don't worry. You're in very good hands here. Another week of recovery, and you'll be ready to go back to Kansas."

"Where are you going?"

"Let's just say the regulations for experimentation aren't quite as stringent in some countries as they are here."

"But . . ."

He lifts a hand, trying to keep my new heart from galloping out of my chest. "I have no intention of following through with Edward Bartholomew's plan. I promise."

"But you said you destroyed the other part of his research, the longevity sequence part."

He grimaces and looks away from a moment. "I did. I couldn't take the chance of anyone finding it. So I deleted the files and smashed the drive they were on. I even burned all his written notes."

"But . . ." I start for him.

His eyes meet mine. "I read through them quite carefully before destroying them. I mean, I had to. As a doctor, as a re-searcher, it would have been totally improper, irresponsible to destroy such research without knowing what I was destroying first."

He settles against the back of the chair, his face moving away from the dim light above my bed.

"You have an eidetic memory," I say, because it makes perfect sense. It's easy to destroy a map to the fountain of youth if you have a photographic memory and the map is stored forever in your brain.

"I'm not going to do anything evil with it," he says. "I promise I'm not going to sell it to the highest bidder. But I think I might know a way to replicate the sequence and deliver it into a person using a ribonucleic acid virus. I just have to find, or create, the right virus to deliver it. Then it replicates itself into the host DNA. I think I'm the perfect research subject to test it on." He leans forward, into the light. "You remember when I talked about us going to the Bahamas?"

"Yeah."

"Screw the tropics. How about we go to Mars?" He stands, his lanky body, unable to contain the excitement rushing through it. "I'm serious, Kyle. Think about how smart we could be in two hundred years. Imagine what we could learn, what we could achieve. The problems we could solve. Screw Edward's plan to kill off everyone because of overpopulation. We'll find a different way, a better way. Maybe we'll even give everybody a chance to live a long, productive, youthful life, and they'll be able to because we'll have made colonies on the moon and Mars, and we'll create giant space stations. I know that you haven't realized your full potential yet. You haven't even begun to, but people like us, we can lead the direction the world's going in. It's going to be amazing!"

He sits back down, and he's breathing rapidly like he's just run through the corridors of that space station his mind is envisioning.

"Think what we can do, Kyle." His eyes are so luminous. "It'd be wrong to waste our intelligence, to waste the opportunity we've been given."

I think of my intelligence, the intelligence that came from a piece of Edward Bartholomew's DNA. I don't want it. I don't want any part of him inside of me, but I can't exorcise it like some demon.

"Have fun," I say, bringing a disappointed frown to Rubenstein's face.

"You'll change your mind," he says, standing and pushing the chair away from the bed. "You're just seventeen. You've got lots of time, lots of it, to figure things out. And don't worry, I'll know how to find you when you do."

I scoff. "You mean you'll be watching me?" My heart, Matt's heart, erupts on the monitor. "Is the fucking GPS still inside me?" I try to get up, to get at him, but the pain stops me. "You've inherited his experiment, and it's never going to end, is it, because there's still a subject left. Me."

"And what a wonderful subject you'll be. I can't wait to see you come into your own. Connor only had eighteen years to be perfect. What will you be like in a hundred?"

"Do what you want. Live a million years. But leave me alone. Leave me the fuck alone!"

"You'll change your mind," he says, standing up and smiling down at me. "Once you've matured a little, you'll be glad to be a part of science, of discovering the possibilities."

I think about Cami and the night we were at Luigi's restaurant when she told me I needed to "mature," to "ripen."

Rubenstein is walking toward the door.

"I'm not very mature."

He turns and looks at me. Then I flip him the bird.

It's early, really early. The cemetery is about twenty miles out in the country, and during the drive, Cami's fallen back to sleep.

I ease the door of the Jeep open and quietly get out. I'm so glad to have the Jeep back, and Cami's glad to have Emma back. After coming home for Christmas, Emma decided to stay. We swapped vehicles again, and while I don't totally hate the Smart car anymore, I love the Jeep. I love sitting where Connor sat, and sometimes when I'm holding the steering wheel, I feel like his hands are beside mine, guiding me because he doesn't want me to get into an accident. He wants me to live my life.

The sun's up, brightening the dark green leaves on the trees growing amongst the graves. I walk past the old tombstones first. Some date back over a hundred and fifty years. They're made of limestone instead of marble, and the dates and names are barely visible. No one puts flowers on those graves. There's no one left to—no one still alive who remembers who these people were.

I follow the path to the newer section of the cemetery, where there are lots flowers, mostly plastic, sitting on the various graves. There are large marble stones with pictures of husbands and wives. A few with only one spouse pictured because the other one is still alive. And solitary stones. One grave has a cradle etched beside the name of the child who lived only a few months. Instead of flowers, a teddy bear leans against the gray marble headstone. Connor's grave is in the last row next to an open wheat field. There's a photograph of him inset between the dates of when he was born and when he died. It's his senior picture. He's wearing a baby blue button-down shirt, but it isn't buttoned all the way up. His hair has that perfect "yeah, I get up in the morning looking like this" appearance. He's standing outside, the sun at his back, and anyone would envy him. Anyone would think the world was his.

"Happy birthday," I say. "Mom and Dad will be out later, but I wanted to give you something first, on my own. It's not wrapped, but . . ." I place the controller Connor gave me one year ago today in the grass just below his picture.

"Kind of cheap, I know—giving you back what you gave me. Truth is, I don't play anymore. Well, I play a little bit with Josh. Kid's getting pretty good, too, but I'm not going to let him become like I was. I'm going to make sure he gets out in the world. Me and Jimmy, we're co-coaching his soccer league. And don't give me that shit that I don't know anything about soccer, because I already know that, but it's kids kicking the ball around outside—how hard can it be? And Jimmy, he's taking it really seriously, reading books on it and Googling plays. I didn't even know they had plays in soccer."

Two robins chase each other across the grass, then disappear, one after the other, into the thick leaves of a maple tree.

"I want you to know how much that night we stayed up playing meant to me. It was the greatest game of my life, and since I know I'll never top that, I don't need the controller anymore. And guess who got a four-point-seven this semester? Yep. I actually started trying, but no sports. I can't deal with those dickhead coaches. I have been running, though. You were right about me liking it. I think Matt likes it too. Okay, I know that sounds totally effed up, but sometimes when I'm running, I get this weird feeling in my chest like his heart likes it. He was a really fit guy, and it's not like he could run the same after he lost his leg, so . . ."

I shake my head because I can't believe how much things can change in just one year.

"I wish . . ." My eyes start to burn like they always do when I come to visit Connor. "I wish I'd looked at you like Mom and Dad and Cami look at me. It's kind of creepy in a way"—I laugh—"but it's also awesome."

I look around at the various graves, each one the resting place for a person, for a human being with a name and a face and fears and aspirations. I wonder how many of them died without knowing how much they were loved.

I guess that's just how people are. We take for granted that we'll always have the chance to tell someone what they mean to us. We take for granted that nothing is going to happen to them, and so we all walk around not realizing how much *we're* loved. How much *we're* valued.

I almost died. Connor did die. Now my parents embrace me with their eyes. They hug me and kiss me, and I know without any doubt how much I'm loved. But the truth is, they don't love me any more than they did this time last year or the year before, or the year before. We've just all learned to show it now. To not take anything for granted.

"Happy birthday, Connor," I say, hoping he can hear me. Hoping that he knows what I never told him.

I look out at the open field. The wheat's starting to lighten from green to gold, the rising sun illuminating it. In the breeze, it rolls like waves on the ocean. A hand touches my back, startling me.

"Why didn't you wake me up?" Cami says, wrapping her arms around my waist.

"You looked too peaceful. I couldn't."

She lets go of me and scans the graves that seem to go on and on just like the stalks of wheat in the field. "We'll never take life for granted, will we?" she says, grabbing my hand and pressing it against her lips.

"Not a second of it." I pull her to me and start to kiss her, but stop. I don't think Connor would mind us kissing on his grave. I know he's happy for me. But still. He can't kiss Emma. Cami seems to understand, and she leans her head against my shoulder.

"Happy birthday, Connor," she says. "We miss you."

She looks at me, sees the tears in my eyes, and gives me an

understanding smile. But she doesn't understand. These tears aren't for Connor. They're for me, because one day I might be standing here young and healthy and Cami will be . . .

Maybe Rubenstein was right when he said I'd come around. He's got people watching me. Not all the time like Bartholomew had, but I see them every once in a while; strangers stand out in small towns. And I recognize the way they suddenly avert their eyes when I look at them. I could tell one of them that I'm ready. That I'm a hundred percent onboard with whatever his plans are. But first I have one request. Change Cami. If he's really figured out how to give himself immortality, then give it to her, too. And then give it to Josh, because she won't be able to stand seeing him get older. And Josh will want it for his someday girlfriend, and we'll all want it for Jimmy and for our parents and then where would it stop?

"Do you have any idea how much I love you?" I tell her, and the sympathy in her eyes turns to concern.

"Are you all right?" The grip of her hand tightening around mine. "You're healthy, right? You'd tell me if you weren't?"

Her deep brown eyes fill with fear.

"I fine. I'm going to be around for very long time." I stare at her, marveling at the way the morning light brings out tiny strands of auburn in her hair. I look into her eyes, and what could possibly be wrong?

I'm alive.

I pull her toward me and hold her as I think about those who didn't survive.

I wish all the years Edward Bartholomew gave me could

be turned into a birthday cake for Connor. I'd resurrect him and all the others, and we'd slice the years up—every person—every superior—getting an equal number. Maybe they wouldn't divide up to be that many, but it wouldn't matter, because we'd make sure they were good years. The best.

I love the thought of all of us together having a party. Triagon could play the piano, and Hannah could dance. Amber could fix up her hair and wear a gorgeous dress, and we'd line up to kiss her, because . . . well, who wouldn't?

Cami pulls away, and she must see the slight smile on my face. "What are you thinking about?"

I smile back, because right now I'm young and she's young, and really, no one knows how much time they're going to have. And if there's one thing I know Connor would like to tell me, it's live. Just live. And I intend to. And I'll hold on to Cami as tightly as I can, because there's one thing I know for sure: it's going to be one hell of a ride.

ACKNOWLEDGMENTS

Writing is such a solitary act. Inside each writer are voices that both encourage us and dissuade us. And when an outside voice sounds, the voice that tells the writer that they've created something worth reading, it's beyond amazing.

Thank you, Arielle Eckstut and David Henry Sterry, for being two of those voices and for not only choosing me as the winner of their Pitchapalooza contest, but for being the first to really believe in Kyle and his story. Thank you for going above and beyond and for introducing me to my amazing agent, Ayesha Pande.

Ayesha, I can never thank you enough for your support and guidance and, most of all, for your belief in this story and in me. Validation is like air to a writer, and after years of holding my breath, you made it possible for me to breathe. I could write *thank you* a million times but in the interest of conserving paper I'll just give you one gigantic "THANK YOU!"

Stacey, I'm so happy your name has an *e* in it. I don't know if you remember our first conversation, but my daughter told me that I should only trust you if you spelled your name with an *e*. For an eleven-year-old, she was very bright. I trusted you with my story and with Kyle. You took both and transformed them into more than I could have ever imagined. You and Kate put me through my paces, and I loved every minute of it. Thank you, Stacey Barney and Kate Meltzer, for teaching me so much about the craft of writing and for making Kyle's world and story an even better one.

Bringing a book to life takes so many people, and I have to thank my entire Putnam team: Lindsey Andrews, Irene Vandervoort, Annie Ericsson, Cindy Howle, Ana Deboo, Rob Farren, Adrian James, and Jennifer Dee.

Robyn Hill, thank you for being the best beta reader a writer and friend could hope for. Thank you for your support and your belief in Kyle's story and for the dozens of red pens who sacrificed themselves so that *Deadly Design* could make it to readers everywhere. And mostly, thank you for the hours you spent with Kyle and Jimmy and all the others. Couldn't have achieved this without you!

Thanks to Julie, Sharon, and Ciera for being my young-adult guinea pigs.

A huge thanks to my family for giving me the space and time I needed to write. Usually it's a parent's job to believe in and encourage their children in their dreams. Thank you for believing in mine. And thanks for doing the dishes and laundry and for figuring out dinner and for knowing that if I'm in a bad mood, it's because I need to write.

And thank you, Mom and Dad, for always making me believe I could achieve anything if I tried hard enough.